The Memoir of
JOHNNY DEVINE

Center Point
Large Print

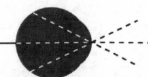

**This Large Print Book carries the
Seal of Approval of N.A.V.H.**

The Memoir of JOHNNY DEVINE

Camille Eide

CENTER POINT LARGE PRINT
THORNDIKE, MAINE

This Center Point Large Print edition
is published in the year 2018 by arrangement with
Ashberry Lane Publishing.

Scripture used in this book, whether quoted or
paraphrased by the characters, is taken from
the King James Version of the Bible.

ISBN: 978-1-68324-681-7

Library of Congress Cataloging-in-Publication Data

The Library of Congress has cataloged record
under LCCN: 2017050999

To Mom, my anchor
a woman of class and grace
a true tender heart

The Memoir of
JOHNNY DEVINE

There is neither Jew nor Greek,
there is neither bond nor free,
there is neither male nor female:
for ye are all one in Christ Jesus.

—Galatians 3:28—

> After all the women I've known and all the illusions of romance I've helped create on stage and film, you'd think I was Hollywood's leading expert on love. In fact, many people not only believed this, but banked on it.
> ~*The Devine Truth: A Memoir*

1

October 1953
Laurel District, Oakland, CA

A tiny cyclone of dry leaves raced ahead of Eliza as she crossed 35th Avenue, urging her to hurry. Or perhaps, more likely, the urge to hurry was coming from her stomach. The warm, leaf-scattering breeze caught the hem of her skirt and swirled it around her knees, quickening her steps all the more. Her heels clicking across the pavement sounded like a tiny horse's hooves.

At the entrance to Lucky's Diner, Eliza stopped and searched her sweetheart handbag—a gift from Betty, of course—just to make sure the money was still there. Eliza didn't care what today's Blue Plate Special was, as long as it didn't cost more than fifty cents.

Inside the diner, her stomach groaned at the smells of coffee and fried food. A waitress Eliza had not seen before worked the window side of the diner. Tugging off the scarf that barely kept her dark, collar-length curls in order; she followed the woman's progress.

The new waitress moved deftly from table to table. Perhaps this one would be friendlier than old Greta.

Eliza hurried to the only empty window seat, then turned up her coffee cup and waited, shushing the embarrassing sounds coming from her insides.

Anticipation must have awakened the sleeping beast.

As she waited, she made a quick study of the other diners. Two young women, one with a toddler and the other with an infant, sat in the next booth. The baby peeked over her mama's shoulder and blinked at Eliza with big, blue eyes.

Eliza smiled until the baby broke out in a toothless grin. She widened her smile and waved her fingers, but the mother glared over her shoulder and quickly shifted the child down onto her lap. Cheeks warming, Eliza returned her hands to her own empty lap.

A man in a long, dark coat, seated at the counter, peered over his shoulder at her.

She turned and focused her attention on the

busy crisscross of traffic outside her window. Busy was good.

"Coffee?" the new waitress asked, carafe in hand.

"Yes, please." Eliza poked her cat-eye glasses higher and read the name *Peg* on the waitress's pin.

Peg handed her a menu and filled her cup. "Holler when you're ready to order, hon."

"I'll have the Blue Plate Special, please." Eliza took a scalding sip of coffee. Black as tar and bitter as always.

Frowning, Peg watched Eliza gulp down her coffee. "Don't you even want to know what it is?"

Eliza set the half-empty cup down and smiled. "Whatever it is, I'm sure it's divine."

As Peg left with her order, the jukebox blared to life.

Eliza tapped her toes to the lively sounds of Les Paul's guitar and Mary Ford's voice singing about her undying love for a boy named Johnny.

Papa would have closed his eyes, tuned out the sounds of traffic and café chatter, and focused on the sound of the guitar. After listening to a song once or twice, he would practice for hours until he could play it note for note.

With a sigh, Eliza shelved the memory. The last time she saw her parents was in 1938, just a week before her high school graduation. They had looked so full of life, waving goodbye from the train as it pulled away from the station, promising to return with pennants from Fresno State for her and Betty, and with any luck, two full-time teaching jobs. Papa had been especially keen on teaching again. Eliza always suspected the lean years following the Great Crash had been harder on him than on Mama. But the only souvenir Eliza and Betty got from their parents' trip was a telegram saying they'd been killed in a railway accident outside of Modesto.

When her meal arrived, Eliza quickly assessed each item. The gravy-coated mashed potatoes and breaded mystery meat wouldn't keep—those she would eat now. The dinner roll and dill pickle spear could wait. The green beans were questionable, but they would also wait.

In the center of the plate, as either an added bonus or a mistake, rested a cluster of plump, green grapes. Since when had the standard bargain fare included fresh fruit? She looked up.

In the long galley window, a toothy grin greeted her. Jimmy was cooking today. Of course.

Eliza checked to see if anyone was watching, then raised her hand in a brief wave of thanks.

Jimmy waved back, still grinning.

Swell. Grateful as she was for the treat, she didn't want to encourage a college boy. For some reason, Jimmy didn't seem to understand that Eliza was at least ten years his senior.

She ate slowly, marveling at the way warm potatoes could reach into the hollowest places. She cut the breaded mystery meat—which turned out to be chopped beef—into tiny bites and made her meal last longer with two more cups of coffee, a trick she'd learned from the girls in steno school. When she finished her allotted portion, she pushed the plate away, then drained her cup and signaled Peg for one last refill.

"Pity you didn't eat all your dinner," Peg said, filling Eliza's cup. She reached for the half-empty plate.

"No!" Eliza grabbed the plate and pulled it close. "Sorry, I'm . . . not quite finished with that."

"Well, that's good. Because just between you and me, doll, looks like you could stand to gain a few pounds." Peg gave her shoulder a soft pat and moved along to the next table.

Eliza tugged four napkins from the dispenser, unfolded them, and piled the rest of the food into the center of each. As she did, she felt eyes on her and looked up.

The man at the counter was staring at her again, sending a tingle along her spine.

She wrapped up the food and stuffed the bundles into her handbag. Whatever the stranger had in mind, she wasn't interested.

Peg returned with her check. "Will there be anything else? Dessert? More coffee?"

"No, thank you." Eliza smiled.

Peg smiled back and waited.

Ah, the tip! Eliza held her smile steady but wanted to slither beneath the table. She had only enough money to pay the bill and not a penny more. Betty would have kittens.

Once Peg had moved on, Eliza dug like mad through her handbag, searching for anything of worth she could leave the woman. Or at least a scrap of paper to write an IOU on.

Was she really so pitiful? No. This was only temporary; things would turn around soon. She just needed a break, a leg up. Perhaps the American Women's Alliance would offer her a regular column now that she'd written a dozen articles for them, and one that paid in double digits for a change.

She could just hear Betty now. *Don't tell me you have no choice, Eliza. Women of our class do not scrape by. Forget those crazy notions of yours and get yourself a husband.*

The trouble was, Eliza had already taken that particular advice, but marriage hadn't been the fairy tale her sister had promised. Far from it.

In the bottom of her purse, Eliza's fingers grasped something cold. She pulled out a nickel.

Her last nickel.

She could buy a cup of coffee with that.

Or . . . she could leave a tip. Peg had to eat too.

She left the nickel beside her plate, then paid her check.

The man at the counter rose and paid his check also. He left the diner a few steps behind Eliza.

She hurried across the street and looked back, but the ogler must have gone another way. Eliza slowed her pace. She was in no hurry to trade the clean bay breezes for her stifling one-room studio.

Since her last freelance job had just ended, the next thing on Eliza's to-do list was to call the employment agency. Inside her building, Eliza ignored the peeling yellow paint in the lobby and looked around.

With any luck, the super was occupied elsewhere and not hovering near the telephone eavesdropping on tenants' conversations.

She hurried to the hall at the bottom of the stairs, fully expecting to wait in line for the telephone, but for once, none of the other girls were using it. She gave the number to the operator and waited to be connected, fingers crossed.

It didn't take the receptionist at the agency long to answer Eliza's query. Still no typist or stenographer work.

Not ready to give up, she headed upstairs to her apartment for her telephone book. There were still a couple of former contacts she could try again. But as she neared the top of the stairs, Eliza nearly tripped on the last step.

Her sister waited at the apartment door.

• • •

Kit-Cat's steady ticking seemed louder than usual—as if to announce that there was an intruder in the room.

Betty must have heard it too, because she looked over her shoulder at the clock and made a huffing sound. "I positively despise that thing."

Eliza sighed. She happened to love that clock. It was *different*.

"It's tacky, Eliza. I hate the way the eyes move back and forth with the tail. It gives me the heebie-jeebies."

All the more reason to love it. Eliza hid her smile.

Betty swept a narrowed gaze across the studio apartment.

Why had she come? With a husband, two neatly groomed kids, and a picture-perfect home surpassed only by Ozzie and Harriet's, Betty was far too busy for drop-in visits. She only ventured down from Richmond Heights when something she couldn't be caught dead without wasn't available there.

As Eliza waited, Betty continued her scrutiny, shaking her blonde head at the narrow sideboard just big enough for a hot plate, electric coffee pot, two saucers, and a cup. She frowned at the small café table in the center of the room where Eliza's ancient typewriter left no room for eating. Which was a moot point.

Betty grimaced at the threadbare chair, the rickety bureau, and lastly, Eliza's twin bed. Which she'd forgotten to make.

She hadn't exactly been expecting company.

Betty shook her head. "Darling, you really need to—"

"Betty, please. Don't start."

"What? I just want to see you happy. It's not too late, you know. You're still young. And ten years of mourning is plenty sufficient."

Mourning? Was that what her sister thought she'd been doing?

"You're throwing away the best years of your life, Eliza. What's all this writing and working yourself stick-thin getting you? Not a home of your own, that's a fact." She frowned, dark-blue eyes seeming genuinely confused. "What kind of a woman doesn't want a home of her own?"

"The kind who would rather have no home than a miserable one," Eliza said quietly.

Betty stared at her, barely masking her disbelief. "Just because your marriage wasn't ideal is no reason to throw away your—"

"Ideal?" Eliza stiffened. The only "ideal" thing about her marriage to Ralph Saunderson was that he joined the army the minute he heard about the war, giving Eliza a chance to lick her wounds in peace.

And then the selfish brute got what was coming to him.

Burning with shame, Eliza went to her bed and straightened the bedding, forcing the awful thought from her mind. A good wife would feel grief, not relief, at the news her husband had been killed in battle. But then, a good wife would probably do many things Eliza had never mastered, like turning a blind eye to his cheating. Or to the fact that he'd named some other woman his beneficiary.

Taking up her pillow, Eliza turned to her sister. "I don't want to argue with you, Betty."

"Good." With a sigh, Betty moved closer, her brow creased. "What *do* you want?"

Eliza fluffed her pillow and lifted her shoulders in a shrug. "I just want . . . to feel complete." She frowned. It wasn't a notion she'd ever entertained, much less voiced aloud.

"Well, *sure* you want to be complete, darling. Hence the need for a husband. Isn't that what I've been saying all along?"

Eliza tossed the pillow to the head of the bed, suddenly weary of the pressure to accept this destiny, to measure her worth by her home and what man she belonged to. Betty seemed so certain, and yet at times it all seemed like pretense, like the silent lie Eliza had lived once and swore she would never live again.

"I don't think a woman should get married just so she can have an automatic dishwasher and a full Frigidaire," she said.

Betty's cheeks reddened, nearly matching her bold, red lips. "You make married women sound shallow."

Eliza shrugged again.

"Please tell me that's not what you think of me."

She looked her sister in the eye. "I thought we were discussing *me*."

Kit-Cat's ticking—which suddenly seemed louder—filled the room.

Rats, the time! Eliza needed to call her former employers again, now that people were getting home from work. Best not to do that with Betty hovering nearby. "The drive to Richmond Heights must be a real bear, especially at this time of day."

Betty gasped at her watch. "Oh, for pity's sake, Ed will be home in two hours, and I don't have meat thawing. I wouldn't have come here if I'd known I'd have to wait so long for you to show up. We'll talk soon, hon." She pecked the air with a kiss and left.

As soon as Betty was gone, Eliza took the bundles of food from her handbag and tucked them between the coffee pot and hot plate. Her stomach piqued a sudden interest in the grapes. But until she got paid again, she needed to make the food last.

A buzz sounded at the door.

Expecting to hear one more piece of sisterly

advice, she opened the door, but it was Ivy from across the hall.

"There's a call on the line asking for *Mrs.* Saunderson." Ivy peered beyond Eliza as if looking for someone. "Sounds official."

"Thank you." Eliza stepped out and closed the door behind her, forcing Ivy and her curiosity to step back on the landing, and dashed downstairs. It had to be the agency. It *had* to.

"Hello, this is Mrs. Saunderson," Eliza said into the receiver, hoping she sounded confident.

It *was* the agency. The receptionist told her about an interview for an opening. "However," she said, "the job doesn't fully suit your qualifications."

Eliza frowned. "But you said the job is for an editorial assistant with typing and shorthand skills. I have extensive experience in all three. It's on my profile. Why do you say I'm not qualified?"

The receptionist apologized. "What I meant was it doesn't match your *specifications*. But I know you're eager for work, so I thought you might want to hear about it anyway."

"Yes, please." What specifications had she listed on her profile?

"The job is a long-term project requiring strong editorial skills."

"Yes, I understand that."

"And it pays very well."

A shiver of excitement raced down her back. "But . . . ?"

"But the employer is . . . a single male, and the job is at his private home."

Ah. Her rule on that item was non-negotiable. "I'm sorry, I don't think—wait, how much does it pay?"

The woman gave her a figure.

"Per month?" It wasn't heaps more than what she'd made on her last freelance job, but was still worth considering.

"No, that's per week."

Eliza gasped. "Per *week?* Are you sure?" She could earn six times her rent in a month. But working for a man in his home? It just wasn't smart. "I'm sorry, but I—"

The super lumbered past in his usual untucked, grease-stained work shirt—ironic, since he never actually worked on anything. When he saw Eliza, he rubbed his fingertips together and gave her that leering look of his. The one that reminded her that the further she got behind on rent, the less pleasant he could be.

Eliza shivered. "Yes, I will take the interview."

2

The bus left downtown Berkeley and climbed into the east hills. The neighborhoods north of the University campus differed from the rest of the city. The homes here were larger, finer, and set farther apart. But what stood out most was how vastly different each home was from the others in design and character, nothing at all like the uniformity of her east Oakland neighborhood.

The bus let her off at Beechwood Lane. It was a good ten-minute walk to the address the agency had given her, which turned out to be the last home on the dead-end, tree-lined street. At least, she assumed it was a house, since she couldn't see any part of a building. A hedge of evergreens formed a tall screen along the front of the property and ended at two thick stone columns supporting a barred, metal gate.

Eliza tugged the hem of her jacket, smoothed her skirt, and pushed the call button. She'd never encountered a locked gate at a residential

24

job before. Tucking a wayward curl behind her ear, she looked over her shoulder at the quiet lane. Only two cars had passed during her walk, another stark contrast to her busy neighborhood. It was almost as if she'd stepped into another world.

The speaker box beside the gate crackled. "Yes?" The female voice was nearly lost in the static.

"Hello," Eliza said, wincing at the natural softness of her voice. She spoke up. "My name is Mrs. Saunderson. I'm here for an interview." She pushed her glasses higher and peered closely at the tarnished brass plaque above the speaker box. *Vincent.*

"Come up to the door and wait," the tired voice said.

The gate buzzed, then opened slowly with a humming, metallic sound.

Eliza stepped onto a cobbled stone drive.

The gate closed on its own.

She followed the drive as it curved to the right, bordered on either side by an overgrown hedge bursting with white blooms. The sweet fragrance reminded Eliza of her mother. Somehow, the passing years had made Mama's favorite scent easier to remember than her face.

Still, the blooming hedge was a good sign. Anyone who would surround their home with the scent of gardenias couldn't be all bad.

Weeping willows obscured Eliza's view of the dwelling until she rounded another bend in the drive. There, nestled between flowering shrubs and trees, stood a house Eliza could only describe as something from a storybook. Dark, decorative trim adorned the white stucco walls, matching the weathered shakes of the roof. Leaded glass windows made up of small, square panes faced west, and smooth, round stones of varying sizes formed an arch above the door.

What really drew her attention was the turret above the entryway, a column rising from the place where two angled parts of the house met in the center. A cone-shaped roof topped the tower, coming to a point like a witch's hat. The turret's narrow window glittered from sunlight hitting the tiny diamond shapes. A small balcony jutted out beneath the window.

Eliza had never seen such a charming villa anywhere but in a book, and certainly not in the middle of a swanky Berkeley suburb. This home looked more like something from *The Hobbit*. Surely a bearded dwarf would round the corner any minute, and then perhaps a hobbit with a long pipe would throw open the tower window and shout a friendly greeting.

To the right of the house, beyond the drive, the grounds ended at a line of dense trees partially obscuring a stone wall. This homeowner clearly valued his privacy.

She couldn't really blame him. Who wouldn't want to keep such an enchanting place tucked away from prying eyes?

From midway along the drive, a moss-entwined stone path cut across the lawn and curved around the left of the house toward a secluded garden, daring Eliza to slip off her pumps and test the cool, green carpet and smooth stone with her stockinged feet. A trellis dripping with clusters of wisteria formed a canopy in the center of the garden, and beneath it, two white, wrought iron chairs and a table beckoned her to come sip tea and spend a leisurely afternoon basking in sweet-scented seclusion.

Hopefully no one was watching her from the house as she paused a moment longer, drinking in the charm with a smile she couldn't contain.

This would be no ordinary typing job.

She followed the path to the house. On either side of the front door, windows overlooked lemon-scented shrubbery and a shaggy lawn.

The front door opened, and a small, colored woman wearing a starched gray-and-white maid's uniform stepped out. She peered at Eliza through round glasses. Her sparse gray hair, pulled back from her creased forehead, tufted in places like a fine mist. Without speaking, she looked Eliza up and down.

"Hello." Eliza offered her most professional

smile. "I'm Mrs. Saunderson. The agency sent me."

The old woman planted fists on her hips and studied Eliza's shoes, then her two-piece navy suit—another hand-me-down from Betty, chosen to accentuate Eliza's dark-blue eyes—then peered up at Eliza with a narrowed gaze. "Ma'am, how old are you?"

Not once had she been asked her age for a typing job. "I'm thirty-three."

The woman continued her scrutiny. If not for the incredible pay and the amount of borrowed bus fare it had taken to get here, Eliza might have turned around and caught the next bus back to Oakland. But perhaps people who lived in enchanted estates—or at least their help—could be expected to be a bit eccentric.

"Do you . . . want to know my typing speed or see my portfolio?"

"No, ma'am. I 'spect you type just fine." The maid studied her face again.

Eliza got the feeling the old woman was trying to decide if she knew her.

Finally, the woman nodded. "All right then, come inside." Leading the way with a steady hitch in her step, the woman took Eliza through a small sitting room filled with an assortment of antique furnishings, past a narrow, curved staircase with a hallway beside it, and into a long parlor. The room was more of a library, the walls inset with dozens of shelves and papered in gold and crimson. The golden glass and wrought iron sconces and quaint furniture looked like they'd been here for half a century, but were spotless and well-kept.

"Have a seat, ma'am."

Eliza sat on a velvet settee facing the front windows and the picturesque view of the bay with the silhouette of the Golden Gate in the distance.

The maid peered at her again, hunched shoulders bringing her face nearly level with Eliza's. "Do you know who live here?"

"I'm afraid I don't."

"Well, he be the one you discuss the typin' with. But before he come, I need to know how you behave around famous folks."

"Famous? I don't know if I've ever—"

"Last girl didn't even make it through her first day." She let out a huff and shook her head. "I knew that red-faced woman gonna be trouble the minute I seen her."

"So, your employer is . . . a celebrity?" Eliza scrambled to think of anyone famous with the last name of Vincent.

"That's right. He been in many pictures, but I 'spect you was just a schoolgirl then."

"Pictures?" Eliza smiled. "How exciting."

The maid's narrowed gaze told Eliza this was

29

the wrong response. "You ever see a celebrity up close?"

Eliza had to think about it. "I saw Eleanor Roosevelt at a press conference once. But I was in a large crowd and didn't get close enough to speak to her."

The maid nodded. "I like Miz Roosevelt. She a smart woman." She studied Eliza as she spoke. "But movie stars is different."

Eliza's curiosity was now fully engaged, but she kept it to herself, since the woman clearly took her screening job very seriously. She looked the old woman squarely in the eye. "I can assure you that I will behave as sensibly with your employer as I would with any other."

"Humph. I be the judge of that." The woman's wrinkly face softened. "I'm Millie."

"I'm pleased to meet you, Millie. Please, call me Eliza."

A buzzer sounded from somewhere across the library.

"Beg your pardon, ma'am." Millie shuffled to a doorway at the far end of the room and picked up a telephone receiver. She spoke in low tones for a few moments, then hung up and came back to Eliza.

"He see you shortly." Millie turned away.

"Oh, wait—before you go, can you tell me who he is?"

Millie shook her head. "No, ma'am. You know

30

soon enough. Besides, I ain't goin' nowhere." Millie tottered to the stone fireplace and stood beside it like a tiny, gray sentinel, her knobby hands clasped in front.

A twinge tingled along Eliza's nerves. How would she react to meeting a famous movie star face to face? Would she get weak in the knees? Tongue-tied?

If it meant getting the job, she could certainly act calm. Though pretense was despicable, it was, unfortunately, something she'd become quite good at. If she could spend three years pretending to be serene and unaffected while a storm of humiliation and hurt raged within her, she could certainly conceal being a little star-struck.

Had she and Ralph only been together three years before he had left for war? It seemed so much longer—long enough to leave his voice forever ringing in her ears . . .

A real woman knows how to keep a man happy. And I'm stuck with one who can't even get one thing right.

Eliza tried to tune out the memory before the last part could—

Should've just gotten a dog.

Something thunked against wood.

Eliza shook off the memory and prepared to meet the employer.

The thunking sound grew louder until a tall, dark-haired man in charcoal tweed slacks, a crisp white shirt, and a tie appeared in the parlor doorway.

Eliza gasped in spite of herself and stood, almost too numb to move. Millie was right—there were probably few who wouldn't recognize Hollywood's legendary Johnny Devine.

He leaned on a cane, but straightened to a full six-foot-plus when his gaze found Eliza.

Her heart thudded. The silver screen had not done his looks full justice.

"Mr. John," Millie said from her post. "This is Mrs. Saunderson."

"How do you do?" Johnny Devine asked in that trademark voice that made far too many sensible women swoon. He eyed Eliza carefully, waiting.

Still numb, Eliza couldn't answer.

Millie's description of her employer as "famous" was an understatement. *Notorious* was more accurate. Louella Parsons's Hollywood gossip column had been the first to dub him "Devilishly Devine." From all accounts, Johnny Devine was extremely fond of women—young or old, rich or poor, married or single, loose or chaste. Rumor had it he could seduce anything in a skirt quicker than he could hail a cab.

Johnny turned to Millie, and the old woman gave him a single nod. He returned his attention to Eliza and studied her for a painfully long moment.

"Mrs. Saunderson," he said finally. "Won't you please be seated?"

Reminding herself to breathe, Eliza found her seat. *He's just a man. Just a regular man.*

While Millie held her place, Johnny Devine limped to the other side of the fireplace and lowered himself onto a chair, squeezing his cane in a white-knuckled grip as he sat. He drew a deep breath and faced Eliza. Then he smiled.

Oh . . . my . . . stars . . . On screen, that smile was a heart stopper. But in person? It could melt the stockings right off a girl.

"I'm writing a book," he said. "A memoir, actually. It's under contract with a New York publishing house, Covenant Press. I have the first three chapters here—"

He began to rise, but Millie tut-tutted at him and retrieved a manila envelope from the fireplace mantel. She tottered over and handed it to Eliza.

Memoir? Eliza stared at the tan packet on her lap, wishing she didn't have to touch it.

"After going over those first few chapters," he said, pointing at the envelope, "my publisher suggested I hire a typist with strong editorial skills. You can see his marks for yourself. He likes the content but wants me to find someone who can do the edits on those chapters and get the project back on schedule by sorting out any other . . . grammatical issues that arise as I write the rest."

Eliza stared at the envelope, thoughts whirling. The last thing she wanted was to read three hundred pages of him boasting about his dressing room adventures, much less fix the grammar. But the pay was so unbelievably good.

And yet there was also the issue of working *with* him. In his home.

Eliza stole a glance at him. He was surely older than he'd been in his last picture that she'd seen, but every bit as attractive. In fact, he was more handsome than a man had a right to be.

She stiffened. Of course, this was a man whose good looks, breathtaking smile, and smooth charm had gotten him anything and anyone he wanted. However, she wouldn't be duped by a sweet-talking liar, no matter how handsome. She'd learned that lesson all too well, thanks to Ralph. "I have extensive editing experience and am confident I can do the work."

"Tell me about your qualifications," Johnny said, his deep voice businesslike.

"I have a bachelor's degree in English." Eliza resisted the urge to lift her chin. Though she'd worked hard to earn it, the degree had done her little good. "With a minor in Journalism."

Wincing, Johnny Devine shifted slightly in his seat. "Impressive. And your experience?"

"During the war, I worked in the steno pool

at McClellan Air Force Base. Since then, I've worked as a freelance editor, writer, typist, and stenographer." Not steadily enough to make a decent living, but that wasn't any of his business. Those good-paying base jobs had been given to men returning after the war, leaving Eliza, and many women like her, jobless.

"Excellent," Johnny said. "Do you have any questions for me?"

"Yes." Why hadn't she inherited Papa's forthright-sounding voice like Betty had instead of Mama's soft tone? She sat up straighter to bolster her nerve. "Do you intend for us to work alone?"

He frowned. "Alone?" But just as quickly as it appeared, his frown dissolved. He turned and stared out the window, his lips pressed tight. "No. I should have mentioned that at the start. Millie is here every day of the week. And my handyman, Duncan McBride, lives on the property, so he's always around."

Millie chuckled. "Well, where else he gonna go? That ol' leprechaun older than me."

Swell. Two ancient domestic workers were Eliza's only guarantee against unwanted attentions. But at least their presence meant she and Mr. Devilishly Devine wouldn't be completely alone. And she'd be nuts to pass up the money. Betty would sermonize about the man's reputation, but Eliza was a grown woman.

She could manage the consequences of her own decisions just fine.

Johnny's gaze was on the hooked rug at his feet and would not meet hers.

She had better not regret this. "Very well, I would like to be considered for the job. But if you intend to hire me, I need to make one thing clear."

"And that is?" Johnny asked.

Eliza forced her voice steady, because what she was about to say stretched every one of her nerves taut. "Any funny business and I quit. On the spot."

Millie's face bunched up in confusion. "*Funny* business? What in the world kinda—"

"It's all right, Millie," Johnny said quietly.

Eliza lifted her chin and waited, heart racing.

"You will not be insulted in this house," he said. "You have my word."

She studied him, heart hammering. "Your word?"

"Yes." Slowly, Johnny Devine looked up and met her eyes. "Though it may be of little worth to you, I am a man of my word."

For now, she had no choice but to take him at that word.

For whatever it was worth.

> 1940 was a record-breaking year in many ways. That year, I put more film in the can and received more awards and nominations than ever before. The line of starlets at my door was longer than Gable's. And the number of times I got so blind drunk I couldn't tell you my name also reached a record high.
> ~*The Devine Truth: A Memoir*

3

After rising earlier than usual but later than planned, Eliza dressed quickly, gulped down two cups of the blackest coffee, and made it to the corner bus stop just as the bus was pulling in, stirring leaves like yellow confetti in its wake. She thanked her lucky stars as she boarded. Being late the first day of her new job would have been disastrous.

Her window seat offered a distant view of the Golden Gate, the flurry of city traffic, and students milling around the Berkeley campus, things Eliza could normally watch for hours. But today, the city and all its buzz was just a passing blur. Her thoughts were on yesterday's interview, her mind reliving every word of it to be sure she hadn't dreamt it. After being in such an enchanting home, who wouldn't suspect it had only been a dream?

But she *had* gotten the job, and though such an amazing opportunity was too good not to be shared, she couldn't tell Betty—not yet, anyway. Eliza wasn't ready for her sister's well-meant meddling, at least not until she had socked some money away. And even if it hadn't been a condition of employment, she wasn't about to tell the girls from the steno pool or her old classmates that she was working for Johnny Devine, the movie star. She didn't dare risk losing the job by drawing a squealing mob of swooning fans.

When Millie opened the door, Eliza greeted her with a calm smile. "Hello, Millie. Lovely day, isn't it?"

The old woman gave Eliza's shin-length navy skirt, white blouse, and coral scarf a once-over. "Yes, ma'am," she said, peering at Eliza with the same scrutinizing look she'd given her the day before. With a nod of approval, Millie motioned her inside.

Eliza reminded herself to breathe. No matter what sort of man Johnny was, she couldn't help but feel awed by the celebrity. She surveyed the front room but saw no sign of him.

Millie took Eliza's pillbox hat and handbag, then shuffled toward the library. "Mr. John say to tell you he workin' in the dinin' room. If you was to have need of him."

Eliza exhaled her relief and followed Millie.

In the library, a small Queen Anne desk and shiny new Smith-Corona typewriter faced the front window, offering her a charming view of the grounds, as well as the city and bay beyond. Perhaps seeing the view as she worked would help keep her imagination from wandering.

The opening chapters of the memoir were stacked neatly to the left of the typewriter, a ream of clean, white paper to the right.

Eliza sat down and picked up the first page of the original draft. Blue marks from an editor's pencil covered so much of the sheet that there was little white space left.

Someone had already begun retyping the manuscript. Apparently Eliza's red-faced predecessor had typed the first page before losing her wits. But did her breakdown have something to do with his story, or was it from being in too close proximity to the movie star?

Ignoring the twisty feeling in her belly, Eliza read the typed preface.

> To you, my friend: My sole aim in writing this book is to take you to a place that I pray will, in spite of much ugliness along the way, give you a sense of great hope. This is not an autobiography, though I will share a great deal of my life. If you are expecting Hollywood gossip, you

will be disappointed. This book is not an insider's scoop, but a confessional. With a purpose. To be honest, I don't relish the idea of traveling back through my life and reliving it. But if doing so will help one person discover what I have found, I will gladly make the journey. I hope you'll stay with me to the end.

And to You, Gracious Father: I thank You for Your endless patience with me. For Your forgiveness, Your help, and Your mercy—Your unbelievable mercy. The only story worth telling is how You changed my life. Without You, I have no story. For Your sake, and for the sake of those without hope, please help me tell it well.

Baffled, Eliza reread the page, trying to make sense of it. This was not the book anyone would expect from a man like Johnny Devine. But then, her job wasn't to speculate about the book or its author—it was simply to type it.

Determined to make herself indispensable, she went straight to work. To her surprise, the book began abruptly with a dark, sobering look at his life at the height of his career around 1940—an odd place to begin if he was planning to cover most of his life. Surely his childhood was the logical place to start.

She read over the editor's marks in the main manuscript, then began the task of retyping the text, noting editorial suggestions and making grammatical changes as she went. But she found phrases that should have been included earlier, requiring her to start over. She slowed her pace and read ahead, making revision notes before she typed. Pencil between her teeth, she read on, typed a little more, then stopped again.

The text needed a transition.

Sunlight poured over the typewriter, warming the gleaming metal. She pressed on.

Pulling out a finished page, Eliza checked the mantel clock. A full hour had passed, and all she had to show for her work was two measly pages. The rising tingle in her spine reminded her that what she accomplished her first day was critical, especially after what had happened to the other woman. Two pages an hour was simply unacceptable. There were plenty of girls ready to snap up this job in a heartbeat.

Eliza willed her nerves to stay calm. Even ten years after Ralph's death, she still expected to be blamed when anything went wrong. Words could be like nails driven so deeply into the soul that, even when removed, they left a lasting hole.

She looked over the manuscript again with a critical eye. No. It wasn't her fault, but that of the writing. It alternated between eloquent and incoherent. Sometimes, in spite of the awkward grammar, his writing had a naturally rhythmic, conversational flow, as if he were telling a story directly to Eliza. But other times, the writing was flat or redundant, the thoughts rambling and incomplete.

The tick of the clock marked the passing seconds. She pressed on, determined to fix each line, one by one, if that was what it took. Yet halfway through the third page, Eliza stopped, baffled. She read and reread the page. What was Johnny trying to say? Even his editor had left a giant, blue question mark in the margin, so Eliza wasn't the only one unable to make sense of it.

She had no choice but to ask him to clarify.

She took the page and went out of the library, then stopped. Where exactly *was* the dining room?

The front sitting room opened into another room at the other end of the lower level, and to her right was a spiral staircase. Beyond that, a long hallway led toward the rear of the house.

She chose the hallway. The click of her heels echoed like a roomful of clocks, probably alerting every neighbor and stray cat of her movements. A good thing, since she could probably get lost in this house.

The hall led to a white kitchen with a long row of windows that drew in sunlight through small square panes, casting a patchwork of light on the wall. Millie was drying a mixing bowl, her attention trained on a television set perched on a rolling cart.

"Luuuuuu-cy!" Ricky Ricardo's voice thundered. Laughter roared from the TV.

"Lord, have mercy," Millie said, shaking her head. "She gone and done it again, fool woman." Millie turned around, saw Eliza, and shook her head again. "The more lies you tell, the more lies you gots to tell to keep it all afloat." She hung the dishtowel on a bar. "I tell my grandchildren the same thing my granddaddy tell me. A lie come back on you like a whip. Maybe not today, maybe not till Judgment Day, but sooner or later, a lie come back and sting you, every time."

The idea of Millie's grandfather making reference to a whip sent a shudder through Eliza. No doubt he'd experienced such ghastly treatment firsthand.

Millie removed a pan of something golden and bubbling from the oven. The rich, sweet scent of apples, sugar, and spices filled the kitchen, rousing Eliza's hunger. Whatever it was, it smelled heavenly. A deep growl rumbled from her insides.

Millie turned around and gave her a squinty look, head cocked to one side as if she was searching for the source of the ominous sound.

"Can you tell me where I can find Mr. Devine?" Eliza held up the sheet of manuscript as proof of her mission and resisted the urge to fan her burning cheeks with it.

"Mr. John? Yes, ma'am. Follow me." Millie set the pan down on the stove and led Eliza back along the hallway. They turned and went into the sitting room, then through a doorway and to their left into a dining room.

Dozens of handwritten pages covered one end of the table like leaves scattered by the wind. Tall-backed mahogany chairs surrounded the table. A large window offered a lovely view of the weeping willows that obscured the lower part of the driveway and front gate, the tree branches rippling like long hair in a gentle breeze.

Johnny Devine stood at the window with his back to her.

Eliza cleared her throat. "Mr. Devine?"

Johnny turned with a jolt. "Sorry, I didn't hear you come in. And please, call me John."

A prickle of unease gave her pause. First names made things decidedly personal. Most employers would not suggest it.

"If you don't mind, that is."

"Of course not," she lied. She wasn't about to call him by his first name. "I saw the name 'Vincent' on the front gate. Was that a previous owner, or perhaps an alias? Or—I'm sorry, I'm being nosy."

"Not at all. This was my grandparents' home.

44

My given name is John David Vincent. I prefer not to use the stage name unless I have to."

"I see."

"How is it coming?" He nodded at the paper in her hand.

As Millie excused herself, Eliza gave the page a scrutinizing glance. Perhaps the pause would give her time to make what she had to say easier. "I'm sorry to disturb you, but there's a passage here that I'm . . . not sure what you meant to say." Eliza reminded herself, again, to speak more firmly. Most people didn't take a soft-spoken woman seriously, and as a female trying to break into a male-dominated literary world, softness was an added disadvantage.

Frowning, he limped closer, took the page, and read it. He towered over her by several inches, even when leaning on a cane. His aftershave gave off a warm, woodsy fragrance. The crease in his brow deepened. "I'll rewrite it. It may take a little while. I hope you don't mind."

"No, not at all."

He glanced at the bottom of the page and frowned again. "This is only page three." He turned to her. The amber flecks in his dark eyes set his questioning look ablaze.

"Yes." Was he upset about her slow progress? But she couldn't simply retype the manuscript as it was—the writing needed significant revision. Surely he knew that?

Would he blame her anyway? Fire her?

John met her gaze. "I'll bring it to you when I'm finished."

Eliza forced a polite smile. "Very good." She turned and headed back through the front sitting room, passing an inviting display of colorful French tapestries and calming woodwork while her insides clenched tighter with each step.

Was this how working with him would be for the entire book?

Back at her desk, she took up a notepad and continued going over the manuscript, making her revisions in shorthand which she could type later, after he returned the revised page.

She was making steady progress when Millie cleared her throat from the other end of the library. "Lunch be served at twelve thirty, ma'am. I 'spect you'll take it in here?"

Eliza turned to answer but hesitated. No doubt that streusel-topped apple dish was to die for. But she hadn't even earned a full day's pay yet. At the rate things were going, by eating his food, she could end up owing *him* at the end of the day.

And owing him anything was out of the question.

She swallowed hard. Twice. "No, thank you, I . . . won't be needing lunch."

Frowning, Millie tilted her head and peered around Eliza's feet and over the desk. "You brought your own, then?"

"I'm quite fine, thank you, Millie." Eliza's smile felt too tight. *As long as you don't bring that miraculous apple thing in here.*

By the time John came back with his page, she had revised two more pages in shorthand.

He set the new sheet of paper on her desk. "Perhaps this is clearer," he said, his deep voice almost a grumble. He stared at the page for a moment, then turned and left.

With a wince, Eliza watched his retreating limp. She had heard he'd been injured in the war, but she didn't know the particulars. Walking seemed painful for him. Forcing herself to focus, she returned to her work.

The rest of the day followed in the same pattern: revision, short bouts of typing, and more interrupting Mr. Devine—or John, which she still couldn't bring herself to call him—when the writing was unclear. Every time she went to him for clarification, his frustration oozed across the room. It didn't help that the sound of her shoes on the wood floor alerted him to her approach. She'd never wished for a pair of slippers more.

At five o'clock, Eliza gathered the wads of paper that had missed the waste can and collected her purse and hat from Millie. Mustering her nerve, she went to the dining room.

John was asleep at the table, his dark head resting on folded arms, his jacket slung over the chair behind him.

Should she wake him or wait? Seeing the film star drooling on his sleeve did help make him a little less intimidating. She cleared her throat.

John awoke with a start and sat up. "Mrs. Saunderson."

"I'm . . . sorry to disturb you, Mr. De—" Frowning, she bit her lip. What in the world was she going to call him? "I'm leaving now. I will continue retyping your opening chapters tomorrow."

He grabbed his cane and rose, expression unreadable. "Do you know how long before you can begin typing what I'm writing now?"

"I'm not sure." Her mind raced for a valid defense. Ralph had never accepted blame for his mistakes. Everything was always twisted into being her fault.

Millie came into the dining room and stood quietly beside the buffet.

Eliza concentrated on keeping her voice as kind as possible. "Because of . . . the kinds of revisions your publisher requires," she said carefully, "it's taking me a bit of time to work through them." With any luck, she was the only one who could hear the dry click in her throat.

"I see. But that may be a problem. I had four months to turn in a completed manuscript, and I'm a month behind schedule." His face churned with unreadable thoughts.

If he wanted to fire her and hire someone else,

couldn't he just say so? She forced herself to speak. "I promise to do everything in my power to meet your deadline."

He studied her carefully, as if sifting her words and weighing each one. "All right, Mrs. Saunderson, you do that," he said. "And I'll pray."

4

Eliza arrived at the villa the next morning determined to disturb her employer as little as possible. She went to work smoothing out transitions and following the editor's notes. But she soon came across more phrases and sections she didn't understand. Who was "Jonesy," and why had John brought up the name only to never mention the woman—assuming it was a woman—again? Were his readers supposed to know who she was? As teenagers, Eliza and Betty had been strictly sheltered by their old-fashioned parents. Though Eliza had later become familiar with Hollywood gossip, perhaps she was still naïve to things that were common knowledge to the general public.

And what did he mean by the phrase "nameless studio starlets assigned to *candy duty*"? She read on, but there was no further mention of the phrase. She had her suspicions about what it meant, but the author still needed to explain the term for his readers.

Since she dreaded interrupting him, she marked problem spots and read on. When she had collected a number of things needing to be fixed, she took them to him all at once. Thanks to heels that announced her approach, every time she went to him, John was leaning back in his chair, watching her enter, with a grim look that deepened with each trip. By noon, it was all she could do to make herself walk into that dining room.

The pay is good, she kept reminding herself. And as she worked, Eliza held on to the hope that John was learning from his prior mistakes and was now avoiding them as he wrote. It was a small hope, but she held on to it all the same.

The sound of Millie clearing her throat from the other end of the room made Eliza jump. "You take lunch in here today, ma'am?"

Tempting as it was, Eliza had no intention of eating away her earnings.

Besides, Joan, one of the girls from her building, had invited her to a card party later that evening and there was sure to be snacks. And payday was coming soon. Life had been either feast or famine for so long she'd grown used to going without.

"No, thank you, Millie." Eliza continued

51

to work, pencil in her teeth and ignoring the rumble in her belly that began the moment Millie mentioned food. By some act of cosmic providence, Eliza had actually eaten supper the night before. On the bus ride home, she'd found a sack lunch containing an apple and half of a cheese sandwich. Normally, she wouldn't eat food someone had left lying on a bus, but the half sandwich had been neatly wrapped in wax paper, the same way Betty would do for Sue Ellen or Eddie Jr.'s school lunch. Both the apple and the sandwich seemed perfectly fine, and since she couldn't afford to faint on the job, she had taken her chances.

At a sound behind her, Eliza turned.

Millie hadn't left the library but was standing at the back of the room with arms folded, watching her.

"Yes, Millie?"

The old woman lifted her chin, sending a flash of light from her glasses, like cowboys in a western signaling each other from their hiding places in the rocks. "Beg your pardon, ma'am," Millie said evenly, voice firm. "But skippin' meals ain't smart. And you seem like a smart woman. That's all."

"Thank you, Millie, but I'm fine." To Eliza's dismay, the growl that came from her middle nearly drowned out her refusal.

Millie's eyes narrowed. She tromped back to

the kitchen muttering something in the same tone she'd used on Lucy Ricardo.

It wasn't long before Eliza came across a page that not only wasn't clear, it was slightly unsettling. John was making strange references to a menacing movie camera as if it had a mind of its own—like something from a Hitchcock film. The thoughts were so vague that she wasn't sure if he meant it as a metaphor or if he meant to convince the reader that the camera was really alive.

Which made him sound crazy.

Which might then explain the red-faced woman's early demise.

She stared at the page again. The penmanship was neat and firmly written. She had once interviewed a graphology specialist at a military base who analyzed handwriting to determine things about a person—hidden things.

Crazy things.

On the other hand, maybe a person had to be a little batty to work in Hollywood. Hopeful, she read it again, but her heart sank as she reached the end of the page. It was complete nonsense.

Eliza took the page and headed toward the dining room. Halfway there, she stopped.

John was clearly growing weary of her interruptions. What if he thought she couldn't do the job?

What should I do?

Betty would tell her to simply do what she was being paid to do: correct grammatical issues and turn in an edited, typed manuscript before the deadline. But since the passage of text was so unclear, she had no choice but to go in there and ask him to clarify his work.

Again.

Wincing at the click of her footsteps, Eliza headed to the dining room.

The rising tone of Millie's voice startled her. "—and that's *twice* now. The woman ain't nothin' but skin and bones already, Mr. John. We gonna find her stone-cold dead on the floor any day now, just you—"

Eliza took an extra loud step and entered the dining room, page in hand.

Millie, bent near John's side, straightened when she saw Eliza.

"So sorry to interrupt, but I—"

"Mrs. Saunderson," John said. A plate of steak and onions and a dish of cobbler topped with ice cream sat in front of him. He examined Eliza's frame with a glance so brief she may have imagined it. "I hope you're not working through lunch?"

Millie stood silent, watching Eliza.

"Thank you, but I don't—"

"Oh no," Millie said, shaking her head at Eliza. "No, I'm sorry, ma'am, but you just bein' unkind now."

"Unkind?" Had Eliza offended the woman?

"All that food I made just gonna be thrown out," Millie said. "Be a terrible, sinful waste. If you don't take some, I could lose my job."

Eliza studied John to make sure she'd heard right, but he was leaning back in his seat with arms folded, watching Millie.

"So if you don't want to see a poor old woman beggin' on the streets, you best take some. You can eat here or take it on home, but you gots to take somethin'."

John turned back to his meal, a faint smile tugging at the corners of his mouth.

"I see." What living soul would dare refuse such a performance? Apparently Johnny Devine wasn't the only actor in the house. Much as she hated to do it, Eliza would just have to accept lunch and have the meal deducted from her wages. "Yes, thank you," she said quietly. "But only if it's not too much trouble."

"No trouble at all," John said, opening a folded napkin. "Millie?"

"Yes, Mr. John." The woman grinned, forcing deep ripples from a lifetime of smiles into her cheeks. She tottered off toward the kitchen.

John indicated an empty chair beside him. "Please, have a seat."

"Oh. I . . . didn't know you meant . . . in here."

John stiffened. He glanced out the window, his face a blank—almost. The discomfort in his

55

expression was so faint that someone passing by probably wouldn't notice it. "Millie can join us," he said quietly. "Is that acceptable?"

As Millie returned, Eliza's gaze followed the steaming steak until Millie set it down on the table. "I . . . suppose that would be fine," Eliza said, her voice barely audible.

As she took her seat, John said, "Millie—"

"Right here, Mr. John." The old woman stood at the end of the buffet, gnarled hands clasped, lips turned up slightly at the ends.

Inhaling the savory aromas of caramelized onions and juicy beef seared to perfection made Eliza dizzy. Her mouth watered as ribbons of steam curled up from the plate. Her stomach rumbled. She swallowed hard and took up her utensils.

"Gracious God," John said, voice solemn.

Eliza halted and studied him.

John's eyes were closed, his head bowed.

She put her utensils down and stared at her lunch, salivating.

"We thank You for this meal and for Your amazing grace and mercy. Forgive us, guide us, and empower us to follow Your way. May we be ever grateful. In Christ's name, amen."

Eliza had never heard such a prayer, and steak, onions, and buttered green beans had never tasted so good. Several times, Eliza had to remind herself to eat slowly, especially when she found

John watching her. Why on earth had she agreed to eat in here? Couldn't she have insisted on taking her lunch in the library?

Millie brought in a small dish and set it beside Eliza's plate.

Eliza breathed in the fragrant scent of apple and spices, warm and sweet. The cobbler had been topped by a dollop of vanilla ice cream that drizzled tiny rivers of cream over golden streusel and pooled around the edges of the dish. Smiling, she took a bite. Amazing, heavenly, far more delicious than she could have imagined. Millie was some kind of saint—she had to be.

Millie came near with a silver coffee pot. "Coffee?"

"Oh! Yes, please," Eliza mumbled, barely getting intelligible words out around a mouthful of cobbler. She covered her mouth and glanced at John.

With a deep frown, he took a bite of his dessert.

Her face burned. Could she be any more uncouth? John was probably accustomed to dining in upper class circles with celebrities and wealthy types. Eliza could almost feel the kick from Betty's shoe beneath the table.

As Eliza sipped her coffee and willed herself to stop blushing, John took his napkin, wiped his mouth, and reached for the page Eliza had brought to him.

She stilled. The tranquilizing effect of a full stomach had lulled her into a stupor, making her temporarily forget her dreaded mission. She swallowed her coffee wrong and lapsed into a coughing fit.

"Are you all right?" John asked, face tense. "Millie, some water for Mrs. Saunderson please."

Eliza put up a hand. "No, I'm okay. Just went down the wrong way." She coughed one more time, poked her glasses back into place, and cleared her throat. "So sorry. I'm fine."

"Good." He glanced at the page, then looked up and caught Eliza in a probing stare.

She braced herself. Time for another gentle, diplomatic explanation about the writing. Time to try to help him understand—

"What does Mr. Saunderson do for work, if you don't mind my asking?"

At the unexpected question, Eliza dropped her gaze to her lap, where she folded her napkin into a crisp square. "He was killed in the war," she said quietly. "In the Philippines." She reached for her coffee and sipped, carefully this time.

"Oh. I'm so sorry to hear . . ." John stared out the window with a distant look, as if remembering something. Then he rose. For a moment, all he did was stand there beside his chair, eyes closed, with a grip on his cane that turned his knuckles white.

Eliza set her coffee cup down. Had he changed

his mind? Maybe his mind had gone entirely elsewhere.

John limped to the window and stood with his back to her.

An old man crossed the lawn, bent nearly double and straining to push a rotary mower.

"So your husband is one of the fallen," John said quietly. "A hero."

Hero. Eliza would never deny that Ralph was a hero for giving his life to his country. It was just that his heroism began and ended with his military service. Somehow that heroism never managed to materialize in his personal life.

John unlatched the window and swung it open, drawing in the scent of cut grass. "Of course you're widowed. I should have known." He muttered something she couldn't quite hear, something about how war robbed families of good men.

No, he wasn't muttering. He was praying.

As he stood at the window, Eliza pressed a palm to her full belly. *Remember what you came to do before you caved in and ate the better part of a steak.* The deed still needed doing, and the more time she wasted, the more difficult her job would be. "When you're ready to look at this page, there is a passage we need to revise."

"Of course." He eased out a sigh. "What mountain of mangled metaphors are we tackling now, Mrs. Saunderson?"

She cleared her throat. Bringing these issues to his attention wasn't easy, but it would be even harder on John in the end if his publisher sent the manuscript back, dissatisfied. "This page . . . I'm afraid it's just not quite clear." She rose and took the sheet to him, then poked at her glasses, which were already as high as they could go.

He took the page and read the marked passage, the furrow of his brow deepening. He read it again and handed the paper back. Slowly, he paced across the room. "I don't know. I suppose what I meant to say was how ironic it is that at the height of my career, with top billing and my name in lights all across the country, I was terrified."

"Terrified? Why?"

"My greatest fear was that one day, when it no longer had use for me, the camera would turn on me without warning. At any moment, the shot would fade to black, then come back into focus from backstage and zoom in with unforgiving clarity—behind the bright lights and makeup and brilliant lines."

Eliza stared at him, the meaning of his muddled passage about the camera suddenly clearing. She hurried to the table, turned the page over, and jotted in shorthand.

John returned to the window. "Then the camera would pan in on the skilled professionals buzzing around me," he said. "The clever set designers, the expert makeup artists, the talented cameramen, the swooning co-stars, the brilliant directors—and the camera would reveal the disappointing truth. It would finally expose the masterfully built mirage, the empty illusion that was Johnny Devine."

She took down every word, working her pencil as fast as she could, and then looked up, waiting for more.

He shook his head. "That was the fear I lived with every minute of every day. At any moment, I would be exposed as the fraud that I knew I was."

When she finished jotting, she stood with paper in hand and read over what she had written. "Yes, that's much clearer." She turned to him. "It's quite good, actually."

Millie cleared her throat.

John turned to the woman. "Did you . . . have something to add, Millie?"

"Oh no. *You* the storyteller, Mr. John, not me." She cocked her gray head. "But I *was* thinking . . ."

Brows raised, John waited. "Yes?"

"Maybe instead of *you* writin' it and then Miz Eliza runnin' all over creation tryin' to straighten it out, maybe you could just *tell* her your story and let her write it. Proper like. Then she can type it up clean as a whistle."

"You mean have him dictate the story to me." A

dozen thoughts vied for Eliza's attention at once.

Millie nodded. "Yes, ma'am." She turned to John. "You dictate your story to Miz Eliza, and she help it come out right the first time. Just makes sense to me, that's all."

John shook his head, his gaze aimed toward the entryway and the library beyond. "It wasn't my intention to . . . work that way."

"Actually, it *is* a good idea," Eliza said, energized by the hope of making better progress. Millie was correct; dictation made far more sense than the way they were doing it now. It would solve much of the needless difficulty of the task and also get the book back on schedule. "I could take shorthand while you tell me what you want to say, and if I need any clarification, I can ask as we go. Then I can type what we've composed at the end of each day. It would certainly speed things up."

John's gaze alternated from Eliza to Millie. "The book *has* fallen behind schedule," he said. "Perhaps dictating would make up for lost time."

Millie and Eliza nodded in unison.

He stared at Eliza. "You realize this means working together."

"Yes," she said, her cheeks instantly on fire. They both knew what he referred to, but she saw no need to address the issue again. She'd made herself quite clear at the interview. "But I'm afraid there's one thing I need to warn you of."

He tightened his grip on his cane, as if bracing himself. "Yes?"

"This kind of editorial work would be considered collaboration, and for that, the employment agency may charge extra."

"Ah." John relaxed. He peered at her with a long look. "I see. And exactly how much *extra* are we talking about?"

Eliza's chest tightened. "I have to check with the agency to be sure, but I believe it would be twenty-five cents more per hour."

John scratched his clean-shaven chin, deep in thought.

Now what had she done? What if he thought she was just using his pressing situation for her personal gain? He could decide to get someone else. Itchy sweat popped out along her brow.

"All right, I'll agree to that. I'll have Duncan move a desk into the library for me. Millie, if you wouldn't mind . . ."

"Yes, Mr. John." Millie glanced at Eliza with a knowing nod. "I know just what to do."

"Swell," he said. "It looks like we've just solved our problem."

"Yes. Very good," Eliza said. She wasn't about to tell either of them that they may have only exchanged one problem for a whole set of new ones.

> If there was a God, I didn't want to know Him. There were already enough people trying to control my life.
> *~The Devine Truth: A Memoir*

5

After lunch, John surprised Eliza by coming into the library carrying a stack of handwritten pages. Pencil poised above the paragraph she was revising, she turned and watched him amble around the room, cane in one hand, pages in the other. He seemed a bit lost.

Did he mean to begin dictating now, even though she wasn't finished retyping his first chapters? "Did you have something you need me to type? *Mr. . . . ?*"

How could she call him John? The man was a famous film star with an Oscar and two Golden Globes, for pity's sake.

"No, I'm working in here now so you can tell me if—I mean *when*—you need me."

Apparently, he was making himself available to assist with the pages she still needed to retype. "That should be very helpful, thank you."

He turned and continued his stroll, pacing the

length of the room while reading back over his newest pages.

Eliza also returned to her task, forcing herself to concentrate on the passage she was revising. The man was clearly unaware of how distracting his presence was, and even more, his aimless movement. If only he would sit down.

But he didn't, so she did her best to ignore him.

While Eliza worked and John strolled, Millie came in, followed by the leathery old man Eliza had seen earlier. She presumed he was Duncan, the handyman. He was no bigger than Millie, but since he stood with a fixed stoop, it was hard to know how tall he really was.

Eliza turned her attention back to her work, but couldn't help wondering why John kept two such elderly workers.

"Mr. John need *this* table in front of *that* chair over there," Millie said in a loud whisper.

Eliza glanced over her shoulder.

Millie was pointing at the upholstered chair near the fireplace where John had sat during her interview.

"So it's just the one table then, Millie?" the man said.

"Yes, just the one," Millie said over her shoulder as she shuffled toward the kitchen.

Duncan lifted the bill of his stained cap and scratched his forehead. "Sure, and the minute I'm up to my elbows in compost again, you won't be calling me back to rearrange the rest of the room?"

Millie turned back and gave him a tight-lipped look. She pointed at a small round table in the corner. "Like I said, *this* table in front of *that* chair."

Biting back a smile, Eliza resumed her task.

Duncan lugged the table over to the chair, but instead of sitting down, John seemed more inclined to wear long ruts in the carpets.

In spite of the ongoing distractions, and thanks to John's availability, Eliza edited and retyped far more pages than she had the day before, to her relief. Yet she still felt uneasy. Though he didn't hesitate to help when she asked, John still seemed put out when she needed him. But at least he was willing.

As the five o'clock hour drew near, Eliza tidied her desk for the weekend and prepared her weekly timesheet for the employment agency, then took it to John for his signature.

He leaned on the mantelpiece and studied the sheet.

Turning, he looked into her eyes.

Her breath caught.

Eliza had been extra careful to keep a good distance from him. But in that moment, standing closer than she'd meant to, she was keenly aware of two things. The first was how unbelievably attractive a man he was. He even smelled good, like warm cedar and leather with a hint of spice. And the second was a reminder to keep her guard up. Now that they were working together, there would be more opportunities for him to beguile her with his infamous charms. Though his behavior toward her so far had been nothing but professional, she knew not to trust a charming, handsome man. Ralph's romantic conquests hadn't ended at the altar, and she'd be a pure fool to let herself get close to a man like that again.

Especially one with the reputation of Johnny Devine.

"Does this include the extra fee for collaboration?" he asked, holding up her time sheet. His intent look and the depth of his voice sent a current thrumming through her.

Eliza took a half step back. Those kinds of sensations would be dangerous for any girl— even one on high alert. "This is only my hours for this week. I still have to tell the payroll department about the new billing rate."

"Excuse me, I'll be right back." John reached for his cane and left.

Eliza waited, confused. If she hadn't seen him on film, she would have a hard time believing the man was capable of being good-humored or sociable.

Not that she had any intentions of socializing with him.

She collected her purse and hat, and as she reached the front door, John met her there.

He held out an envelope. "Good night, Mrs. Saunderson. We'll see you Monday, Lord willing."

Frowning, Eliza took the envelope. "What is this?" When he didn't answer, she looked inside.

The envelope contained a ten-dollar bill. Ten dollars was food and bus fare for a week, plus payback of Ivy's loan, plus some to spare.

"What is it for?"

He opened the front door. "It's the difference you're earning now. Twenty five cents per hour for a week. Sounds like you won't get a paycheck right away, and I wanted to be sure you were paid now. For . . . all your extra work."

Eliza calculated the increased difference, and he was correct. "But I haven't worked a full week yet. This is too much." She tried to give it back, but John shook his head.

"Please take it. You've earned it."

"But . . . I haven't, really." Her confusion shifted into unease. Her pulse sped. She tried again to hand it back. "I can just have the billing department collect it from you, like usual." *Because I'm wondering if there's something else you're expecting to collect from me. . . .*

"Consider it a bonus, then." Even his faint smile produced dimples, the same ones that had earned him the title "Dreamiest Man Alive" by all the girls in school.

Her pulse drummed in her ears. "But employers don't usually pay for this kind of work in advance." *Especially not in cash.* "So . . ." Eliza mustered every bit of boldness she had. "So this *off-the-books* cash is only for my collaboration work and nothing more?" The truth was, it wasn't romantic advances from him that Eliza would find so unwelcome. It was the lying attentions of a flattering cheat. She wasn't stupid. She may not have love, but at least she had her dignity.

John studied his feet, jaw tightly set. "This is simply for your hard work, Mrs. Saunderson, nothing more." With a sigh, he looked outside. "James one, twenty-seven."

"What?"

"It's from the Bible," he said.

By the time Eliza arrived home, the sky was growing dark.

Someone had tacked two notes to her door. One said a man called but left no name and said he would call again.

That was odd. A man who had any legitimate business with her would leave a name.

The other note said that Betty had called.

Still frowning at the first one, Eliza took down the notes and opened her door. Hot, thick air rushed at her, making her cough. She went to the sliding glass door that led onto her tiny balcony, opened it, and turned on the ancient fan. The annoying sound it made, like the chiming of a hundred tiny bells, meant she couldn't leave it on at night unless she wanted to endure broom handle thumps from below all night and get an earful about it from the other girls in the morning.

Today was a feast day, thanks to her good fortune. She opened the jar of Skippy she'd bought on the way home, took out a slice of Wonder Bread, smeared peanut butter on it, folded it in half, and took a large bite. As she chewed, she made a second one and took her dinner to the tiny table. The beginnings of an article on ethnic injustice waited in the typewriter. She took another bite and leaned closer to read what she had written.

> Japanese families, sent to internment camps, had been not only forced to leave their homes, but forced to sell them far below market value, or in some cases, to simply give them up. How could people have turned a blind eye to such injustice? Why is such oppression accepted in society simply as—

Something furry tickled her shins.
Eliza screamed and nearly fell off her chair.

A skinny, black cat with a white chin sauntered out from beneath the table.

The stray tom must have come in from the balcony. She had seen him out there a few times in recent days, but he'd never ventured inside before.

Chuckling at losing her wits over a cat, she crouched down to pet him, but the cat shied away. She coaxed him closer with a piece of her sandwich, then scratched him between the ears.

There was a pronounced kink near the white tip of his tail, a nick in one ear, and the outline of ribs showing through his fur.

"Poor old tom, looks like you're hungry too. Guess you'd better stick around, because we've got pennies from heaven today. Although you never know how long the bread's going to last around here, you're welcome to share what I've got."

The cat rubbed alongside her leg and bumped her with his bent tail.

She stroked his head.

The cat lifted his chin for an under-the-jaw scratch. The coloring on his neck and chest looked like a tuxedo.

"Well, aren't you the gentleman now," she said with a laugh. "So, all this sudden attention has nothing to do with my groceries, huh?"

The cat sniffed her fingers.

"All right, here you go. I'm a pushover, I

know." She fed him a few more pieces and stroked his fur. Pets weren't allowed in the building, but maybe if she fed him and put him out during the day, he would come back when she returned home at night.

"If you're going to hang around, I guess you need a name. How about Mortimer?"

With a yawn, the cat stretched.

"No, too stuffy. Truman? Eisenhower?"

The cat stepped around the chairs and stared suspiciously at the closed lavatory door.

"Not much of a politician, hmm? No, I think you have more of a bookish look about you. Whitman? Burns? Scott? No. I don't see you as the poetic type either. Maybe a literary hero. Mr. Darcy? Now there's an aloof chap who's impossible to read."

Speaking of hard to read, what made John Vincent/Johnny Devine so aloof?

But then, shouldn't she prefer him aloof to the alternative?

She gave the cat a light stroke, forcing her employer out of her mind.

The cat shied just out of her reach, but continued to purr. Contradictory little fella.

Eliza smiled. "Yes, Darcy suits you perfectly." She broke the rest of her sandwich into pieces and set them down for the cat, then went downstairs to wait for the phone.

It seemed Joan was rescheduling her card

party due to a last minute date. As soon as Joan finished her call, Eliza gave Betty's telephone number to the operator.

Sue Ellen answered.

"Hiya, doll," Eliza said with a smile. "How are you? How's school?"

"Oh, Auntie Liza! I'm swell. But I hate sixth grade! The boys are such drips!"

Eliza heard some muffled talk, then Sue Ellen huffed into the phone. "Eddie Jr. has a friend over to watch *The Lone Ranger*. His family doesn't even have a television. What a square. Just a minute, Auntie Liza, I'll get Mother for you, hold the phone. Mother! It's Auntie Liza!"

Eliza waited several long seconds as the eleven-year-old got a gentle scolding that shouting wasn't ladylike, similar to the ones Eliza and Betty's mama had given them as girls.

At least *someone* was carrying on Mama's legacy.

"Eliza?" Betty sounded relieved. "Darling, I've been so worried. Why didn't you return my call?"

"I'm sorry, I got in late. I work across town, and it takes three buses to get home."

Betty sniffed. "Oh. Well, I'm glad to hear you're alive, anyway. But why do you have to ride so many buses? What sort of job is it?"

Eliza described the editing and typing part of the job, but left out the part about whom for and where—for the time being. What Betty didn't know, she couldn't fuss about.

"I don't understand why you put yourself through all that for a temporary job, I really don't."

"It's a long-term, freelance job. And it pays very well." In cash sometimes, it seemed.

"Long-term?" A huff reached across the miles as if Betty were standing beside Eliza. "Really, how long-term could it be?"

"A few months, probably. It's hard to say at this point. If the publishing house sends it back for revisions, it could be even longer."

"But, darling, you know that won't do. It might put some food on the table—such as it is—but it's not a permanent plan. It's just not . . . responsible. Or proper. A respectable woman's place is in the home, making sure her husband succeeds. You understand, don't you?"

Yes, Mother. Eliza winced and quickly shook off her attitude. Betty was all she had left, and her sister really did care, in her own way.

"And since you brought it up, I have to say I really worry about you. About your future, I mean. *Someone* has to think about it. Now what about that nice man, Stanley, that Ed invited over last time you were here? He owns two appliance stores. In fact, he sold us my new Hotpoint Automatic Laundry Pair. Stanley does *very* well, Eliza. Did he ever call?"

Eliza grimaced. It wasn't that she was opposed to dating a pudgy bald man who sweated more than he talked about himself—which was a lot. It was the idea of marrying someone simply for security and identity while pretending to the poor man and everyone else that she was happy.

"Well, I suppose you didn't really encourage him, did you."

Why would Eliza encourage a man to call her if she wasn't interested in marriage?

And why *wasn't* she interested in marriage?

For three very good reasons: cooking, cleaning, and smiling. Smiling while listening to complaints and demeaning insults. Smiling while cleaning a shattered dinner plate and tomato sauce from the wall where Ralph had thrown it. Smiling while eating her dinner alone because Ralph had gone over to Bruno's for something that didn't "taste like dog food."

Smiling while pretending she wasn't dying on the inside.

"Eliza? Did you hear what I said?" Betty's voice had risen half an octave.

"Sorry, what?"

"I said you can't do this forever, darling. You're thirty-three. You *have* to think about your future. I'll have Ed talk to Stanley again."

Couldn't Eliza work on getting her books published and freelance in the meantime? Was it irresponsible to want to make a way for herself that didn't depend on someone else? Were women really only good for helping men succeed with their dreams and nothing more?

Maybe Betty was correct. Maybe it was foolish to want to be a person in her own right, to entertain her own hopes and dreams, to believe she could use her skills to make a difference. Maybe she should do what Betty wanted and date Stan, the Hotpoint Man.

But what about Eliza's wants? Did they not matter?

A tear slipped down her cheek. She brushed it away, surprised at herself. Tears had never solved anything.

Joan was back with a pinky and thumb at her ear and an apologetic smile.

Eliza wiped her cheek and held up a finger. "Listen, Betty, I have to go. Let me think about it, okay? Tell Ed hello and give the kids hugs and kisses for me."

"Well, all right," Betty said with a sigh. "Take care."

"You too, Betty. 'Bye now." Eliza headed up the stairs and back to her room.

Mr. Darcy was gone—no surprise.

She massaged her stiff neck, then planted herself at the table and reread her half-finished article. But words like *racial* and *sexes* and *oppression* only made her heart heavy.

What did she want, really? Independence?

Well, that was obvious, since she was willing to go hungry rather than ask a man to support her.

What about love?

She shrugged. What about it? Aside from her parents, love had been a struggle to earn—as if what she and Ralph had could even be called love. She'd never been pleasing enough. Was there such a thing as love that wasn't based on performance or on a momentary whim of approval? Could she ever be loved simply for who she was, without the constant pressure to be something more?

Did such a love exist?

In the movies, maybe. But she lived in the real world. Real world love, as she had found, was conditional. It took constant work to earn it and kept her in constant fear of losing it. The trade-off just wasn't worth it. Not to her.

Eliza put a stick in the balcony door so she could safely leave it open a crack to let in the cool night air. She turned off the clanging fan, reached for the light, then stopped when she saw the spines on her bookshelf and remembered John's quiet, parting words. She hunted through her bookshelves for the secondhand Bible she'd bought for a class in college. She found it, then leafed through it to the book of James and read until she spotted the chapter and verse.

Pure religion and undefiled before God and the Father is this, to visit the fatherless and widows in their affliction, and to keep himself unspotted from the world.

Wanting the exact definition, Eliza looked up the word "affliction" in the dictionary.

An instance of grievous distress; a pain or grief.

She frowned. Did John think she was a grieving widow in distress?

Of course. He probably couldn't help but notice how she inhaled her lunch like a pig.

Eliza read the passage again. He had insisted she take money she hadn't yet earned. To which she responded by suspecting his motives. To which he responded by suggesting he was obeying a Bible verse about helping widows.

The peanut butter in her stomach turned to sludge. Was the man simply being kind? At the beginning of his book, he claimed to be a changed man. Eliza hadn't given much credence to those words. She'd become an I'll-believe-it-when-I-see-it kind of gal.

Was it possible that she had read him wrong?

Maybe. But even if she had been wrong, that

didn't change the fact that she needed to stay on her guard. Johnny Devine was an award-winning actor. She'd seen him on the silver screen and knew exactly how convincing a liar he could be.

> The camera lies like a flattering lover. I should know—I've been both the pursuer and the pursued. No one can spot ruthless flattery better than I can.
> ~*The Devine Truth: A Memoir*

6

At noon on Saturday, Eliza gave up on Mr. Darcy. She'd placed a bowl of water on the balcony and left the door open all morning as she washed and hung her underthings, hoping the cat would come back and make her studio a regular stop on his rounds. Maybe even come to think of her place as home. But there were probably other balconies where he fared better than peanut butter, bread, and water.

Swell. Stood up by a cat.

She finished her article, proofread it, then placed it in a large manila envelope. The American Women's Alliance had agreed to consider it for a paying spot in their national magazine, *A.W.A.R.E.* There had also been some discussion with Eliza of an opening for a regular column, for which she intended to apply. The AWA had published a number of her articles in their weekly newsletter, and though those had earned only meager pay, she had the great satisfaction of reaching out to oppressed women who needed to know they weren't alone. The newsletter's readership wasn't huge, but it was growing.

Unfortunately, Eliza wouldn't enjoy much in the way of publishing credits, because even though she was writing primarily for women, the editor suggested Eliza use a non-gender-specific pen name for protection. She had decided on E.J. Peterson—the initials for *Eliza Jane,* and her maiden name. It had a strong ring to it, like the name of someone who ought to be taken seriously.

Eliza smiled as she sealed the envelope. This article could be just the break E.J. Peterson needed.

She donned a red-floral chiffon scarf over her hair and tied it beneath her chin, then grabbed her article and handbag and set off for the post office.

Leaves lined the gutter at the curb like a long orange-and-brown boa, shuddering with the passing traffic. Autumn was dessert, in Eliza's book. After the heat of summer, autumn came with clean, fragrant breezes like a scoop of sorbet after a spicy meal.

Passing the corner bus stop, she kept going. Nothing sounded better than an invigorating walk and some fresh air. The post office was an easy ten-block stroll, and she'd planned for it by wearing her old saddle shoes.

She hurried past shop windows with signs promising more kinds of automatic household equipment than she'd ever seen. Everything was automatic now, even dishwashers. Mama had taught Eliza and Betty to work hard, to never spend a penny when one could make do with elbow grease, and not just because times had been so lean. Although Eliza's parents had been fortunate to find work during the Great Depression, they continued to do things the frugal, old-fashioned way, even after the economy had improved. Mama had often hummed a little tune while she scrubbed laundry in a tub, an old-world sort of tune that Eliza had never heard anywhere else. Maybe it was something Mama had made up. Or perhaps something Mama's mother had taught her as a girl—*somewhere* in Europe. Somewhere too insignificant to show the curious young Eliza on a globe or map.

By the time Eliza was in high school, she'd finally given up asking her parents where they'd come from. Laura and Wesley Peterson were just quiet, boring literature teachers from some quiet, boring place. But when Eliza was a child, the vague way Mama and Papa had referred to their younger years had often sent her imagination running wild. She'd imagined they were in a band of horse thieves and were hiding from the law. Or royalty ousted by a coup and living in exile. She had always preferred that fantasy, daydreaming about how, one day, a string of white Rolls-Royces might stop at the door of their small Sacramento bungalow and whisk the Peterson family away to a castle in another land.

But after years of living with the couple who spent more time with their noses in books than anyone she'd ever known, Eliza finally accepted the fact that something far less exciting was likely to account for her parents' lack of interesting history and gave up asking. With such a dull home life and the prevalence of so many books, it was no wonder Eliza had developed such an imagination.

She greeted folks passing by on the sidewalk, and as the Laurel Theater came into view across the street, she smiled. Now she could afford to treat herself to a nickel movie. The Laurel ran old, reissued films in a program they called "Yesterday's Favorites," which was a growing trend with the smaller movie houses.

Maybe she'd stop on the way back from mailing her article, since Saturday matinees were a double feature and still just a nickel. She'd missed most of the first picture. That was fine. It was probably an old B western, which she wasn't over the moon about anyway.

As she neared the marquee, she smiled again. *Empty Saddles*—clearly a western. She might still catch the tail end of that one, and then see the A picture which was—

Nothing to Say but Goodbye, starring Marlow and Devine.

Eliza halted, causing another pedestrian to jostle her elbow.

Blonde bombshell Deborah Marlow and Johnny Devine. What were the chances that "Yesterday's Favorite" would be one of John's pictures?

She stepped off the sidewalk to get out of the way of passersby and stared at the marquee. On second thought, it wasn't so surprising. The growing popularity of television was causing a drop in box office sales, so houses like the Laurel would run a popular older film for a few days, then switch to another. They went through a couple of old films a week that way. And John had starred in many films. In fact, she'd seen his name on the marquee before. Still, it *was* an odd coincidence.

She mailed her article and then walked back to the theater, curiosity growing with each step. She'd seen a few of Johnny Devine's pictures when they released, but that was years ago. At the time, she had no idea she would one day meet him. What would it be like to see him on the big screen now?

With her ticket and soda in one hand and a bag of popcorn in the other, she slipped through the curtain and into the dark theater. Her eyes took a moment to adjust to the dark. Scanning the rows, she saw an empty spot about midway down the aisle, so she made her way to the wooden bench and ducked onto the seat.

The lady beside her greeted Eliza with a smile.

Minutes into the first scene, Eliza stiffened. According to a close-up shot of a newspaper headline, the story was set in 1938. Perhaps seeing a movie wasn't such a good idea after all. The less she remembered about the year she turned eighteen, the better. But then, she hadn't treated herself to a movie in a while, and it wasn't as if the worst year of *her* life would be on the screen. She could leave at any time, if she wanted to. She focused on the rueful strains of saxophone in the opening score.

The heroine was a cynical young heiress with no one she could trust. Desperate for a break from the boardroom, she set sail on a cruise ship and disguised herself as a working-class girl, much like Eliza. But the similarity began and ended with the girl's work status. Even in a plain overcoat and felt hat, the woman was gorgeous. Bold, self-assured. A woman who knew her worth and would never let anyone tell her otherwise. Was it the actress or the character exuding such confidence, or both?

The heiress explored the ship but kept to herself until she noticed a group of men playing cards in a smoke-filled room off the lower deck. She asked to join them, but none of the men looked happy about a woman interfering with their game. Especially the handsome man with a cigar clamped between his teeth—played by Johnny Devine.

"No dames allowed," he said in that deep, trademark rumble.

Eliza's breath caught.

"Oh, I know what you mean, he does the same thing to me every time," the woman beside her purred, gaze fixed on the screen. She sighed. "I could watch him all day. Isn't he positively divine?"

The heiress had somehow talked the men into letting her play a round of poker. If the cigar smoke and shots of whiskey bothered her, she didn't show it. After she won several hands, the heiress thanked the men and said she needed to leave. Johnny's character—Geoffrey—excused himself and offered to escort her to her room. "After all," he said in her ear, "that's *my* money you're carrying, and I want to be sure you still have it tomorrow night so I can win it back."

The blonde played it cool with a shrug and let him escort her.

Eliza could see where the storyline was going. It didn't take long for the sparks to ignite between them, and soon Geoffrey and the heiress were spending more and more time together. One night, bathed in milky moonlight at the ship's railing, with waves churning in the background, Geoffrey lifted the woman's chin, looked deep into her eyes, and leaned in slowly for a kiss, his eyes closing . . .

The lady beside Eliza throttled her bag of popcorn, sending a shower of kernels all over the floor, but Eliza couldn't take her eyes from the screen. It was the longest, most heart-stopping kiss she'd ever seen. She checked on her neighbor, who was fanning herself and trying to clean up the mess she'd made.

Then the ship docked and Geoffrey was on the telephone in a dark little room at the back of a seedy café. "Sure, I'm sure. She's hooked all right, and by the time we get back to New York, I'll have her reeled in." Geoffrey listened and checked around him.

Eliza's heart sank.

"Don't worry. She's so head over heels she won't know what hit her until after the share-holder's meeting . . . sure, I'll remember. Just make sure *you* remember to bring the other half of my dough."

Eliza stopped breathing. *It's just a movie.*

Her neighbor patted her arm. The woman was watching her intently, nodding. "This part always gets me too," she whispered. "Have you seen it before?"

Eliza shook her head.

"He's really not a bad man. But don't let me spoil it for you."

With a nod, Eliza resumed watching, but with

growing regret over her decision to see this film. So many thoughts and sensations flooded through her. Hearing the sound of a younger John's deep voice coming from the screen and seeing him without a cane was so strange. And of course, a ten-foot image of his smoldering eyes and handsome face was now permanently burned into her memory.

That wouldn't be helpful come Monday morning.

And seeing him portraying a man so convincingly in love threw her for a loop—and how. But the most difficult part was watching how skillfully Johnny the Actor depicted a man playing such a duplicitous, unscrupulous role. A man pretending to be a man pretending. A multi-layered lie, one that he pulled off with disturbing authenticity.

The thought of all that deceit and believable sincerity made Eliza's stomach twist, popcorn and all. She wasn't sure she could finish watching. She hunted in the dark for her handbag and slipped its handle over her arm.

"You're not leaving, are you?" her neighbor whispered. "You have to see what happens next. It's the best part!"

"Well, maybe a few more minutes." Eliza sat back and tried to relax.

As the story went on, the couple became inseparable, spending every remaining moment together. By the time the ship docked, they were making ardent promises to each other to meet again. They parted and headed in separate directions, but then Geoffrey turned back, forced his way through the crowd, and found her.

In a softly lit close-up, he pulled her close and told her he loved her like he'd never loved anyone. He kissed her, and the heiress melted into his crushing embrace.

Eliza's insides lurched. So convincing, and yet, such lies. Similar to the lies Ralph had used to woo her. Too bad Eliza hadn't been warned of Ralph's duplicity the way this audience had been warned about Geoffrey's.

Back in New York, Johnny's character went to meet the man who had hired him, sweating and fidgety as he waited. When his contact arrived, Geoffrey said he wanted out. Not only did he refuse the rest of his "fishing" money, but he also gave back the money he'd already been paid.

It turned out poor Geoffrey the snake had fallen in love—for real.

Eliza was not surprised by the storyline; she had already guessed where the plot was going. It had been done before and would be again. The way she had it figured, the heiress would now discover that Geoffrey had been sent to "fall in love" with her as a decoy, a way to detour some important investment decision she was about to make, and the poor woman, who thought she had finally found someone to love and trust, would realize it was all an act, and worse, a means to use her for gain.

The pain and humiliation of such betrayal hit too close to home. With teeth gritted, Eliza held on a little longer, just to see if she was right.

In a penthouse office, the heiress was paid a visit by a terse-talking private eye who had proof that her company's competitors had hired a decoy in an attempt to manipulate her and railroad her investors. She didn't believe him at first, but then the detective said he had a photograph of the decoy. He took out an envelope, but the heiress stopped him, saying she needed a moment. She squared her shoulders as if bracing herself, and then took the envelope. She pulled out the photo, gave it a brief glance, then slipped it back inside. Her eyes glistened, but only for a moment. Chin up, she handed the envelope to the man. "Good work, Mason," she said. Something in her expression changed. Hardened.

Eliza could feel the woman's embarrassment coming straight off the screen in waves.

"Do whatever you need to do," the heiress said evenly. "I don't ever want to see that face again."

Eliza had also had enough. She stood.

"Oh, but you'll miss the ending," her neighbor said. "You'll never guess how, but it all turns out, I promise. Are you sure you have to go?"

"I'm afraid so. Nice chatting with you." Belly

churning, Eliza dashed out of the theater and kept going. There were better ways to spend a nickel, ways that wouldn't upset her stomach and remind her of her own humiliation. Perhaps the less she saw of her employer, the better—

A weird tingling on the back of her neck made Eliza stop and look over her shoulder.

People were walking the sidewalk in both directions. A man in an overcoat a block away was going the same direction as Eliza. Watching her.

The man from the diner.

You've seen too many detective pictures. Snap out of it.

She ventured another look back, but the man was gone.

> I knew I was being lied to and yet chose to believe it. What's sad about self-deception isn't that it makes a fool of you—though it does—but that sooner or later you wake up and realize there's nothing worth believing in.
>
> ~*The Devine Truth: A Memoir*

7

As the gate closed behind Eliza Monday morning, her cheeks burned, in spite of the gusty breeze that whipped across her skin and tugged at her uncovered curls. She'd spent the morning in such a dither that she'd forgotten a scarf. Preparing for work reminded her of last Friday and what she'd implied to John about the ten dollars. If her mama had been there, she would have offered Eliza gentle words of correction. She would likely say that, while being *mindful* of her feminine intuition was always wise, a lady didn't always have to *speak* what was on her mind.

This learning-to-assert-herself scheme wasn't turning out quite as planned.

When Eliza arrived at the house, Millie was cleaning a window but set down her cloth and went to the door ahead of Eliza, humming a tune.

"Good morning, Millie."

"Mornin', Miz Eliza."

Eliza smoothed her curls and followed Millie inside.

John appeared from the hallway, looking dashing in a white shirt, tweed slacks, and a silk tie.

Eliza smoothed her hair again.

He motioned Eliza into the library. "After you, Mrs. Saunderson."

While John headed toward his chair by the fireplace, Eliza settled at her desk. She went straight to work, resuming where she'd left off on Friday. Knowing he was in the room made the back of her neck tingle, similar to the way it tingled after leaving the theater and sensing she was being followed.

After the *movie*.

The one in which John kissed a woman speechless. Which Eliza did not care to think about—ever. And especially not when she needed to concentrate.

"Mrs. Saunderson, may I ask you a question?" John said.

She turned to face him. "Yes?"

He was seated in his upholstered chair with a Bible open on the table beside him. "I don't mean to sound impatient, but do you have an idea how long before we can begin with the dictation?"

The rigidity of his posture made him look as if he were in pain.

"As a matter of fact, I should finish your opening chapters this morning. I think what we have so far should meet with your editor's approval."

"Fine."

Eliza couldn't decide if he was suffering pain or some other disturbance. He seemed engrossed in his study, so she put her curiosity aside and returned to her work.

Millie passed the library with a feather duster, humming. She broke into the words, "Oh, I need Thee . . . every hour I need Thee . . ." She moved slowly through the sitting room, giving a little stroke here and there to a lampshade or the top of a perfectly clean chair.

By the time Eliza had completed the opening chapters, John had resumed his habit of pacing the library, pages in hand. "Okay, John, I think we're—"

John?

He pivoted slowly and gave her an inquiring look.

Well, she *had* been thinking of him as John, which actually went a long way in helping her forget that he was *Johnny Devine*. Which she needed to do all the more now, after seeing him in that film. And she had to call him something.

"We're ready to proceed," she went on, cheeks

warm. "Where would you like to start?" She turned her chair to face him with her pencil and steno pad and waited.

"Could you please read me the last page you typed?" He came toward the desk.

She did as asked and then looked up.

"We'll begin with the heading *The First Years*," he said.

Eliza wrote quickly. "Do you want to start off by reading me what you have written?"

"Oh. I assumed . . ." His brow furrowed slightly. "Is that what you would prefer?"

"Sure. We can see how that reads and go from there."

John opened his mouth to speak but hesitated. He looked at her ready pencil as though it were a spoonful of bitter medicine. "Yes, about that. In case you haven't noticed . . . which is absurd since you've obviously noticed by now, my . . . writing skills are only about as good as a ninth-grade education can provide."

She didn't mean to stare at him but couldn't help it. As far as the way John carried himself, she would have never guessed he was a high school dropout. He seemed so polished, so cultured. But as far as the issues with the writing, this certainly explained a lot. It also explained the man's frustration at her many inter-ruptions to correct his work. She winced. What an absolute heel she was. No one liked being constantly reminded of his or her shortcomings.

She of all people should know that.

"I left school at fourteen to find work. The Great War changed things for me. Drastically." When he looked up, something was buried deep in his expression. Something like pain or shame or a mix of the two.

"I imagine a lot of people found their lives in upheaval at that time," she said lightly. She had long suspected that her parents had been scarred by the First World War, though they had never discussed it.

John studied the page in his hand. "Well, luckily for me, in spite of my lack of formal education, I learned valuable language and storytelling skills through script reading, director's cues, and grueling practice. But there's a big difference between delivering captivating lines to an emotionally engaged audience and putting my personal story down on paper."

"I understand. Writing a book is much harder than most people realize."

He studied her. "You've written a book?"

She nodded. "Several, but . . . they haven't been published. I write on a topic most publishers aren't too eager to print."

"Which is . . . ?"

She chewed her lip. But it was too late to take back what she'd started. "Oppression."

He lifted a brow. "What sort?"

"Racial, ethnic, and . . . gender, mostly." How would he react? Usually people either tuned in to the plight of the oppressed or tuned it out. Hers were certainly not entertaining stories of Hollywood, although John's depiction from behind the bright lights painted a darker-than-average picture of the glittering town.

"What sorts of things do you write about oppression, if you don't mind my asking?"

She lifted her chin. "I write about Americans of Japanese descent losing their homes during internment. Colored musicians and singers who aren't allowed to dine or stay in the hotels where they've performed to sold-out crowds. Women forced to give up their only livelihood when men returned home from war. Things like that."

John studied her carefully. Perhaps he was trying to decide how a woman like her would know of such things. "And yet you still write about this even though no one will publish your work?"

She met his gaze. "Yes, I still write about it. And I *have* published several articles with the American Women's Alliance and the League of Women Voters. Because, whether or not people are willing to listen, some things still need to be said."

He frowned. "But if you know people won't listen, doesn't that make the writing more challenging?"

Eliza smiled, feeling like the teacher of a student who understands far more than he realizes. "Yes, it does. But nothing of real significance is gained without a challenge, is it?"

John locked eyes with her.

Something told Eliza he was dissecting her words. It seemed to be a habit of his.

"You're right," he said finally, studying his cane. "You sound like my editor, Fred Wharton. He told me not to be afraid to write the hard stuff. He said the things my readers will find most compelling will be the things I find the most difficult to write."

Eliza smiled. "Mr. Wharton sounds like a wise man."

John nodded. "He is. You'd like him." He looked at his pages. "Now, where were we?"

"*The First Years*," Eliza said.

He stared at what he had written, but his lengthening hesitation reminded Eliza of the reason for his discomfort.

"Perhaps you could just . . . tell it to me?"

His gaze rose above the pages. A faint smile softened his handsome face. "That's the best news I've heard all week." He tossed the papers onto the table, then leaned against it. "I was born in 1904 in Cincinnati to an Italian shipbuilder and a Welsh immigrant. We were a close family. My childhood memories are good ones, but there were two things I loved most. Visiting the shipyards with my dad, and having my hero always at my side—my older brother, Will."

As Eliza wrote, John strolled toward the window. "Will was six years older than I but never treated me like a little kid. He always let me tag along, always watched out for me. But when the U.S. entered the Great War, my father and Will joined up and shipped out. I was thirteen. I . . . I never saw either of them again."

Eliza glanced up.

John pulled the curtain back and faced the window. "The war robbed me of my entire family," he said. "Not only had a battle in France claimed the lives of my father and Will, but within a year, it claimed my mother's life too. Her grief won the battle for her mind, and she died in an asylum." His voice faded away.

No surprise. He was reliving the sudden loss of his entire family, and worse, as a teenager. She knew that feeling all too well.

"When Mom and I first learned of their deaths, I did everything I could to join the army. I lied about my age repeatedly, but I always got caught. I was just too young. At the time, I didn't care that, by trying to run off and avenge my dad's and Will's deaths, I was only adding to my mother's grief. All I could think about was how the Vincent men were heroes—all but one."

In the silence that followed, Eliza finished writing, shaken by the pain of his loss. No, it wasn't his pain that shook her, but his shame. Shame that was undeserved.

Unlike hers.

She felt such relief at the news of Ralph's death that she may as well have fired the shot that killed him. That relief had haunted her dreams ever since.

As John ambled to the fireplace, Eliza wrestled her shame back to the shadows where it had come from.

He toyed with the knickknacks on the mantel. "But perhaps I don't need to include all that about my family in the book."

"Why not?" Eliza said. "I think it's important—it shows your readers who you are."

John ran a finger over the glass covering the clock face. "Talking about losing my entire family in one year—it might sound like I'm trying to excuse . . ." He shook his head. "It's not my intention to paint myself in a sympathetic light, Mrs. Saunderson. There's no excusing the life I chose, the things I've done."

As he tinkered with the clock, Eliza let his words sink in, wondered at his hesitation. It didn't make sense. "If I were reading this, I wouldn't think that."

"A lot of people suffer. It's no excuse for living a reckless life."

Stunned, Eliza stared at the loops and curves of shorthand in her lap. "I also lost both of my parents when I was young," she said. "In a train accident. I was eighteen. I don't think anyone who suffers such a loss can ever be the same. Especially a young person. It changes who you are. It changes a great many things."

Things like the survival options Eliza had to choose from upon graduating high school: marry Ralph or move in with Betty and her new husband—an option Betty had not encouraged.

John turned and studied her, incredulous. "You lost your parents *and* your husband?"

She nodded. Why had she inserted herself into the conversation when they had a book to write?

"I'm very sorry to hear that," John said, voice soft.

"Thank you. And if you don't mind my saying, I think you should leave it in."

"Well, perhaps. For now." John turned and paced the room. "Where were we? When my mother passed, I was fourteen and on my own. I wasn't the only one hopping trains, looking for work, but I was probably one of the youngest. The need to stay alive brought my high school education to an early end. I hadn't meant to ride the rails as long as I did. I only meant to sock away enough money so I could finish high school and maybe go to college. But when train hopping led me to New York in '22, my plans changed. I no longer cared about school—I had discovered the theater. At eighteen, the thrill of the stage claimed my dreams, both waking and sleeping. And then, along came . . ."

Eliza finished the line and looked up, waiting.

"Scratch that last line." He stood in front of a bookcase, face stony.

She continued to wait, but John remained silent. "What came along?" she ventured.

He sighed. "It's not something I'm proud of, Mrs. Saunderson. I'm . . . not eager to see it in print."

Something in his tone made her sad, though she had no idea why. At least he was honest with himself. But wasn't it his aim to be honest with his readers as well? "What do you want people to come away with after reading your story?"

His gaze met hers. "That with God, there is hope of redemption—for all of us. Even for the worst of sinners."

Redemption? Of course she expected to hear of his religious conversion at some point in the book. She just didn't understand why he was so intent on telling others about it. "Well then, I think that in order for people to appreciate your . . . message of hope, you need to show us what hopelessness looked like."

John closed his eyes, then nodded. "Yes, I believe you're right."

A sound from the sitting room made Eliza aware of someone's presence.

Millie hovered at a lamp near a sitting room window with her feather duster, flicking at a spot here and there, still humming.

John blasted out a breath. "And then along came Stella."

Eliza turned away from him and wrote at her desk. Perhaps not looking at him as he spoke would help him say the more difficult things. "Who?"

"Stella Beatty."

The name seemed vaguely familiar, but Eliza couldn't place it. "Who was that?"

"Stella was a retired actress, a widow twenty years my senior. She was many things. She was my acting coach, my mentor, my banker, my foot in the door, the one who pulled strings and got me screen tests. She had important connections. She came up with my stage name, my look, my walk, my voice—everything."

Eliza finished writing.

John remained silent.

"And . . . ?" She peeked over her shoulder. Surely there was more, but she wasn't sure she wanted to hear it.

John stared at the book spines on the shelves. "We were lovers. I'm sure the relationship is no secret, thanks to Louella Parsons and her gossip column."

And so begins the sordid details. Eliza wrote, and when she finished, she glanced up.

He fiddled with something on the bookcase, looking like he needed something—a drink perhaps. A strong one.

"Go on," she said lightly, trying to picture the woman. She would have been beautiful and fascinating and glamorous, of course.

John shook his head. "It's not a pretty story."

Eliza studied him. What did that matter now? There was probably little John could reveal to his readers that wasn't already known. After all this time, he was worried about what people would think of him?

No—he said he didn't want to paint himself in a sympathetic light, and she believed him. He wasn't looking to impress anyone. The book was some kind of confession, as he had claimed.

Duncan appeared in the library doorway. "Beg your pardon, Mr. John. I have today's mail." He handed a stack of letters to John, then tugged his cap at Eliza and ambled away.

John shuffled through the mail. He stopped at one point and drew out a small, pink envelope. He slipped it into his pocket, then went to his chair and tossed the rest of the mail onto the table. "Where were we?"

She read back over what she'd written. "You said Stella was twenty years your senior. How old did you say you were?"

"Eighteen." He picked up a piece of mail, then went to the fireplace and opened it.

Eliza's stomach did a little twist. "She was thirty-eight?"

"I know how it sounds."

"Do you?" Eliza bit her lip.

He flashed her a look. "You don't think I know how much more disgusting that makes it?"

In spite of his rebuke, Eliza's thoughts whirled. Disgust was only part of what she felt, but what could she say? It was none of her business.

John studied her and then turned away. "I'm very sorry, Mrs. Saunderson, I shouldn't have snapped at you. I'd just . . . rather not mention the relationship, because even though it's true, some people might find it too sordid. And others will just find it entertaining."

She wasn't the least bit entertained. The idea of an older woman involving herself with so young a man sickened her, no matter the reason. Maybe Eliza was naïve to the ways of the industry, but getting mixed up with someone young and impressionable was wrong in any social sphere.

"Why did she do it?" she asked. "I mean, why did she help your acting career like that?"

He shrugged. "I guess she saw something she thought was worth gambling on. A sure way to make a name."

Eliza huffed. "A name for whom?"

"For us both, I imagine."

"So she used you." Had she just said that aloud?

"That's how things work in show biz." He turned and glanced at her notepad. "You're not writing that, are you?"

"No." Why was getting information out of him like coaxing a stray cat inside? "It just sounds to me like Stella was a greedy woman who took advantage of a kid who really needed—" Eliza's breath caught. She'd probably just spoken her mind right out of her job.

"Sure, I was little more than a kid, but it's not as if I wasn't willing." His words sounded flat.

Was John taking the blame for the relationship? *It's none of your business, Eliza, let it go . . . Don't be foolish . . .* "No," Eliza said, shaking her head, marveling at her own audacity.

"No?" He frowned.

"She held a position of power over you. She *used* you."

John threw her a look, then limped to the window and opened it. He kept his back to her. "You're right, but I've forgiven her. And while I intend to be truthful, I don't intend to cast blame on others for things I've done."

"But I believe it's important to give the whole story. It explains—"

"It excuses."

Millie cleared her throat from the doorway. "Lunch is served, Mr. John, Miz Eliza."

John mopped his brow with a handkerchief and

gestured with it toward the dining room. "After you."

She could hear Betty now. *Stop getting yourself mixed up in his story, Eliza. You're only here to type a book.*

> It's easier to believe you're running a race than it is to admit you're just running.
>
> ~*The Devine Truth: A Memoir*

As Eliza entered her building that evening, Joan met her on her way out. "Heya, toots, there was a telephone call for you earlier." She pushed the knot of her neck scarf to one side. "Some man. Didn't sound too promising, though. I'd give that fella the heave-ho if I were you."

What man would call her, unless . . . John? No, he would have no reason to call her after hours. But wouldn't that be something if it *was* him, and Joan had talked to a famous film star without knowing it?

She stifled a smile at the idea, then realized Betty had probably given Eliza's telephone number to Ed's friend Stanley. She grimaced. "Did he give his name?"

"Nope. He just said he'd be in touch. Oh, and he said he hoped you enjoyed the matinee." She winked.

Joan sauntered out, leaving Eliza alone with her numbness.

So she *was* being followed outside the theater.

By whom? And why? Thoughts whirling, she climbed the stairs. How had the man gotten this number? Did he know where she lived?

At her door, she froze. What if he was in her room now?

With fumbling hands, she unlocked her door and peeked inside, staying out on the landing just in case. Why would he be following her? She'd heard of men who targeted women. Especially single ones living on their own. Too bad she didn't have a brother or an uncle. Of course, there was Betty's husband, but Ed Cunningham was a placid, preoccupied man, whom she couldn't picture fighting with some trench-coated masher. Besides, Ed and Betty lived an hour away. No, if she was going to prove that women were complete and capable in their own right, she would have to deal with things like this herself.

Fortunately, the only male lying in wait for her was one hungry tomcat.

When Eliza arrived the next day, John was on the telephone at the other end of the library. As she waited for him to finish, she read over her typed pages and tried not to listen in on John's conversation, but his tone made it impossible not to.

"No," he said with slow, deliberate patience, as though he were speaking to an unreasonable child. "As I said, I only know what I've already told you. I don't know any subversive anti-Americans. In fact, I've never even met one. Are you sure there are any?"

Eliza met his gaze inadvertently.

John opened his mouth to speak but then clamped it shut, lips pressed tight as he listened. "Now you're twisting my words. You know that's not what I meant." He listened for a few more seconds, shaking his head. "Look, I'm sure you have far more important things to do. I know *I* do, so let me make it easy for us both and say goodbye. That's right. You have a good day now." He hung up the telephone, but he stared at the receiver as if he wanted to toss it across the room.

Eliza turned to her typewriter, curiosity swelling.

John came to her desk. "Still typing yesterday's notes?"

"It's finished, I'm just looking it over. Was that something about the book?" *And that's the best you could do? Surely the man can spot a nosy female a mile away.*

"It's this McCarthy fiasco. Ever since the Rosenberg executions, there's been a pack of bloodhounds at the House Un-American Activities Committee devoted to sniffing out communists in Hollywood." He shook his head. "They even have a small deputation in Berkeley. They've set up a temporary headquarters at the

110

Shattuck Hotel. Apparently, they can spy on entertainers *and* intellectuals from there."

Even though he no longer worked in film, could John be affected by the heightened scrutiny on Hollywood?

"I don't know why Eisenhower puts up with McCarthy's nonsense," he said. "The man accused the entire Truman administration of being communists. And he's still running around like a lunatic with the authority to accuse anyone who sneezes of being a commie."

The execution of Julius and Ethel Rosenberg earlier that summer had sent a fearful hush rippling out across the country. Eliza had heard about it in the newsreels. And the papers reported that a growing number of citizens were afraid of the suspicious eye of Senator McCarthy and the HUAC. With actors being blacklisted, many in Hollywood feared they would be next.

"Have any of your friends been affected?" she asked.

"Just about everyone I know is being questioned, and I've known a lot people in this industry. People whose political interests are none of my concern. Did you know they blacklisted John Garfield? I worked with him and never heard him say a word about being a communist."

Eliza had read about Garfield. "I heard he died of a heart attack last year."

John nodded gravely. "People think his death had something to do with this whole Red Scare debacle." He shook his head. "He was only thirty-nine."

How could the government continue to support such paranoia? Rumor had it many people questioned whether or not Ethel Rosenberg was even guilty of her husband's crimes. If they could convict and execute someone on weak evidence, what did that mean for others under scrutiny?

"Are they going to accuse you too?"

John strolled to the window. "I don't care if they do. I'm not a communist. They've been trying to get me to name names, but I've already told them everything I know, which isn't much." He turned to her. "Listen, I'm sorry. I shouldn't get so hot under the collar. I'm sure McCarthy's witch-hunt will run out of steam eventually." Muttering, he added, "I'm praying it does."

Millie came in carrying a tray. "Such a fine day. I thought you two might wanna work outside. Enjoy the last of that warm, sweet breeze 'fore it gone."

"Excellent timing, Millie, thank you." John exhaled a long sigh. "Here, let me get the door." He ushered them outside to the garden.

He and Eliza each took a seat, while Millie set a plate of golden macaroons on the wrought iron table and poured two glasses of lemonade. She left the pitcher with them and hugged her empty tray. "Anything else you two be needin'?"

"This is perfect, Millie." John leaned back, his smile relaxed. "Thank you."

Millie shuffled into the house, humming a lively tune.

Eliza grinned. That old woman had to be an angel—if there were such a thing. She tucked a tickling curl behind her ear. With her notepad and pencil in hand, she turned to John.

His eyes were fixed on her. He quickly looked away. "So, where did we leave off, Mrs. Saunderson?"

She cringed inwardly. It was good that he addressed her formally; it kept things professional. But still, something felt so aloof about it, as though he were pointing out that she was from a different social class, someone outside his celebrity sphere.

She read the last page back to him.

John began with how he tried to move on with his career after Stella left.

"When? How?" Eliza put her notepad down. "It's your story, but you can't just skip over *that*. Which one of you broke it off?"

John lifted his gaze slowly and studied her from beneath those dark lashes.

Something in Eliza's chest fluttered. *Cut that out. Next you'll be swooning.*

"*I* ended it. And let's just say she wasn't ecstatic about it."

"Why did you break it off? I mean—" Eliza set her pencil on the table with great exaggeration. "If you don't mind my asking."

He looked at her pencil. "Off the record?"

She nodded. His readers may forever wonder what happened, but she wasn't writing another word until she knew.

John sighed. "All right. I finally got fed up with her using me to line her pocketbook."

"Wise decision." Eliza took up her pencil, biting her lip to hide a smile. She took notes as John went on.

After Stella left, he continued to audition on his own as "Johnny Devine" and failed every audition—no surprise, since Stella had taken her clout and left unhappy—but then in 1925, he got a lucky break with the American Laboratory Theatre in New York. Former Moscow Art Theatre members Richard Boleslavsky and Maria Ouspenskaya took Johnny under their wing. There he learned Stanislavski's system, known later as Method acting, a style that helped create some of the world's most renowned stars.

When an MGM scout spotted him performing at "The Lab," he invited Johnny to Hollywood to audition. Johnny went west, and though he failed that screen test, he found enough bit parts and odd jobs on studio sets to stay alive. Also, he discovered a new hero: Charlie Chaplin. By this time, Johnny was passing screen tests, and agents had begun to take notice. Working at DeMille Pictures, as it was known at the time, he met Cecil B. DeMille one day while working on a set.

After giving Johnny some tips on making it in pictures, DeMille cast him as an extra in *The Godless Girl*. From there, he started working in other silent films, then graduated to talkies in the 1930s at a time when many big name male stars were washed up because they didn't have the voice to make the transition to sound. Johnny Devine's face and voice suddenly landed him better parts. He began working with top-billed stars, and though he wasn't yet a household name like Douglas Fairbanks or Clark Gable, he was becoming known well enough to be recognized in public.

John leaned back with glass in hand, as though thinking about what to say next.

In the silence, Eliza took a moment to reread her notes, all the while marveling at this inside glimpse of Hollywood. John was eating one of Millie's cookies, so Eliza reached for one and took a bite. She hadn't had a macaroon since Mama was alive. The toasted outside and soft, chewy inside melted in her mouth. Eliza closed her eyes and savored the taste of coconut and almond. "I can't cook worth beans, and I don't have a grandmother," Eliza said between bites. "I may just have to adopt Millie." She reached for her lemonade.

John chuckled. "Sorry, but her twelve grand-children might have something to say about that." He looked across the garden to the tree line bordering the south side of the property. His face sobered. He turned and pushed the plate of cookies toward Eliza. "Say, why don't you take these home? Millie always makes far too much. It would cheer her up to know someone will use them."

Eliza pushed her glasses higher and eyed him. "Millie needs cheering up about her cookies?"

"Sure. She's adamant about not letting anything go to waste. She single-handedly saw her entire family through the Depression."

"Did she? What an amazing woman," Eliza said. "So then . . . why does she keep making too much?"

John took a moment to think about that, then he chuckled. "You got me."

Eliza hadn't forgotten Millie's speech about being thrown out to beg in the street. "In danger of losing her job, my foot." She laughed. "You know, you're not the only actor in this house."

"You're right. That *was* an Oscar-worthy performance if ever I saw one."

Eliza looked down at her notes but couldn't help smiling. Millie was something else. And if given a choice, Eliza wouldn't have her any other way.

When she glanced up, John's eyes met hers and held, as if seized by some unseen force.

Her heart skittered double-time.

With a frown, he reached for his glass but didn't raise it, just stroked away beads of condensation. "Now then, where did we leave off?"

John dictated and Eliza wrote until they had composed another page.

She was still jotting the last few lines when John reached for his cane and stood. "If you'll excuse me, I have some things to attend to. I won't be long."

"Of course. I'll just go inside and type these pages."

John nodded and left. Instead of going into the house, he passed the front door and continued along the stone path toward the driveway. Perhaps he was going to see Duncan.

Eliza headed for the house, but as she reached the door, she heard John's voice and stopped. She peered around the bushes but didn't see anyone with him. Strange.

When John came into the library a little later, Eliza had finished typing his notes. "Where were we?" he asked, taking his seat by the fireplace. He placed a small notebook on the table. He looked spent.

"Hollywood, the early 1930s. You were fast becoming a recognized name."

John stared into the water glass Millie had left for him. "I'm not sure what to talk about next."

"Why don't you start with some of your films?"

He stared across the room. "Yes, I suppose that's about when things really began to unravel."

Eliza turned away and worked at her desk. Perhaps that would make it easier for him.

"My first big break was on the film *The Pearl of Kuri Bay*. Fans went bananas over what Louella Parsons dubbed an 'explosively passionate couple' in her article—along with a few other nicknames she coined for me."

Eliza tried but couldn't contain her pesky curiosity about the other half of this *explosively passionate couple*. "I'm not familiar with that film," she said, her cheeks cooking. "Who was your co-star?"

John took a sip of water. "Deborah Marlow."

Heart thumping, Eliza wrote the actress's name, but in her mind's eye, she saw the gorgeous blonde from the matinee—her charisma, her raw emotion. Eliza might have guessed Deborah Marlow was the one. And the columnist was right. *Explosively passionate* described that toe-tingling kiss between Deborah and John, right down to the—

"Mrs. Saunderson?"

With a jolt, she turned. "Yes?"

"I said, 'Are you ready for me to continue?' "

"I'm sorry, yes."

John went on and listed a number of films and directors, stopping at times to look in his notebook to check his dates.

"Is that an earlier draft of your book?" Eliza nodded at the notebook.

"No, it's my journal," he said. "Some thoughts, reflections, a few prayers sprinkled in. But in a way, I suppose it's like a draft. Most of what's going into my memoir comes straight from this."

"I kept a journal after my parents' deaths," she said. "My way of breaking reality down into more manageable pieces."

"The reality of all you'd lost."

She glanced up. "Yes. Actually, it was more of an ongoing letter to my mama."

Until Ralph tossed it in the trash. Because, according to him, anything that took Eliza away from attending to his needs was a waste of time.

She swallowed the sting and readied her pencil. "What next?"

"Yes. Well, in spite of my growing success, something was off-kilter. And getting worse. I'd never gotten over how Stella had used me, and now, others were lined up to do the same. Two-timing agents. Dames who only wanted to be kept in high style. Studio owners who wanted to control my every move, my life. I no longer knew who I could trust. On top of that, I worried constantly about my acting. I wondered if I was being sought after for my talent or just for the

119

image the studio had created. Any time a critic doubted my talent, I pushed myself to the limits to prove I was either a superstar or a complete fraud, one or the other. I started drinking and staying out all night. I'd show up on the set at the last minute, wearing last night's clothes, hungover and scrambling to remember my lines. Honestly, I don't know how I pulled it off, but somehow, I did. I wasn't going to let anyone tell me I was no good. I was the only one allowed to do that." John swirled the water in his glass. "And throughout all that, there were women."

Eliza kept her expression even. *You're just here to type a book. And you're being paid well to do it.* She gripped her pencil and waited.

John rose and went to the window. "But that's all I'm going to say about that for now."

Exhaling her relief, Eliza nodded.

"About that time, I met Oscar Silva." John turned toward Eliza. "From the moment he signed on as my agent, I gave that man a steep uphill run for his money. He could barely keep up with all the scandals. Oscar saved my backside more times than I can count, and he saved the studio a lot of bad press. They didn't want to lose all those ticket-buying fans by letting it leak that I—"

Air hissed from between his gritted teeth, and he returned to the window.

She kept her eyes on the page in front of her.

Avoiding eye contact kept things comfortable. And not just for John.

"That I never slept in the same place twice."

She wrote it exactly as he said it, but the marks on the page could not convey the shame in his voice.

"Anyway," he went on, "I was a louse. I still don't know why Oscar stayed with me as long as he did."

It seemed John was no longer dictating, but talking to her. She looked up.

"As a matter of fact, we're still friends to this day, though I certainly don't deserve his friendship. Shows you his caliber. He's a good man." He let out a sigh. "A very good, honorable man."

Her gaze locked onto his, and something tugged in her chest. The idea of John admiring another man for his goodness and honor made her heart heavy.

Everyone knows a realistic actor is either a very good liar or a very poor one.

~The Devine Truth: A Memoir

9

By the end of the week, Eliza and John had fallen into a working rhythm. Friday afternoon, when they had finished their dictation for the day, Eliza read back over her notes, then turned to John. "Can I read this last section back to you?"

"What am I listening for?"

"I'm thinking we should insert a little more detail, give the reader the feeling you're inviting him or her into your inner circle, so to speak. That's what you want in a memoir." She tapped her pencil on her pad, ideas already forming for a couple of spots where he could engage the reader more.

"Mrs. Saunderson . . ."

She met his gaze.

John leaned forward in his chair. "I don't believe I've thanked you for all the hard work you've been putting into this." He looked into her eyes and smiled. "I'm beginning to think your name should be on the cover, not mine."

Eliza had often made a point to avoid those

penetrating dark eyes, especially when they probed hers like this, and she had succeeded— most of the time. But she couldn't ignore his words of praise, which spread through her now like warm cocoa. She'd always been a sucker for a kind word. There hadn't been an overabundance of them lately.

Who was she kidding? There hadn't been any at all.

"I'm just putting your words on paper," she said, easing the words carefully around the sudden lump in her throat. "And I know you're just pulling my leg. Your name alone will sell a million copies. I bet as soon as this book hits the shelves, everyone will be clamoring for you to make a comeback."

With a harsh laugh, John shook his head. "Not interested. In fact, just between you and me, sometimes I wish God would make the fame disappear. But then I remember I should be grateful, because that fame will probably help get this story into more people's hands."

"That's guaranteed." Eliza put her notepad down and rubbed her neck. "Must be nice to have a name that sells books before they're even written." She gasped, cheeks instantly on fire. What a thoughtless thing to say. "I'm so sorry, that was incredibly rude—"

"No, please, don't apologize. I completely agree." He reached for his cane and examined the smooth, curved handle. "If it were a matter of my writing merit alone—well, we both know there's not a publisher who would touch it."

She couldn't look at him, but from the corner of her eye, she saw John rise.

Millie came in with a tray of iced tea and molasses cookies. Quietly, she set it down and headed back to the kitchen.

John watched Millie leave, then turned to Eliza. "Have you been paid yet?"

She set her notepad down. "I pick up my first paycheck today," she said. There had to be something else they could talk about, something besides being paid to write.

"Your agency is billing me, so I'm sure they'll take care of it," he said. "But I'd still like to be sure they're giving you the proper rate for collaboration." He looked into her eyes. "You'll let me know if they don't?"

"I'm sure I won't need to trouble you, but thank you."

He turned his gaze in the direction Millie had gone. "She's been widowed many years. Her life isn't easy. But she says, because of her family, she couldn't ask for a single thing more."

Eliza simply nodded. What was on his mind? This was the time of day when she usually switched to typing the day's notes, leaving John free to go about other business. Yet today, he didn't seem to be in any hurry to go.

"Do you have any other family, Mrs. Saunderson?"

Why did he want to know that? But at least the topic was better than talking about scratching out an existence as a no-name writer. "I have a sister." Eliza turned, put a sheet of paper in the typewriter, and propped her notepad on the easel. "And she has a family."

A perfect family. And she keeps a perfect home and throws perfect lawn parties and wears perfectly matching pearls and a perpetual smile in perfectly correct social circles.

Eliza looked over her shoulder at John. Surely he was only being attentive to be polite.

John nodded. "I'm just curious, of course. I mean, why a kind, intelligent young woman such as yourself would choose a career instead of . . ." He shook his head. "My apologies. It's none of my business."

She silently agreed—it *was* none of his business. And yet, society deemed a woman's role as a housewife to be implicit and, therefore, everyone's business.

"I'm sorry, I meant no offense," John said. Without waiting for a response, he headed out of the library, the steady *thunk* of his cane echoing on the wood floor.

Was it really so strange for a woman to *choose* to work instead of making a home and serving a husband and family?

Of course it was strange. When television portrayed Harriet Nelson as the happy modern woman, who would consider doing anything else?

Eliza wasn't opposed to family. It was just that, during the past fifteen years, she'd forgotten what family felt like.

Almost forgotten. Some longings hovered like a shadow, close but untouchable. *A baby would have made being married to Ralph worth it.*

A lump formed in her throat. No one knew of her silent longing, not even Betty. Closing her eyes, she forced the thought away. No, she wasn't opposed to family. But family meant marriage, and she certainly didn't want marriage if it meant a life of shackles and lies.

After stopping for her paycheck, Eliza got off the bus at the market near the Laurel Theater and picked up a few groceries. The feeling of money in her pocketbook was sweet, almost as sweet as the Nestlé bar she'd bought for later. She also bought a can of tuna for Mr. Darcy, just in case.

The stray tom must have had some kind of feline sixth sense, because when she arrived home, Darcy was on her balcony drinking from the water dish she'd left out. He looked startled to see her, but he stood still, watching her movements through the glass.

"Pickin's must be slim if you're back for bread

and water, huh? Well, I've got something I think you'll like a whole lot better." She dug through the sacks until she found the tuna, opened the can, and piled the meat high onto one of her two plates. With slow, even steps, she took the plate to the door, being careful not to frighten him.

He watched her approach, wary but curious, nose lifted high as if trying to smell through the glass.

Eliza chuckled. She set the plate down, stepped aside, and slowly opened the door.

The cat sniffed the air again, ducked his head a few times and listened, looked around the doorway, then ventured inside. He gave Eliza's pumps a glance, then went straight to the dish and dug in.

"We have to stick together, Darcy," she said. "Everything isn't served to us on a silver platter. We have to look out for each other." Humming, she unpacked the groceries, stacking coffee, cereal, and canned milk around the sideboard. In addition to the Nestlé bar, she'd also splurged on a couple of oranges.

A girl just needed something fresh and juicy once in a while.

While her coffee pot perked, she checked on the cat.

His bent tail quivered in little circles as he ate his fish.

Eliza got to the end of the song and laughed.

She'd been humming one of Millie's hymns. Had the old woman intended to get "What a Friend We Have in Jesus" stuck in Eliza's head? As she put away the rest of her purchases, she thought about Millie and her steadfast calm and wise words.

Why was she so content? Was it because she had family surrounding her, as John had said? How had Millie managed all those years working as a maid while taking care of her family—by herself, no less—and despite the kinds of societal oppression she must have faced as a colored woman? Was being a maid the kind of life she'd always wanted, what she'd dreamed of as a little girl? She must have been born in the 1870s. Would a young girl like Millie have had big dreams for herself in those days? Or had she grown up simply accepting her lot in life and knowing no other choice but to make the best of it?

Had she found religion useful?

Eliza's parents had never said much on the topic of religion. They had neither supported nor renounced Christianity or any other forms of faith. They were of the mind that people were morally accountable to their own beliefs, and that good morals were important to strong families and a well-functioning society.

But where had they gotten their morals? Eliza never had the opportunity to discuss such things with them.

128

A knock on the door startled her. When she opened it, the super stood on the landing.

"You got a caller on the line. I said I'd get you this time, since I seen you come in, but just so you know, I ain't no answering service. Especially when your rent's past due."

"I have the rent," she said. "Just a minute." Eliza retrieved her handbag, counted out twenty-five dollars, and handed it to him. While he counted it, Eliza eyed the cat to be sure his feline curiosity didn't bring him to the door, where he could be seen.

The super stuffed the money in his pocket. "Well, I still ain't taking no phone messages, and I sure ain't climbing these stairs every time you got a call."

Eliza stepped past him, closed her door, then headed for the stairs.

"I ain't no receptionist, and this ain't no sorority house," he hollered from the landing.

She hurried down the stairs to the telephone, biting her tongue. No one would ever mistake this place for a sorority house. "This is Mrs. Saunderson," she said into the receiver.

"What's your other name?" A man's voice.

A chill prickled her spine. Theater man—she was certain of it. "Who is this?"

"Don't bother, I already know who you are. Just giving you a chance to come clean."

Eliza frowned. "About what?"

129

"About who you *really* are." He drew out each word. *"E . . . J . . . Peterson."*

Her jaw dropped. Only a few editors knew that Eliza Saunderson was E.J. Peterson. "Who are you?" she asked again. A little zap cinched her nerves. "And why were you following me?"

"I'll ask the questions," the man said. "Who's funding you? An underground group?"

"Funding me for what?"

"How long have you been writing propaganda?"

How had he gotten her telephone number? Eliza looked around.

The entry door at the end of the lobby opened.

Her heart raced.

Ivy came in with a teenybopper in a pink poodle skirt.

"Look, you've got things mixed up, so I'd appreciate it if you'd stop—"

"You write articles about equal rights for minorities."

Eliza gasped. "What?"

"The sad plight of dames, Japs, and coloreds. Isn't that right?"

Eliza tried to answer but couldn't get air past the anger in her throat.

"You sneak around in the shadows—spreading subversive ideas—long enough, and we'll find you. Now why don't you make it easy on us both and admit you're E.J. Peterson and you're writing commie propaganda."

The hallway swayed, and Eliza took a step back to steady herself. "You're mistaken. I'm not a communist."

Ivy and the other girl stopped talking and stared at Eliza.

"How did you get my—?"

"The AWA has longstanding commie ties. Tell me who's paying you to write this stuff. I want all your Red contacts."

"The American *Women's* Alliance? They are no more communist than . . ." Eliza had to stop and think. If this man was from the HUAC, he probably thought *everyone* was communist.

"You're forgetting I've done my homework, *E.J.,*" he said slowly.

He had found her through her articles, somehow. "Well, you didn't do a very good job, because I don't write propaganda and I sure don't know anything about the AWA having communist ties."

"I have a stack of files on my desk that says otherwise."

How was that possible? Did these people make this stuff up? If so, then it would be best to deny anything that could be twisted and used against her. "I'm afraid you're mistaken about me. So, please—"

"You're going on record as a hostile witness?"

She heard the sound of a pencil scratching on paper. "No, I mean I'm not—look, whoever you are, I don't know what you're talking about. Don't call again." She hung up.

The girls whispered to each other, eyeing her.

Propaganda? How was writing about injustice considered communist propaganda? Was this a joke? Or was she truly coming under suspicion?

The newsreel picture of Ethel Rosenberg's grim face just before she and her husband went to the electric chair flashed through Eliza's mind.

No. There had been some kind of mistake, that was all there was to it. A mistake that would sort itself out as soon as this man realized the AWA was an organization that supported women. Nothing more.

> Even with all that fame, all I had to show for my life was a stack of films and a long line of women who wished I'd never been born.
> ~*The Devine Truth: A Memoir*

10

On Monday, dictation went slower than molasses in winter. John sat in his chair, head back, staring at the ceiling. He started a few times, but then took back what he said, saying "scratch that."

Eliza basked in the warmth of the sun pouring in from the window behind her and waited, giving him time to think. Yet, after nearly half an hour of pondering, John remained silent.

"What about your film awards?" she prompted. "Which picture earned you your first?" She sounded more like a journalist than a typist, but it would be good to get him talking.

John leaned forward in his chair. "I won an Academy Award and Golden Globe for the film *Sweet Revenge*. My fourth major film." He heaved a tired sigh.

Why was he so reticent today? "I saw that one. You played an angry lawyer, if I remember right."

John huffed out a laugh. "Yes, an example of

133

Stanislavski's influence. I played the role of a defense lawyer who became disillusioned with the whole court system when he found out that justice was never intended for his client."

"I remember," Eliza said. "She was on trial for killing her husband."

John nodded. "She was a battered wife and was completely candid with the courts about what happened and why she finally did what she did. But the judge didn't want to hear her side. He only wanted to make an example of her. He was a chauvinist. With a gavel."

Ralph's red, angry face came to mind, but Eliza forced it away. She wrote the title, glad her gaze had somewhere to be, thankful that John couldn't see the heat flooding her cheeks.

Of course, relief over someone's death wasn't the *same* thing as actually killing him. But sometimes, when the nightmares came, Eliza couldn't tell the difference.

John turned a letter opener over and over as he recounted more of his films, then put the silver-handled tool down and leaned back with a sigh. "I'm sorry, I really don't want to hear about myself right now. Let's talk about something else. What about you? You're an author taking months out of your life to write someone else's book, every day, week after week."

Eliza glanced at him. Had he forgotten he was on a tight deadline? "Yes?"

"Doesn't it interfere with your life?"

What life? "I'm thankful to have a job."

John picked up the opener again and worked on a piece of mail. "Do you have to work? I mean, surely you have other income."

What an odd question—of course she had to work, like any other single, working-class girl. Unless she inherited wealth or received royalties, like John probably did, a girl had to work. Or get married. "Yes, I have to work."

"I'm sorry, it's probably none of my business, but I'm curious as to why. A soldier's death benefit should be more than enough to take care of his widow."

Eliza doodled on the notepad, making boxes inside of boxes until there was no room left at the center. "I am unable to receive Ralph's death benefit."

"Why?"

Not only was it none of his business, it was odd that he was so interested in her personal affairs. Eliza started another nest of boxes. "Ralph named someone else as his beneficiary." She glanced up.

John stared at her, his face a mask of disbelief. "How is that possible? Who?"

Millie stood in the other room holding a candlestick holder in one hand and a polishing cloth in the other. She was staring at the cloth, but seemed to be waiting. Listening.

135

Swell—an audience to witness her humiliation. "The beneficiary was a . . . woman with whom he'd fathered a child."

The candle fell from the holder with a thud.

John stared at Eliza, his frown deepening.

Eliza readied her pencil. Perhaps John had detoured long enough to get back to his manuscript. She didn't want to talk about herself either.

"So you've been supporting yourself on your own for eight years?" John asked.

"Ten. Ralph died in forty-three, two years after he went to war." She hoped the words hadn't sounded as bitter as they tasted.

John's gaze fell to his open Bible. "A man takes care of those he's responsible for. If he's any kind of man." He rose and limped to the window.

Eliza stared at John's tall frame. Who was this man? By his own admission, he'd been a selfish, irresponsible louse. But whatever he had once been, he clearly wasn't now. In fact, the more time Eliza spent with him, the harder it was to believe that the man at the window and Johnny Devine had ever been the same person.

Tuesday morning, John resumed his pacing and pondering. At least, Eliza *hoped* he was pondering, because at the end of the first hour, she was still staring at a blank page.

The scent of baking apples wafted into the library, rousing Eliza's hunger. She'd eaten breakfast, but corn flakes in canned milk was like eating a bowl of sand compared to Millie's cooking. Which John had insisted Eliza accept as part of her pay.

John stopped at a bookcase, pulled out a book, examined the flyleaf, put it back, and got another.

"Writer's block?"

John's head snapped up. "Sorry?"

Eliza lifted her pad and showed him the blank page.

He studied her notepad for a moment, then went to his chair and eased himself onto it. He leaned his cane against the table. "I didn't want to tell you at the time so as not to alarm you," he said, "but I sent the chapters you've typed so far to Fred Wharton, my editor."

Heart in her throat, Eliza stared at him. "And?"

"I just heard back, and he loves it." John leaned back in his seat. "In fact, he wants to meet you."

Her heart raced. "Your New York editor wants to . . . *meet* me?"

John smiled. "Of course. But I told him you're a very busy, in-demand writer and would have to check your calendar."

Eliza could only stare at his handsome smile. Was he mocking her? No. With a strange certainty, she knew he would never do that.

"He's traveling to San Francisco soon and asked if you'd like to join us for lunch. I think you'd enjoy meeting him. But it's up to you. No harm done if you don't."

Duncan came in and left a stack of mail on the edge of Eliza's desk, then touched his cap and nodded at Eliza. Sniffing the air, he tromped off in the direction of the kitchen.

"Did Mr. Wharton say why he wanted to meet me?"

"No, but I'm sure it's because he knows the difference between a ten-thumb hack and a real writer. He noticed a 'phenomenal improvement' and said the writing was 'exceptional.' "

Did John resent that? No, his face was only calm and composed. "Perhaps I could meet him," she said. What was she setting herself up for?

"Excellent. Did I mention he's soon to be the publisher at Covenant Press? The business has been in the Wharton family for generations."

She gasped. *"Publisher?"*

John nodded. "His father will retire at the end of the year and will pass it down to him."

Eliza stared at the blank page, thoughts churning. The fact that John's editor wanted to meet Eliza wasn't what was slowing John down. She met his gaze. "So, what else did Mr. Wharton say about your manuscript? The part that has you stalling now?"

John studied her for a moment, then rose and came to her.

Her pulse sped.

He reached down and took the stack of mail Duncan had left on her desk and sorted through it. "You're very intuitive. Yes, Fred wants me to slow down and delve deeper into the difficult things. The things that drove me to the edge."

Eliza waited until he returned to his chair, then readied her pencil out of sight. Maybe if he thought he was only talking to her, he wouldn't let his worries about how things sounded interfere with his spoken thoughts.

"Deep down, I knew I was just a shooting star, a flash in the pan, a momentary light on the verge of burning out and disappearing without leaving a trace of anything to show for my existence. And the clearer that became, the harder I worked to be the biggest reprobate I could."

She wrote quickly. "So . . . if you can't be good, then be good at being bad. Is that it?"

John was staring at something far beyond the room. "Something like that. Yes." He turned to her. "I want people to understand that God gave me a second chance in spite of all that I'd done. I don't think it's coming across. I was aiming for rock bottom as hard and as fast as I could, and yet, in His mercy, God took hold of me and lifted me out of that pit. He forgave me. For the first time in my life, I felt real peace. I didn't get there on my own—I couldn't. It was purely God."

Eliza nodded and wrote it all. "That's good. And I know you're eager to express that message.

But I think you're getting ahead of yourself. Perhaps we should build up to that."

"You're right. I suppose I just want to hurry up and put all this behind me."

"I know."

He looked at her, expression softening. "You do?"

"Yes."

John studied her for a very long time. He sighed. "Will you please read back what you last wrote?"

As Eliza read it aloud, John closed his eyes. This was not a lying cheater. This was a man reliving things he desperately wanted to forget.

"Everything was about indulging myself," he said after she finished. "Keeping my name at top billing, playing the game but hating it, using and being used, running before a woman got too serious—or, if I'd been honest—before she got any ideas of ditching me. I tramped from one relationship to another like a stray dog, never staying in one place long for fear of being trapped. Boozing it up every night until the demons disappeared. It was as if the hounds of hell were chasing me, and I wondered how long—no, I *knew* I couldn't stay ahead of them much longer."

Eliza looked up.

John was staring at her notepad. "I'm not trying to make any excuses. I hope that's clear."

"I'm sure it will be."

"No, I mean, *you* know I'm not trying to justify what I was, don't you?"

Eliza nodded, warmed by his concern about what she thought of him.

"I accept full blame for everything I've done."

"I know," she said softly. This certainly came as no surprise.

John picked up his glass of tea and swirled it, making the ice spin. "There were women. Married, single, engaged—it didn't matter." His words came out tight, laced with regret. He set his glass down slowly, as if to give the memories time to scatter. "I married twice even though I knew it wouldn't last. There was no real commitment on my part. Both marriages ended badly."

He lapsed into silence again, giving Eliza's mind a chance to wander. With all those relationships, it was odd that John had never fathered a child. Perhaps he was infertile. Eliza had never become pregnant and had always supposed it was Ralph who was infertile. But, of course, he later proved that theory wrong.

"The sad thing is," John said, "everyone knew what I was. Including the studio. And yet everyone turned a blind eye, because reviewers adored me, other studios made competitive offers, and critics raved about the 'Devine' magnetism and charm."

"The studio turned a blind eye?" Eliza said. "But I thought your agent was always bailing you out of scandals because it looked bad for the studio."

He shook his head. "By that time, I was getting truckloads of fan mail and my fame skyrocketed. The studio ate it up and gave me a huge raise. As long as the lines at the box office were growing, studio owners looked the other way. But I guess the truth is not everyone turned a blind eye. Vivienne, my second wife, divorced me in 1940."

"Second? What about the first?"

John sighed. "I married co-star Veronica Neumann in 1934. Then in 1938, while filming *Back Alley Business*, I met another co-star, Vivienne LaPlante. Veronica didn't appreciate my habit of collecting co-stars. As soon as my divorce to Veronica was final, I married Vivienne."

Eliza started to write, but paused and looked at John.

"Yes, I suppose you should write that," he said, voice weary. "Surely everyone knows. Unfortunately, by the time my second marriage ended, I didn't even care. I was getting stone-cold drunk every night. From then on, my address was the Hollywood Roosevelt."

With another sigh, he rose and went to the fireplace. "I'd lost all sense of honor. A real man strives to leave a lasting mark in this world, you see. Make it better somehow because he was here. But I had no such ambitions, not by that time. I was topping all the charts, but even with so much fame, all I had to show for my life was a stack of films and a long line of women who wished I'd never been born. Even if I'd wanted honor, you couldn't find a trace of it in me. If there was ever a time in my life I'd longed for true significance, it was long past."

Eliza's pencil froze. True significance? The words echoed, taunting her. She had believed everything John said so far, but his last statement struck her as ludicrous. Could a Hollywood star with scores of fans truly have any concept of the quest for significance? Could a man whose name had emblazoned every marquee in the country understand the void that she—a penniless nobody—had so long struggled to fill?

Don't think, just write.

She finished his lines, then waited.

John paced the floor. "I felt vacant, no matter how much I tried to fill the emptiness with women and booze and night life. Deep down, I knew I had become something completely opposite of what my father and Will had been. I was completely careless about anyone but myself."

Eliza glanced at him.

John looked away. "There was a young starlet in 1940—Jeanette Lovell. She was pretty, eager, full of life and raw talent, but she was green. She had no insider savvy. I . . ." He crossed the room and stood at the window, leaning hard on his cane as if braced for whatever he was about to say. "It should have mattered that she was a newlywed, married to her high school sweetheart. It *would* have mattered to any kind of *real* man, but . . ."

Her eyes were clamped shut, perhaps in some childish attempt to block out what was coming next.

"Dear God," he whispered. "I can't do this."

Eliza opened her eyes as John left the library, his awkward gait more pronounced in his hurry. He headed through the sitting room and disappeared.

11

Eliza watched him leave, thoughts whirling.
What else did John have to confess? And how
much more would she have to hear?

Millie stepped into the library from the kitchen,
drying her hands on an embroidered tea towel.
"Miz Eliza? I got a small favor to ask. Might you
step in the kitchen a minute?"

"Of course." Eliza followed Millie.

At the stove, Millie picked up a dish containing
a golden, round pastry oozing with sticky syrup
and topped with sparkling sugar. A half dozen
more sat in a pan on the stove. The scent of
cinnamon filled the room.

"Somethin' funny with this batch. Could you
taste it?" Millie nudged the dish into Eliza's
hands.

Eliza took a spoonful of the pastry, tasted it,
and closed her eyes to savor the tangy blend of
spiced, sweet fruit and flaky pastry shell. "Millie,
this is marvelous. There's nothing wrong with

it." She cut another spoonful and popped it in her mouth, eyeing the old woman. "What are you trying to pull?"

Millie shrugged. "Just needed a woman's opinion, that's all."

"Mm-hmm," Eliza said, chewing. "You know what they say about lies coming back to get you later, don't you?" She licked her spoon and scooped another bite.

"Yes, ma'am."

"So you're trying to tell me you honestly think there's something wrong with this—what *is* it, by the way?"

"Apple dumplin'. All right. Truth is, this here my grandmama's recipe, and it won more blue ribbons than you can shake a stick at."

Eliza's brows rose. "Impressive. I can't even peel an apple without destroying it." She chuckled and took another bite.

"Oh, I 'spect you can, ma'am. You just need to stop listenin' to voices sayin' you can't."

Eliza swallowed hard and studied the woman who only looked frail, because anyone who knew Millie knew better. "What do you mean?"

Millie nodded at the television at the other end of the counter.

Harriet Nelson was taking a full plate of food away from Ozzie. The audience roared.

"Do you like that Ozzie and Harriet program, Miz Eliza?"

Eliza shook her head. "Not especially. I mean, I'm sure it's entertaining, but I'm afraid it encourages women to believe that they are of lesser value to society just because they're women. So many forms of oppression are not only accepted in this country, they're encouraged." She took another small bite, pondering. "I've been trying to get people to recognize the injustice of racial and gender inequality, and to show the need for change by writing about them. I don't know if I'm doing any good, but I have to do something."

"Ah." Millie nodded at the television. "But what if a nice home and all the latest things is all Miz Harriet wants?"

Eliza hesitated. Had Millie never dared to want more for herself? "But there is more to life, don't you think, Millie? Surely a nice home and fancy appliances isn't all a woman—if she's honest with herself—wants out of life?"

Millie peered into Eliza's eyes. "They's plenty worse things, ma'am."

The ridiculous irony of their conversation suddenly struck Eliza, igniting heat in her cheeks. "Millie, you don't have to call me ma'am."

Millie lifted another apple dumpling from the pan and placed it in a bowl, then added a spoon. "Maybe *you* not offended when a colored woman neglect to address you as *ma'am*, but the next white woman I meet just might be. I appreciate you want to see change. And I believe change is comin'. But it gonna take prayer and lots of grace for those folks not mature enough to accept the kind of change you want. The Bible say we not to flaunt our freedom in front of those who are weak and who may stumble and have a guilty conscience on account of what we do." Millie set the bowl on a serving tray.

Stunned, Eliza set her bowl on the counter. "Are you saying . . . the Bible tells you to be submissive to people who are too selfish or ignorant to know how wrong it is?"

"The Bible tell me many things, Miz Eliza. It tell me to be like Christ, be His aroma. Some folks find Jesus a lovely, sweet fragrance. Others run from Him like He a terrible stench. Not up to me to change folks, that the good Lord's job. The Bible also tell me 'the Lord is the portion of mine inheritance and of my cup, Thou maintainest my lot. The lines are fallen unto me in pleasant places; yea, I have a goodly heritage.' "

"If you don't mind my saying, Millie, I don't see how you can say your lot has been all that pleasant. You've suffered more than your share, I think."

Millie took a cup from the dish drainer and poured a coffee. She handed it to Eliza. "Well, if you don't mind *my* sayin', I 'spect your lot ain't been all that pleasant either. Cheatin' husband a hard thing to forgive."

148

Eliza opened her mouth but nothing would come. *Forgive?* How could she ever forgive all the lies, the cruel put-downs, the shame? Not only had Ralph humiliated her by taking up with other women, he'd fathered a child with someone else. The child that Eliza was supposed to have. What could be more painfully unjust? And to top it off, his infidelity had left Eliza penniless. Who could forgive that?

"Miz Eliza, many things in life gonna be hard to forgive, but the only thing unforgiveness give you is a burden too heavy to bear. The burden of other folks' sins *and* ours. Too many folks carryin' a load they need to get free of but can't."

"Yes, I know."

Millie tilted her head for a closer look. "Do you?"

Eliza nodded, nerves crackling at the thought of actually saying aloud the things she'd never spoken of. Living in the shadow of Ralph's cruelty had changed her, made her question herself. What was worse, he'd made her hate, and that hate had done something to her. Feeling only relief when he died wasn't the worst of it. A horrible, recurring dream had burrowed in and drove its black truth into her heart: she'd *wished* him dead. When she first heard he had died, guilt seared her at once and left a mark on her conscience like a branding iron. Yes, she had become a different person, or perhaps the truth was she had lost the better part of herself. She'd become a shell of the good person her parents had raised. "I can't forget about . . . something I'm ashamed of, and it weighs on me. Gives me nightmares sometimes."

"Precious child," Millie said softly, "you can always tell it to Jesus."

Eliza shook her head. "Oh, no. I can't even say it to myself."

Shaking her head slowly, Millie poured a second cup of coffee and set it on the tray beside the dumpling.

"Thank you for the dumpling," Eliza said. "I'd better get back to work. I'm sure he's wondering where I've gone."

Millie turned and laid a crinkly hand on Eliza's arm. "That shame you carryin'? I 'spect it too heavy for me, so I *know* it too heavy for a slip of a girl like you. The only thing strong enough to bear the weight of all we done wrong is a cross on a hill at Calvary. And not just yours and mine. Every shameful thing done by every soul that ever lived can be placed on Jesus. And He took it willingly, so you could be free, because of His great love for you, child."

Tears stung Eliza's eyes. It was an appealing idea, being loved and accepted for who she was, not *if* she improved, not *if* she became something more. But it didn't make sense. Especially when she thought about John and his story. "But if John is a Christian," Eliza said, "and he believes God has forgiven him for the things he's done, and if God takes away shame, then why does John still carry it around?"

Millie's lips pursed. She turned and placed a napkin between the dumpling and coffee cup, then picked up the tray and faced Eliza. "Couldn't say, ma'am. I 'spect he got the idea he need to punish hisself a while yet."

Over the weekend, Eliza took in a Barbara Stanwyck picture, *Christmas in Connecticut*, thankful the Laurel wasn't showing one of John's pictures this time. Then she spent most of Sunday trying to decide what to wear to her upcoming lunch meeting with John's editor. Though she was fond of red, it probably wasn't a good choice for a business meeting. She decided to press her navy suit and hang it in a bag with a few gardenia sachets—one of Betty's tips. She could always count on her sister to be the voice of etiquette in her head.

Thinking of Betty reminded Eliza she still needed to give her sister an answer to her Thanksgiving invitation. She'd been stalling, which was silly. It wasn't as if she had many options. Getting takeout from Lucky's for herself and Mr. Darcy was the alternative. But Sue Ellen and Eddie Jr. had asked if Auntie Liza would be coming, so that settled it.

Monday morning, a November chill sent Eliza back inside her apartment for a longer coat. As she walked to the bus stop, she smiled, remembering walks to school in winter with her sister. Betty had always been the first to don a longer coat and would tell Eliza to go back and get hers. To which Eliza always responded by ignoring Betty and suffering the chill all the way to school. Even then, Eliza had wanted to prove she didn't need anyone making up her mind for her.

The willows in front of John's house had turned a soft, creamy orange and were thinning, the flowing branches swaying softly like an island girl's grass skirt.

John was seated at his spot by the fireplace when she entered the library, a small book in his hand. He began speaking of the many fleeting things in life that promise heaven but don't deliver.

Eliza scrambled to put down her handbag, then picked up her notepad and wrote quickly.

"Oh, sorry, I wasn't dictating," John said. "I was just reading C.S. Lewis. Have you read him? This is his latest book." John held up the thin volume entitled *Mere Christianity*.

"I have read his novel *The Lion, the Witch and the Wardrobe* several times, but no, I have not read his religious works."

John rose with his cane and strolled toward

the hall. "Vacancy longs to be filled. It doesn't matter who you are or how full you think your life is. We all have vacancy of some kind." He glanced over his shoulder at her.

"Oh—I'm sorry, is that you now?"

A half-smile softened his face. "Yes, but you don't have to write that—I was just musing. Happens whenever I read Lewis. He has a great deal to say about life and death, the pursuit of God. Forgiveness."

Had he been talking to Millie? Eliza sat taller and readied her pencil.

With a sigh, John returned to his chair. "All right. Where were we?"

Since their last dictation session had ended so abruptly, it hadn't taken Eliza long to type what little they'd composed. And since John had never returned for the rest of the day, she'd gone back over the manuscript and made notes for building the direction of the memoir, though the details that remained were still a mystery to her.

"When we left off, you were talking about your past relationships. Particularly . . ." Eliza looked at the last page, although she didn't need to. "Jeanette Lovell."

John lowered his gaze to the Oriental rug. His expression hardened. "Perhaps we can come back to that another time. I . . . some things are . . . difficult."

When he didn't finish, Eliza nodded. "I understand. If you want to go back and insert things later, we can simply revise."

"Revise my life." John huffed. "Wouldn't that be a swell trick? If only we could." He shook his head and glanced at her. "What would you revise about your life, if you could?"

Eliza put her pencil down. "I can think of only one thing."

"Let me guess," he said. "Marrying Ralph."

"No." She shook her head and met his eye. "I wouldn't let my parents get on that train."

John numbed her with that look of his.

"That's all," she said lightly. "From then on, everything else would have turned out differently. I'd just let the rest of my life rewrite itself. Maybe even get a happily-ever-after out of it."

John's dark eyes pierced her with an intensity that made her forget how to breathe. "I'm sorry," he said.

Swallowing the ache in her throat, she picked up her pencil.

Leaning an elbow on his knee, John rested his chin in his hand. "I suppose everyone has regrets. This book is forcing me to remember every last one of mine. I have to remind myself that God has both forgiven and forgotten them all. Trouble is, people don't forget. Why is it easier to remember the bad things than it is to forget them? I wonder if it's because absolute forgiveness—all records erased—is so foreign to our nature. It's still hard for me, especially now that I'm reliving the past. I have to remind myself of all the ways God has helped me, changed me, shown me grace even though I don't deserve it. But then, no one does."

"No one? But surely there must be some who are deserving," Eliza said. "What about people who lived good lives? My parents were the kindest and most morally upright people I've ever known. Surely God values that." Her voice had risen slightly.

Millie's head popped around the doorway, probably over the pitch of Eliza's tone.

John studied her as he formed his words. "Knowing you, it's clear that your parents were very good, kind people. But no one is sinless. And God is holy. Holiness and sin can't coexist, and that creates a chasm between God and us. He is a just Judge. Yet He is also a loving Father who wants us to enjoy eternity with Him in heaven. So He made a way to for us. By trusting in Christ, we receive God's full pardon."

"Trusting in Christ?" Eliza's heart thumped. "So . . . what you're saying is that someone like *you* will be in heaven one day, but my good, honorable parents won't?"

Grimacing, John transferred his gaze to the handle of his cane, jaw muscles tensing. She'd just insulted him, but in that moment, she didn't care. If there was a heaven, her parents had more right to be there than anyone.

"We don't know what happens in a person's life during their final moments," he said, voice quiet. "None of us knows if a person is in heaven or not. But God is merciful and gives us every possible chance to surrender our lives to Him."

"Surrender?"

Surely her parents wouldn't have known about the need for that.

She fought to keep angry tears from forming. She couldn't let a man see that his words had any power over her. She'd developed superb control when Ralph was alive. Yet the tears continued to pool and now threatened to spill. In a panic, she stood and looked around the room for escape.

Millie stood near the kitchen doorway, hands clasped at her bosom. Eliza's options were Millie, the washroom, or the front door.

"God truly *is* merciful," John said. His tone beckoned like a cool stream in summer. There was a peculiar gentleness in his eyes.

"Excuse me," Eliza whispered. She darted to the front room, passed through it, and reached the dining room before the gathering tears spilled. She took off her glasses and searched for something to dry her eyes with, but there were only table linens. As she wiped her cheeks with the heel of her shaking hand, she pictured her parents waving from the train, happy, oblivious to what lay before them, both on the tracks and beyond. Where were they now? If surrendering to God and trusting in Christ truly *was* the way to heaven, had they known that?

A rustle in the room made her heart skip. She turned and met Millie's tired, kind gaze.

Without a word, Millie came closer and gently patted Eliza's shoulder.

Eliza could only stand there trembling, trying to collect her wits, oddly comforted by the old woman's silence.

John, who must have followed her, cleared his throat in the next room.

She gave her cheek another brisk swipe.

Millie handed her a small, lacy-edged handkerchief and lifted her chin to peer up at her. "You remind me of my youngest girl," she said. "She's a strong, tender heart too, just like you."

Eliza stole a glance at John as he approached and prepared herself for another blow.

He stopped at the edge of the dining room. "I'm so sorry if I upset you," he said, his voice especially deep. "I didn't mean to—"

"No, you only spoke what you believe. You needn't apologize for that. I'm the one who owes you an apology. I'm sorry for what I said to you. I . . . didn't mean that."

John glanced at Millie, then back at Eliza. "Say, would you . . . ?" He hesitated, the look on his face strangely conflicted. "I attend a small church in Kensington. It's a bit different, as it meets in the minister's home. More private that way. I'm sure you understand my need for that. Anyway, I'd like to invite you. Maybe it would help . . . answer some of your questions."

After all she'd heard about God and heaven in the past few days, she couldn't possibly hear any more.

This job was turning out to be quite the emotional roller coaster. The woman at the agency really should have warned her.

Eliza put her glasses back on and lifted her chin. "To be honest, I'm not sure I'm ready for that. Perhaps I could think it over."

John eased out a sigh. "Yes, of course. Take your time."

Millie shook her head at Eliza. "But not *too* much time. I ain't gettin' no younger."

Hollywood promises fulfillment and happily-ever-afters, but it never delivers. Yet no one seems to notice or care—we always come back for more. At times, even I bought the fantasy, and I was partly responsible for creating it.

~*The Devine Truth: A Memoir*

12

Eliza blew ripples across the surface of her coffee as people passed by on the sidewalk outside the diner. When was the last time she could order anything she wanted on the Lucky's Diner menu without first checking to see if she could pay for it? She ordered a grilled tuna and cheese on rye with extra tuna—Mr. Darcy would appreciate the leftovers—and a slice of peach pie à la mode, which couldn't possibly be anywhere near as good as Millie's.

Maybe when she was finished with John's book, she could get Millie to teach her how to—

What was she thinking? When the book was finished, the job would be over and she wouldn't see Millie again.

Or John.

Heart sinking, she sipped her coffee. It burned going down, adding to the ache that was already forming in her chest. She needed to be more careful with these temporary jobs. Not let herself get too used to things—like Millie's cooking. And steady money. Things would get tight between jobs. She needed to be better about watching her pennies, even while money was coming in. Take nothing for granted.

Someone put Nat King Cole's "Unforgettable" on the jukebox just as Greta delivered Eliza's meal. She pulled her plate closer and sipped her coffee, savoring the velvety sounds of Cole's smooth voice.

A man in a long black overcoat and fedora approached her table. The man she'd seen here before. "Mind if I join you?"

That voice—it was also the man who had telephoned her. And followed her from the theater.

Eliza shook her head, but the man slid into the seat opposite her and took off his hat, revealing short-cropped, red hair.

"No, I meant you may not join me."

"Expecting someone? One of your Red commie contacts, perhaps?"

She swept a glance around the diner and lowered her voice. "I'm not a communist, so I'd appreciate it if—"

An older woman in the next booth turned and stared at Eliza.

Unbelievable. She could end up under suspicion simply by association with this man. "Who are you, anyway? Do you have some identification?"

The man took out a wallet and showed her a card with a government emblem and the initials *HUAC*. "Bert Robinson, Field Agent." He pursed his lips and put the card away.

Eliza was not at all comforted by his credentials. "Why have you been following me?" she said, lowering her voice to a whisper. "I told you I'm not a communist. There's no reason you should think I am."

His bright-blue eyes locked onto hers. "You're mistaken. Your family is communist, and blood ties run deep." He eyed the ice cream melting on her pie.

"My *family?* Now I know you're mistaken. I'm alone." She winced at her blunder. That was the last thing she wanted a strange man to know.

"And Russian family ties run *especially* deep. Did your parents give you their contacts in the Soviet Union? You can spare yourself a lot of difficulty and embarrassment by giving us names."

"I don't know what you're talking about. My parents are dead. And they were European, not Russian." At least, not that she knew of. "And they certainly weren't communists." Her appetite had completely disappeared. Signaling to Greta for a doggy bag, Eliza grabbed her purse and stood.

The man didn't even have the decency to rise for a woman.

"I'm leaving. I'd appreciate it if you would stop bothering me."

The lady in the next booth and her husband were both fully tuned in now.

"How did they die?" the man said, ignoring her last remark.

Eliza pulled her handbag against her abdomen and wrapped her arms around her middle. "Don't you know? I thought you knew everything about me and my family."

The agent shook his head. "Just giving you a chance to shoot straight. They died on a south-bound train headed for Fresno."

"What do you know of my parents' death?" The coffee turned her stomach sour.

Greta came by with a bag and slapped it on the table. "Oh. I suppose you want your check now too." She left muttering.

The agent kept steady, narrowed eyes on Eliza. "The biggest underground commie faction on the West Coast at that time met in Fresno every year in May. When did your folks take that trip?"

She couldn't believe what this man was suggesting. Her parents were no more communist than she was. "It was May."

162

He took out a small notepad and pen. "And where'd they say they were going—family reunion?" He puffed a little nose laugh.

Eliza glared at him. "They had job interviews at Fresno State College. I'm sure it can be verified."

"Wouldn't mean much. The well-trained ones are slick."

"Well-trained in what?"

"Espionage."

"What? This is ridiculous! My parents weren't spies. They were literature teachers." Eliza glanced around the diner. Everyone was staring at her now, even Jimmy in the kitchen. She lowered her voice. "You're wrong, and you'd better get your facts straight. You have nothing but conjecture, no proof." Fumbling with her purse, Eliza took out money for her check and slammed it on the table. "Leave me alone!" She left her meal behind and walked out, willing her knees not to buckle.

"Betty, we need to talk." Eliza wrapped the telephone cord around her wrist and checked over her shoulder for eavesdroppers in the lobby.

"Oh, Eliza, I'm so glad you called. Stanley was just asking Ed about you. I think he's still in-tres-ted . . ." She sang it with a lilt in her voice.

Eliza closed her eyes. "Listen, Betty, I need to ask you something." She looked over her shoulder again. "Do you know anything about where Mama and Papa lived in Europe? Did they ever tell you where they were from?"

A hushed silence. "I know as much as you do. Why do you ask? What's this all about?"

Eliza hesitated at the odd tone in Betty's voice. How *had* that agent found Eliza? "Betty, has anyone called you or approached you about . . . me or our parents, or about anything else? Men in suits?"

"Men in suits? Darling, are you feeling all right?"

She eased out a sigh. "So you haven't talked to anyone, given them my name or telephone number?"

"Of course not. Now you're scaring me. What's going on?"

Eliza told Betty about the harassment by the HUAC agent, starting with the day she was followed at the theater and ending with his visit at the diner today.

"Oh, Eliza! How do you know he's not some lunatic or—" Betty gasped. "A peeping tom? Did you see his badge? Does he know where you live? Maybe you should stay with us for a while."

Stay with Betty? She wasn't in the habit of inviting Eliza to stay. Something wasn't right. "Betty, is there anything you're not telling me about our parents?"

"Me? What a thing to say. I only know what you know. And ditto—is there anything you're not telling *me?* Did he say why he thought you were a communist? He must have had some reason."

"No. I mean, yes, he knows about the articles I've written, even though they were under a pen name, and he has this crazy idea that they're propaganda. He thinks a couple of harmless women's magazines have communist ties."

"What? Darling, I *told* you no good would come from writing those things, didn't I? Oh, Eliza. I know you want to be a writer, but why did you have to actually publish that stuff? What were you thinking?"

Eliza closed her eyes. Counted to ten. Twenty. Thirty.

"Eliza, darling. Now listen, when Ed gets home, I'll bring it up to him. Maybe he'll have some ideas."

She nodded. "Yes, all right."

"This is all very distressing. I'm really worried about you."

"I'll be fine, Betty, no need to worry. I can take care of myself."

"Well, all right then. You're coming for Thanksgiving? Should I find out if Stanley has plans?"

Ugh. "Can we just keep it family?"

"Well . . . sure, hon, if that's what you want. You take care now, and I mean that."

> I don't think any actor sets out intending to trick people into believing lies. Ironically, we are most convincing when we bare our truest, most naked soul.
>
> ~*The Devine Truth: A Memoir*

13

Sunday morning, Eliza stared at the number she'd written on her notepad, then at the telephone. John *had* said to call if she wanted to go to church.

Well . . . did she?

Since John's talk of heaven, Eliza's anger had given way to doubt, and her doubt, to questions. Was God truly kind and forgiving, as Millie said, or a tyrant who demanded surrender? In her experience, nothing could be more demoralizing than forced submission. If that was what Christian faith was about, she was not interested. But she couldn't forget Millie's words. What if it was true? What would unconditional love and total acceptance be like?

She picked up the telephone. What would it hurt to attend a service and get a few answers? Was it wise to be seen in public with John? And what was his church like? The only time she'd attended a service was in college to see a friend in a Christmas pageant. She could just imagine John strolling into that little neighborhood church. How long before the entire place would be in an uproar, with people flocking in to see the Hollywood star?

Did Johnny Devine have to worship in disguise?

She shook off her worries and dialed.

"Hello?" John's deep voice sent a tremor through her that ended with a twist in her belly.

"Hello, it's Eliza Saunderson. I'm wondering if your invitation is still open. For church, I mean." She winced. What other kind of invitation would he offer her?

"Yes, of course. Would you like to meet there, or would you prefer to have my cab pick you up?"

Eliza pushed her glasses higher and checked her watch. Buses didn't run on Sunday, and taking a cab as far as Kensington would be very costly.

"Sharing your cab might be best, if you don't mind."

"Fine. Ten o'clock?"

Once he had her address, she hung up and climbed the stairs in double time, starting a mental list of possible outfits and matching hats suitable for church . . .

In a minister's home . . .

Where was Betty's voice when she needed it?

167

She finally chose a slim-fitting, red with white polka-dot dress, a white cardigan and gloves, and a red pillbox hat with a matching net, and then worried that her ensemble wasn't smart enough.

When John's cab pulled to the curb in front of her apartment, Eliza reached for the car door, but John got out and held it open for her. She glanced around before getting in. Luckily, none of the girls in the building were early Sunday risers.

On the way, John told her she might recognize a familiar face or two.

"A face from where?—the *movies?*"

"Yes, but don't worry," he said. "I'm sure you'll feel right at home."

She wanted to believe him, but it depended on whom she saw. Would Deborah Marlow be there?

The cab stopped at a sprawling house set back from the road. John ushered her into the house and introduced her to the hosts, Pastor Ted and Sondra Moore. Sondra hugged her tight, which was a bit of a surprise but not unwelcome.

The service was held in the Moore's large den, where plush couches and chairs formed a large circle and more chairs formed a row along the back wall. A panoramic window stretching the length of the room offered a view of a flower garden behind the house and a glimpse of the shimmering bay beyond.

Eliza glanced around the room at the twenty or so faces, doing a quick double take at every

168

blonde. John introduced her as Mrs. Eliza Saunderson to a lovely couple named Miller. When she met an older actress whom she recognized, it took Eliza a moment to find her tongue. Goldie Simons had been one of her favorites as a teen. In Goldie's younger days, she had played sweetheart roles similar to Doris Day's.

Goldie smiled. "I'm so pleased to meet you, Eliza. Won't you sit by me?"

Eliza looked at John, who offered a reassuring smile. Perhaps it was his way of turning her loose, but into what, she wasn't sure.

She listened through the hymns, rich with harmony, followed by a prayer. Then Pastor Ted read from the Bible. The story about an adulterous woman about to be stoned to death by an angry mob of men touched Eliza in an unusual way. Hearing of the woman's humiliation and Christ's compassion toward her brought tears to Eliza's eyes. In the midst of such hate and disapproval, the woman found forgiveness and acceptance from Christ.

After the sermon, the congregation sang another hymn, one Eliza had heard Millie sing. Eliza sat still and listened to the words.

"Because the sinless Savior died,
my sinful soul is counted free;
For God the Just is satisfied
to look on Him and pardon me."

At the end of the service, everyone moved to a large dining room for a buffet lunch. Glancing around, Eliza realized an older man in the group was also a film star from a few decades ago. It made sense, of course, that celebrities who wanted to attend church might find a quiet setting like this easier to manage. She would have to ask John later why a number of actors were living around the East Bay. Perhaps, like him, some film stars preferred not to live in Hollywood and found this area a pleasant getaway, but not too far from L.A.

Eliza followed Goldie to the buffet and searched the room for John. She finally found him off to one side talking to a handsome, silver-haired man with a goatee and a lean, athletic build.

The man placed his hand on John's shoulder and closed his eyes, saying words she couldn't hear, but with a fervor she could see.

John's eyes were also closed and he nodded as though listening.

Was the man praying for John?

"Ted and I are looking forward to reading John's book, Mrs. Saunderson."

Turning, Eliza met Sondra Moore's friendly face and smiled in return. How much was she supposed to say about the book? "It's an incredible story. I am sure you'll find it very intriguing." Eliza glanced in John's direction to keep sight of him, but he and his friend were already heading her way.

"Mrs. Saunderson," John said. "I'd like you to meet my good friend and agent, Oscar Silva. Oscar, Mrs. Saunderson is working on my memoir. And she's sharp, so be careful what you say."

Eliza smiled at the man. With any luck, he wouldn't notice how flustered she was at being put on the spot. "Mr. Silva, it's a pleasure to meet you. I've heard such good things."

Oscar turned to John with a sigh. "So you've taken up lying, John?" He winked at Eliza. "Do I get to preview the manuscript, or should I just call my lawyer now?"

"What? Does someone need a lawyer?" a man said, leaning back from the nearest table.

Oscar laughed. "If I do, I won't be calling you, Lester. I can't afford you. In fact, I don't know anyone who can."

Eliza kept a polite smile fixed on her face, but her heart sank. As she went through the buffet line, listening to the friendly chatter in the room, all she could think about was how these people lived smart, glamorous, completely foreign lives. Holding her food-laden plate, she looked across the small sea of prominent people.

She was so out of place here.

John came to her side with a plate in one hand and stood close enough for her to catch the scent of his tantalizing cologne. "Where would you like to sit?"

Oscar approached them, balancing his plate and a Bible. "Mind if I join you two?"

"Please do," Eliza said.

Dining with film stars, agents, and lawyers? Eliza shook her head to clear the sense she was dreaming and tried to eat her lunch, but with a handsome man seated on either side, her attention was anywhere but on her plate.

"Well, what do you think of our little church, Mrs. Saunderson?"

Eliza returned Oscar's kind smile. "It's lovely. I've only attended church one other time, so I'm no expert, but I'm guessing this one isn't typical."

Oscar laughed. "Good! Shows you've come with an open mind." He unfolded his napkin. "I hear you're making great progress on John's memoir."

Eliza glanced at John. How much he had confided in his friend about the project? "I think it's coming along nicely." She nibbled on a slice of dilled cucumber.

John ate in silence. Rather, he toyed with his food. "You've also got a book in the works, Oscar. Maybe she'd like to hear about yours."

"Oh, I'm sure she would." Oscar smiled at Eliza. "*How to Win the Press* is probably just the book you were looking for, Mrs. Saunderson, am I right?"

Eliza laughed. "Yes, how did you know? And please, call me Eliza."

John grabbed his cane and stood. "I need to talk to Pastor Ted, and I see he's alone right now. If you'll excuse me." He left, weaving awkwardly between the chairs and diners.

Eliza watched him go, her heart burdened by his discomfort. Some days he seemed to be in more pain than others. She returned her attention to her plate, her waning appetite now gone. When she looked up, Oscar was watching her intently.

"So, Eliza, I'm curious. What's it been like for you, writing John's story?"

How much should she say? This man was John's good friend, but even if Oscar knew him better than anyone, perhaps he didn't know everything. "It's certainly different from anything I've written."

"No surprise." Oscar nodded. "It must be difficult, isn't it? I mean, being a woman and hearing some of the stories?"

Eliza studied him. Oscar seemed genuine, and from John's account, he was a man of admirable character. "To be honest, yes, sometimes. But I think his story is important, especially in its entirety. I'm glad he's writing it, and not just for the reason he states—to share the hope he's found—but also because I think people need to understand who he is now. For his sake."

Leaning forward, Oscar met her gaze squarely. "Thank you."

"For what?"

"For seeing John for who he is. Not what he was."

Eliza's throat tightened. She hadn't always seen John in a positive light. The day she met him came back in a rush, her mistrust of him, her assumptions. She swallowed hard. "It's just . . . the religious part of it is not something I'm familiar with—an invisible God who can change a person inwardly. It's so opposite of . . ."

Oscar rested his chin on his hand. "Of what?"

"Of the pressure in society to look perfect, to conform, or at least to appear that way. Everyone in their proper place doing exactly what's expected, all the while turning a blind eye to oppression. It's . . . I'm sorry, I'm getting on my soapbox now."

"No, please, go on. I'm interested in hearing what you think."

Eliza looked around to be sure no one was listening. Why was she telling a virtual stranger the inner battles of her heart? "There's an unspoken pressure to conform to the American ideal—happy and prosperous in appearance, but sometimes all I see is an empty façade. Empty and also unjust, because you can only fit the American ideal if you are of the right economical class and ethnicity. And for those who do fit the criteria, I suspect some seek fulfillment by conforming outwardly, but are only fooling themselves and growing emptier by the day."

"That's rather profound, Eliza. You've thought about this quite a bit?"

More than you know. "Yes."

"And you see John's experience as a genuine change, then, rather than simply the appearance of change?"

"Yes." Eliza pushed her plate away and leaned her chin on her hands. "Yes, I do."

"Or a person who's been truly transformed, instead of conformed?"

"Exactly!" She'd spoken too loudly. She glanced around.

Goldie met her gaze with a smile. John looked at her from across the room, then quickly resumed his conversation with Ted.

"So you know about John's conversion experience, then? How he found Christ?"

She shook her head. "We haven't gotten that far yet."

"Hmm." Oscar nodded, studying her. "That's interesting."

Eliza twisted a grape from its stem, more out of a need to escape his scrutiny than from hunger. "Why do you say that?"

He shrugged. "Oh, I don't know." Oscar leaned back and folded his arms loosely across his chest, the picture of a man perfectly at ease. "So, do you think I should buy a copy of *The Devine Truth*?"

With a smile, Eliza popped the grape in her mouth. "You should buy cases of them."

Oscar laughed long and loud. "Ouch. I guess John won't be needing his agent. Sounds like you've got that covered."

Eliza smiled. "I believe his is a very powerful story that can touch many people." She glanced across the room and found John watching them carefully. "I can't wait to see how it ends."

Oscar nodded slowly, studying her with a thoughtful look. "Neither can I."

> Oscar often said he was praying for me, but I told him he could keep his prayers. I was a rational creature. A careless, drunken creature, to be sure, but rational enough to know my perfectly happy life needed no interference.
> ~*The Devine Truth: A Memoir*

14

Monday morning, Eliza made it to the street corner long before the bus arrived, a notable first. It was unfortunate that Pastor Ted hadn't finished the adulterous woman's story in his sermon. Had she gone on as before, or had Christ's pardon changed her? Perhaps John could tell Eliza what had become of the woman.

At John's house, she gave her coat and scarf to Millie, then entered the library.

John was on the telephone near the kitchen. He smiled and beckoned her in.

Her question would have to wait. Perhaps she could ask Millie when she had a chance.

"I'm sorry," John said to Eliza, pressing the telephone receiver to his chest. "I have to take this call. But listen, I had a boatload of ideas last night and jotted them down. Maybe you can salvage something useful from it. It's on my table."

Eliza went to the table beside his chair and found a notebook with writing in it. He'd actually written a lot. And on further inspection, it wasn't bad. In fact, it was quite good. Perhaps her input had been rubbing off. Or, more likely, John was a better writer than either she or John had realized. Maybe he'd just needed a little encouragement and practice. Maybe soon he wouldn't need her help on the composing at all. Maybe—

Maybe things would go back to the way they were. Him writing elsewhere, and her typing in the library, alone.

Eliza stared at the typewriter, then out the front window. A dull fog obscured the bay. Dead leaves dotted the grass at the base of the trees, their usefulness at an end. Winter was coming.

She sat down to work. John had written enough that she worked on it until five o'clock, stopping only for lunch.

Tuesday, John gave her more pages, which were also fairly well-written, so she spent the entire day working alone, again. By Wednesday afternoon, they had made more progress on the book than they had the entire previous week. John seemed more focused, less reticent. His story had now circled back to the point where it had first begun, in the final year of his film career. It shouldn't take much more to finish that phase of his life. After that, Eliza didn't know where his story was going, or how much of his life after Hollywood would be included in the book. Surely there was much more to his story. There had to be. Whatever it was, she couldn't wait to hear it.

But the mystery would have to wait. John was leaving the next day to help Oscar with some kind of Charlie Chaplin Silent Film tribute in Los Angeles and would be gone through the weekend, giving Eliza a couple of extra days off.

When she arrived at home on Wednesday evening, the super blocked her path to the stairs and handed her a slip of paper. It read *Agent Bert Robinson, Berkeley 3549.*

Eliza wadded up the telephone number, tossed it in the waste can, and continued around the super and up the stairs. Halfway up, she stopped and turned. "If that man calls again, there's no need to take a message. I don't want to talk to him. And if he comes around, he's not welcome here."

"Lady, butler duty ain't part of my job description."

"Just don't let him in." She left him muttering and went to her room in search of Mr. Darcy.

An hour later, Ivy knocked at the door. "Phone for you. I mean, I *think* it's for you. The guy asked for Eliza Peterson. I said the only Eliza here was Eliza Saunderson, and he called me

a doll face and said I was right on the money."
Grinning, she twirled a curly lock behind her ear.

"Thanks, but I'm not taking any calls from him."

Ivy cocked her head at Eliza. "You want me to tell him to buzz off?"

Eliza smiled. "Sure, thanks."

"Okay, but what's he look like? Mind if I ask him if he's single first?"

"He's not your type, Ivy. There's only one thing he's interested in." Which was true, but Ivy didn't need to know what it was.

Ivy's eyes narrowed. "Ohhh! I'll tell him to buzz off all right—and how!"

At six forty the next morning, another knock on the door nearly sent Eliza into a screaming fit.

Joan, in curlers and a robe, leaned on Eliza's doorframe as though the walk up the stairs had been too taxing. Tendrils of smoke curled up from her cigarette. "Telephone for you, toots."

Eliza groaned. She needed to leave a *No Calls for Eliza* note on the phone. "I'm not taking his calls."

"Boy, that fella must really like a girl who plays hard to get. So what's he look like?"

Once she finally convinced Joan that Agent Robinson definitely wasn't her type, Eliza bathed and dressed, fed Mr. Darcy the rest of her canned milk, then headed to the bus stop.

It was time to take action.

• • •

"Darling, why didn't you call first?" Betty reached through the doorway and gave Eliza a perfunctory hug. "But it's lovely to see you." She tugged Eliza inside the house. "Sue Ellen?" she called out. "Eddie Jr.? Look who's here!"

A number of things had changed since Eliza's last visit to Betty's home, including a larger console television set and two new pieces of impressionist art above the fireplace. Of course, the view from the front room window hadn't changed. A person could still look down on the entire East Bay from the Cunningham home, which stood at the pinnacle of Richmond Heights in a neighborhood made up of nearly identical homes lined up in perfect uniformity.

Eddie Jr. thundered in from the hallway. "Say, what are you doing here?" he said, his freckly grin missing a few teeth.

Sue Ellen came running in. "Auntie Liza!" The girl nearly knocked Eliza over with her embrace.

"Sue Ellen," Betty said, raising a brow.

"Oh." Sue Ellen stepped back and held out her hand. "How do you do?" She tucked her lips in, barely stifling a smile.

Eliza took her hand and gave her a wink.

Sue Ellen burst into giggles, then turned to her mother. "Why doesn't *she* have to wear gloves?"

"Oops," Eliza said. "I forgot."

"Really, dear. There's no need to be sarcastic.

I'm sure I don't have to tell you how filthy those buses can be. All those people." She shuddered. "I wish you wouldn't take public transportation. Well, come in. You're staying for lunch?"

Eliza dropped her handbag on the sofa. "Sure. Can I help?"

Betty opened her mouth, but then smiled the smile she used on her children when she wanted them to understand how patient she was being. "You've forgotten. We have Odella now."

"Oh, that's right. How is Odella?"

"She cooks a lot better than Mother does," Eddie Jr. said, eyes glued to the television set.

Betty's nostrils flared, replaced by another crisp smile. "Come into the den, Eliza. Ed won't mind us using it. I'll get us some tea."

Which meant she would order Odella to make it and serve it to them.

Eliza followed Betty to the den, done up in the latest style with dark wood paneling, stark furniture, and thick plaid curtains that blocked the light.

"Make yourself at home," Betty said. "Back in a jiffy."

Eliza studied her brother-in-law's cave-like den. The armless brown sofa didn't look at all comfortable with its hard, straight lines and flat seat, and the white plastic chairs looked cold. But it was the latest style, and that, of course, was what mattered.

Eliza shook her head. What a stark contrast to John's home. The furnishings in John's storybook house pre-dated the turn of the century. The famous film star lived amongst old-fashioned things and didn't seem to care.

She was still musing on the differences between the two homes when Betty returned.

"For goodness' sake, Eliza, sit down. You look like a long-tailed cat in a room full of rockers. Now then," Betty said, settling on the hard sofa. "You didn't ride a smelly bus all the way from Oakland just for a cup of my tea."

You mean Odella's tea. Eliza sat on the edge of a chair, feeling the cold through the fabric of her skirt. "Betty, the man who's been bothering me is an agent with the House Un-American Activities Committee. He thinks our parents were communists."

"That's ridiculous," Betty said with a sniff. "They weren't, of course, but what difference would it make if they were? They've been dead fifteen years."

"Not only that, he thinks they were Russian spies. He insists they had some kind of contacts in Russia."

Betty's brow gathered into a frown. "And you told him they weren't, right?"

"Of course, but he didn't believe me. I don't know where he gets his information, but he knows about the train accident and where they

183

were going. He said there was a large communist gathering in Fresno at the same time they were traveling there."

Betty's frown deepened. She lowered her voice. "So, now you think Mama and Papa were *spies?* How could you even think such a thing?"

"I don't know what to think, Betty! This man shows up out of nowhere and seems to know more about my parents than I do. It's a little unsettling."

Betty leaned forward. "What's unsettling is hearing you even entertain such a notion." She shook her head. "I knew this would happen. It's all that gibberish you've been filling your head with, your fixation with coloreds and all that nonsense about oppression—"

Odella, wearing a gray dress and stiffly starched white apron, stood in the doorway holding a serving tray. "Tea's served, ma'am," she said in a flat tone.

As the maid came into the room, Eliza studied Betty, wondering if her sister even cared that Odella had heard her last remark, but Betty's expression was fixed in prim hostess mode.

Odella handed Eliza a teacup. Eliza thanked her and tried to see what was in Odella's eyes, but the woman would not meet Eliza's gaze.

Betty waited until Odella left and then spoke. "Is that why you came here?" Her words were slow, deliberate. "To see if there was something to the rumors you could use, regardless of how it would harm our family name?" Betty tossed her head, but her short blonde curls were sprayed so tightly they didn't budge.

"What are you talking about?"

"I may not be a college graduate, but I know how these things work, Eliza. You're planning to write about this, aren't you? Are you so desperate for material that you would dig around in our own family's private affairs just for a byline? Don't you even care about ruining our parents' good names?"

Heat rushed to Eliza's face. "Of course I'm not writing about our parents. What on earth makes you think that?"

"Because that's what you do. You stir up waters that are best left alone. Don't you see? You're always going against the flow. No wonder they think you're anti-American."

Eliza shot up from her seat, stomach in knots. She looked down at her sister, not believing what she'd heard. "I came here to see if you could help me sort this out, not get into a debate about my convictions. At least I *have* convictions and am not hiding behind an apron and a garden club membership." Her breath caught, but too late to stop the words—they were out, hovering in the air between them like a cloud of yellow jackets.

Betty stood and glanced at the doorway, toward the sound of cowboys and Indians on

185

the television. She turned to Eliza, chin high. "There's nothing wrong with wanting to belong to the best circles," she said in a low, even tone. "It's not as easy for me as you think."

"Is that all you want, Betty? *Circles?*"

Betty's lips pressed together into a thin, scarlet line. "I want to be respected, Eliza. Is that so terrible?"

Eliza shook her head. "I didn't say it was."

"But I see it on your face. Which is ironic, because *you* don't even know the half of it. You have no idea what it's like to live in fear of losing the place in respectable society you've worked so hard for. Even with all your . . . eccentricities, *you'll* never have to worry like I do."

Betty's words echoed in Eliza's ears. "Why? What do you mean?"

Her sister stared at Eliza. "Come with me."

Eliza followed Betty out of the den and into the dining room, then down a hall and into Betty's bedroom.

Betty opened the closet and took down a photo box. She leafed through photographs of her children as babies, then pulled out a folded blue paper. "There. Does that make you happy?"

Frowning, Eliza unfolded the official-looking paper and read. "Nadia Petrovich." She turned to Betty, confused.

"Read the date."

January fourth, nineteen nineteen. Betty's birthday. "What is this?"

"It's my birth certificate, Eliza. Unlike yours, which leaves no doubt that you're a full-blooded American."

Eliza glanced down the page to the lines listing the infant's mother and father. Instead of Laura and Wesley Peterson, as were listed on Eliza's birth certificate, the parents' names on Betty's read *Lara* and *Vasily Petrovich*.

So her parents *were* Russian.

> I finally had to admit that Oscar's faith wasn't just a fad. Eventually, his patience and persistence wore me out, so I fired him. Repeatedly.
> ~*The Devine Truth: A Memoir*

15

The first thing Eliza did when she returned to her apartment was to tape a note beside the telephone that said *Absolutely NO Calls for Eliza*. And if Agent Robinson showed up at the apartment building, maybe the super would send him away. She could hope, anyway. She couldn't endure any more questions, not until she sorted out what she'd discovered about her parents. Unfortunately, Betty knew nothing more than what was on her birth certificate. Eliza had asked several times until she was satisfied her sister was telling the truth.

Why had Mama and Papa kept their real names and nationality a secret? They must have worked hard to leave so little trace of an accent. How had they hidden being Russian so well?

Were they communists?

Thursday night, Eliza sat at her typewriter, stroking the cat with her feet, picturing Papa's broad shoulders and Mama's gentle smile. And her dark-blue, almond-shaped eyes, which Eliza had inherited.

Spies?

Mama and Papa had been such quiet people. Though they had never spoken of their lives before Betty and Eliza were born, there had been no pretense with them. They were genuine; the same people every minute of every day. If they truly did have some kind of secret involvement or ties with communism, they would have had a very good reason for it.

But she still had too many questions that needed answers. Perhaps, by some miracle, she would find those answers before Agent Robinson did.

Because of John's out of town trip, Eliza had four days off in a row, and it felt strange. She already missed the story and the dictation, the discussions.

On Friday, she spent most of the day on the telephone, hunting for numbers to establishments that might offer some information about her parents' immigration. She needed to find a lead on their background or a clue about them—a ship's log, a hospital record, a person who knew them, anything. The trouble was, she was searching in the dark and didn't even know what for.

Saturday began with a drizzle that turned to steady rain, so a matinee was out. She was trapped in her tiny apartment. And alone, since Mr. Darcy hadn't come around for his morning milk. He'd been coming to see her so faithfully, even staying inside a few nights. What could be important enough to a tomcat to interrupt his homey, new routine? But then, he'd probably been a stray for a long time and wasn't accustomed to being a cherished pet.

She worked on editing an article on women's equality, but the Bible story about the woman and Jesus kept creeping into her thoughts. Perhaps Pastor Ted was telling the rest of it in tomorrow's service. Eliza certainly wouldn't be going. She would probably be welcome, but she wasn't about to go there on her own. She didn't belong.

But she *did* have a Bible, and it wasn't as if she couldn't read the story for herself.

Eliza took the Bible from the bookcase, belly-flopped down on her bed, stocking feet crossed in the air, and leafed through the Gospel of John—a name hard to forget.

She read several chapters, stopping to look up unfamiliar words in the dictionary the way her parents had taught her. She went on until she found the story of the adulterous woman. She read it carefully, touched again by Christ's compassion and by his words, *"Neither do I condemn thee: go, and sin no more."* But after Jesus rescued the woman, there was nothing more said of her. The story went on to Jesus teaching judgmental men about Himself and about truth.

Another line stood out: *"And ye shall know the truth, and the truth shall make you free."*

So how was it that the sinful woman had been set free, but the so-called righteous men still clung to their binding way of thinking?

As far as Eliza could tell, Christ came to change people and liberate them from man-made rules that only changed how a person appeared outwardly. The men in the story, on the other hand, wanted this woman ridiculed and made to conform to their rules. They had no interest in helping her truly change.

Eliza read the next chapter as well, but there was no further mention of the woman. Had she changed?

Was true change even possible?

If you let Me, I will make you new.

Eliza stilled. It was as if she felt the words rather than heard them. They were just *there,* like the memory of a familiar voice.

Mr. Darcy howled at the glass door. Eliza hurried to open it before he changed his mind.

Would John know more about the woman in the story? Perhaps she could ask him the next time she saw him.

Which wouldn't be for another dreadfully long day.

Monday arrived with a stiff breeze that caught the hem of Eliza's skirt and sent a mild chill up her legs. The sight of John's house and of Millie waiting for her at the door was a relief.

Millie tut-tutted, ushering Eliza inside like a mother hen. "That wind gonna blow winter right in on top of us, Miz Eliza. You best bundle up from now on. Catch your death if you don't."

Eliza removed her scarf, smiling. Millie had been polishing with lemon wax again. This house always smelled wonderful and so right. Like home ought to smell.

Millie tilted her head up and narrowed a gaze at Eliza. "You done somethin' different with your hair?"

"No, same hair."

The sound of John's cane approaching gave her a huge case of the jitters. As he came near, he looked tense, but even so, it did her heart good to see him. She couldn't contain her broad smile.

The tension on his face gave way to surprise. His eyes searched hers, questioning. Then just as quickly, his hard expression resumed. "I hope you had a good weekend. You've been working hard and certainly deserved a break."

"Thank you. I visited my sister. How was your benefit event?"

"Long. And a bit of a shock, to be honest. I haven't been to L.A. in more than a decade. Brought back more memories than I'd bargained for. But it was for a good cause. Oscar cooked up this event to help a group of his long-time clients. He thought my name would lend some draw power."

"And did it?"

"The turnout wasn't bad, especially for a first-time event."

She smiled again, pleased for his success. "So, you're glad you went?"

His gaze shifted away from her and toward the library, as if he would rather be in there. "I'm grateful for any chance I can help Oscar." He gestured toward the other room.

Millie left them and Eliza went to her desk, but John didn't join her in the library after all. Odd. Shaking off her disappointment, she reviewed the last few pages of his manuscript, then glanced at John's table for new pages. She didn't see any. Perhaps he had gone to get them.

Millie brought a tray with two cups of coffee and offered one to Eliza, then looked around the room with a frown. "This room feel chilly to you? I'll have Duncan lay a fire."

"I'm fine, Millie, but I don't mind if you think a fire is needed."

Still frowning, Millie set the other cup of coffee on John's table. Duncan entered, mail in hand. Millie stopped him and asked about a fire. With a sigh, Duncan dropped the mail on Eliza's desk and trudged out.

John was still nowhere in sight. Maybe he'd

left pages or his notebook and she just hadn't seen them.

Eliza went to his table and searched more closely, but found nothing. Strange—no pages and no John. She returned to her desk and looked again, finding nothing there either. Her eye caught something pink peeking out of the stack of mail.

A small, square, stationery-style envelope.

Checking around to make sure no one was watching, she leaned closer.

The corner with the return address poked out, but not enough to see who it was from.

Knowing full well that she shouldn't, she reached over and tugged the envelope out a little more.

The return address read "D.M." with an address in San Diego. In a feminine hand.

Something in the center of her chest turned to ice.

A sound in the hallway made her jump, and she returned to her seat, heart thumping. She was no gumshoe, but wasn't it obvious? John was receiving regular mail from a woman with the initials D.M.

It's none of your business, Eliza.

She inserted a clean sheet of paper into her typewriter. Betty would also tell her it was none of her business. Even Mama would say it. But as Eliza waited, heart still pounding, Deborah

Marlow's beautiful face flooded her mind like a movie screen. Glamorous, alluring, confident.

Though tabloids had paired Johnny Devine and Deborah Marlow romantically in the past, he had never talked about her.

Not yet, anyway.

Appalled at the childish direction her emotions were headed, Eliza straightened the stack of manuscript pages, then glanced at the stack of mail. It was rather odd that he never talked about Deborah when he had been candid about other women. Perhaps John had been more in love with this woman than anyone else. Which wasn't hard to imagine. Perhaps he still carried deep feelings for her—why else would he be so secretive about their relationship?

John's cane tapped as he approached.

Foolish girl. You're an employee. This is a job. A temporary job that will end soon.

It was just that her lungs wouldn't work, and her heart fluttered like a caged bird.

What's wrong with you? Stop acting like a child.

Eliza put on the most composed look she could, hating the fact that she was forced to hide behind a mask yet again.

But she had no choice. Allowing John to see that she had fallen in love with him was out of the question.

> Vacancy demands to be filled. It's basic physics. Only a pure fool would ignore or try to deny it.
> ~*The Devine Truth: A Memoir*

16

Eliza looked up at the sound of John's cane.

"So sorry to keep you waiting," John said.

Duncan came in from the kitchen carrying a long-handled basket of wood, which he hauled to the fireplace with shuffling steps.

John eyed him. "Expecting a freeze, Duncan?"

The old man set the basket down. "Millie wants a fire."

"Seems warm enough to me, but if Millie wants it, I won't argue."

Duncan placed wood in the fireplace, muttering about what Millie wanted.

John took his seat and set his cane beside him. "Where did we leave off, Mrs. Saunderson?"

Eliza took the last page of manuscript from the stack and held it up to read. Her pulse still hadn't returned to normal. "It was 1941, and you suspected that your looks and popularity were the real reason you were cast in so many films." She peeked at him. Oh, yes. He still had the looks. She dropped her gaze and readied her pencil.

"Yes. I figured the only thing the director expected from me was to show up. It didn't even matter if I could act. And I did want to act. I wanted to do a good job, or at least I did at one time. I suppose by then, however, I had lost my love for the art. I was convinced that all they wanted was to put me in a film and showcase me with all their staging wizardry. I told Oscar that producers chose specific roles to bring out my . . . bankable charms." He sighed. "Sex appeal is like gold in Hollywood. Never mind my desire to act and connect with the audience. Which was what I really wanted. I never felt close to anyone after my family died. Losing them, and losing the connection with the audience left me feeling detached. No matter how many . . . people I spent time with."

Eliza's shoulders stiffened as she prepared to hear something she would rather not. But hadn't she told Oscar how important it was for John to tell his story, in its entirety? These things needed to be said.

"I want people to understand there was a deep, aggravating void in my life. I hope readers will recognize such a feeling, no matter their specific circumstances."

She finished jotting the last lines. "I am sure many people know the feeling. And I think your readers will be eager to read on and see if you ever found a . . . a lasting way to fill that void."

"I hope so."

He went on with stories of friends who felt the same way about being cast simply for their sex appeal or screen image and then drowned their disillusionment in drink. "Jonesy took it much harder than the rest of us did."

Eliza paused her writing. "Who is that?"

"Gina Jones, but we all called her Jonesy. She could drink like a whale and slip right into character like nobody's business. I don't know how she did it. But the drinking took a deadly toll on her health. She died in a hospital, broke and diseased."

Eliza remembered the actress all too well. Just before Ralph went into the army, when he spent most of his time out with friends, Eliza would slip out for an occasional Saturday matinee, more for the newsreels than the picture. She'd heard about the actress's death. By that time, Eliza knew full well who the woman was because Ralph kept a life-sized pin-up poster of her in the hall closet. Gina Jones: every red-blooded American man's dream.

Eliza had burned that poster the day Ralph shipped out.

"Disillusionment can destroy our soul, if we let it," Eliza said.

John nodded thoughtfully. "That's good. I wish I'd said it."

"Use it. I was only rephrasing what you said."

John smiled. "No, that was all you."

His smile and the deep tone of his voice sent her heart knocking. She tore her gaze away.

He rose and strolled across the room. "And you're absolutely right. I gave my disillusionment over to every kind of destructive vice. I was cursed to follow the path of the disenchanted, or so I believed. Sliding down a greased slope, unable to stop until I hit bottom. Or oblivion, because I'd been aiming for bottom so long I feared there was no end to it."

"Did you ever wonder about God?" *And did He ever speak to you in a strangely familiar voice when you were alone?*

John nodded. "I did. Do you remember that one of my first bit parts was in a silent picture called *The Godless Girl*? The story was a romance between an atheist girl and a Christian boy." John huffed out a laugh. "Ironic, isn't it? My first introduction to God was during production of a fictional screenplay. It got me wondering if there was a God, and if there was, why He'd allowed things to turn out as they had. Why He took good men from the world, like my dad and Will, and left a lug like me to tramp around making a mess of things. I wasn't interested in a God whose logic made no sense."

"Which I suppose you later discovered isn't true."

John shook his head. "No, His logic still

doesn't always make sense. But I know without a doubt that His logic is good and right, no matter how it feels to me. The Bible says His ways are higher than my ways, His thoughts higher than mine. And do you know what? I find great peace in that."

Eliza studied him, confused by the many God-ironies she kept discovering. Was God fickle? Was He compassionate, as Christ had demonstrated, or was He a tyrant? Because if there was one thing Eliza knew, submitting to a bully of any kind was something she would never do again.

> I still don't know if holding on to
> one's last shred of pride is admirable
> or just plain pathetic.
> ~*The Devine Truth: A Memoir*

17

The lunch meeting with Fred Wharton was set for Friday at the Claremont Hotel, by far the ritziest place in town. As the weekend drew near, Eliza found it harder to remain calm. Why did he want to meet her? What sort of a man was Mr. Wharton? What would he have to say to her?

And what would it be like to dine with John in public?

Friday morning, she again read the story of the adulterous woman. She still didn't understand John's blind surrender to God. But a woman in need of redemption, hope, and freedom—this, she understood.

She took out her navy suit and dressed with more attention than usual, adding a splash of perfume and a touch of lipstick. Perhaps red wasn't too bold for a business meeting. Of course, Betty wore red lipstick seven days a week and insisted a woman's lips were meant to be seen. Eliza wasn't sure she agreed.

She studied her reflection in the mirror, then

removed her glasses. Without them, she looked so much like her mama. But though Mama was a kind, lovely woman, there had always been a hint of sadness to her, constant but faint, like the steady sound of a distant stream. Neither Eliza nor Betty had inherited Mama's subdued manner, but rather their papa's lively one.

On second thought, she dug through her wardrobe for her red scarf. She knotted it at her neck, added red gloves and her red sweetheart handbag, then took another look at herself. She smiled at the touches of color.

Eliza arrived at John's house at the regular time, even though the meeting wasn't until noon. John was eager to get as much writing done as possible. Thinking about the approaching deadline tightened the knot in her stomach, but she ignored it and headed for her desk.

John was seated by the fireplace, reading a book. When she came in, he looked up and fell back against his chair as if a gust of wind had pushed him.

"Good morning," Eliza said.

His dark eyes studied her.

"I wasn't sure what I should wear to the meeting." But then, she could have asked Betty. "Is this all right?"

His gaze roamed her outfit, then lingered on her face. He quickly shifted his focus to the framed art on the wall opposite the fireplace. "Yes.

Millie isn't feeling well and took the day off, so I've asked Duncan to work inside today. I hope that's agreeable to you?"

Duncan? Oh. John still thought Eliza didn't trust him. How she longed to tell him not to worry, that she knew what an honorable man he was. "It's perfectly fine with me either way."

John nodded, still studying the wall. Memorizing each picture, apparently. "Shall we get started? We only have about an hour and a half before the cab arrives. Or *cabs,* that is. I've called for two."

Eliza stared at him. Was he worried about the propriety of traveling together? Or how it would look if they went in and out of a hotel in the same cab?

That was it.

Her face warmed. "You want to safeguard your new reputation. I understand."

John returned to his book. "It's not *my* reputation that needs safeguarding," he said, almost beneath his breath.

The Claremont Hotel stood long, tall, and bold against the wooded hills overlooking the East Bay. A dazzling sight with its multifaceted architecture and miles of decorative white trim, it looked more like a sprawling, white castle than a hotel.

As her cab made the final ascent to the main

entrance, Eliza marveled at the grand structure, soaking it all in. Cinderella couldn't have been more enthralled upon seeing the prince's palace. This certainly wasn't Eliza's low-rent neighborhood, favorite haunt of spinster writers and stray tomcats.

She entered the lobby, struck instantly by the polished, dark wood floors and thick, round pillars that spanned from floor to lofty ceiling, gleaming white trunks in contrast to the rich moss-green-and-merlot-colored wallpaper.

John met her at the base of a broad staircase. As he escorted her up, she could just imagine what Betty would say if she knew Eliza was dining here. One lunch at a place like this would probably cost more than an entire month of lunches at Lucky's. *With* tips.

In the red-velvet dining room, a host wearing crisp white tails and a bow tie escorted John and Eliza to a round table where a stout bald man was seated.

He stood as they approached, then shook John's hand.

"Fred," John said, "I'd like you to meet Mrs. Saunderson, author, and collaborator of my book. Mrs. Saunderson, this is Fred Wharton, Senior Editor and soon-to-be Publisher of Covenant Press Publishing."

Fred took her hand. "Good heavens, Johnny makes me sound like some kind of potentate."

His jowly face stretched into a beaming smile. "How do you do?"

"Very well, Mr. Wharton, thank you."

"Please, call me Fred. Thank you for joining our meeting. Although I must say you certainly don't fit in *here*." He pulled out a chair for her.

Eliza slid onto the seat, stung by his comment. Surely he was teasing. Even if someone *thought* she didn't belong at the Claremont with celebrities and publishing executives, who would actually say it aloud?

Fred gave her chair a polite push and then took his seat.

Eliza fanned her cheeks and glanced across the table at John.

He opened his mouth but hesitated, then turned to his editor. "I wonder, Fred, if you could explain. I'm afraid Mrs. Saunderson may have missed the meaning of your . . . compliment."

"What? Oh, so sorry. I only meant you've just brightened up this stuffy room like a fresh bouquet, and then you choose to sit with a couple of drab, old duffers like us."

John looked down to unfold his napkin, a faint smile emerging.

"Oh. Thank you." Eliza willed her nerves to relax. "But if you two are drab, old duffers, then I'm the Queen of Sheba."

Fred laughed and winked at John. "Smart *and* diplomatic."

After placing their orders, the three of them made polite, easy small talk over the sparkling strains of jazz playing nearby and the hum of dining conversation. A lively trombone solo stood out above the chatter.

John cocked his head as if listening carefully. "Is that who I think it is?" he asked.

Fred closed his eyes. "I believe that is none other than Tommy Dorsey, the Sentimental Gentleman of Swing."

Eliza used to listen to the Dorsey Brothers on the radio whenever she could. She smiled, tapping her toes to the rhythm. "Too bad Tommy and his brother don't perform together anymore. I always hoped they'd work it out and play together again."

Fred shook his head. "It's really a shame. If brothers can't get along, then who can?"

John nodded slowly, but by the way the glint in his eyes faded, his thoughts were far away. Perhaps on a different pair of brothers, many years ago.

She didn't realize how hungry she was until the waiter placed a golden chicken à la king in front of her. As the guest at this meeting, she waited for her host's cue.

Fred thanked the waiter and inhaled the ribbons of steam rising from a dish of beef bourguignon, then bowed his bald head, eyes closed, and began to pray.

John closed his eyes.

Eliza did the same, offering God the only thing she had—her ever-increasing questions. *God, did that woman in the Bible 'go and sin no more'? How is it that Christ showed her such love, and yet You want people to submit to You? I've known tyranny, and there was nothing loving about it. Can You really change people, like You did John Vincent? If You changed him, can You remove the anger from my heart? And remove feelings I have no business feeling for a man who sees me as a bookish nobody, who probably still cares for someone from his own world who is so much more—*

An odd silence enveloped her.

Eliza opened her eyes.

Fred and John seemed to be patiently waiting for her.

"Oh. I'm sorry," she said, cheeks burning. "I'm . . . new at this."

John tilted his head and studied her.

"No need to apologize, my dear." Fred's voice boomed across the dining room. He looked at his plate with a happy sigh and started shoveling meat and noodles into his mouth with more enthusiasm than she'd seen in a long time. Apparently New York publishing houses never fed their editors.

Loud whispers and giggling in the far corner of the dining room drew Eliza's attention.

When John turned to see where the sound was coming from, the giggles turned to muffled squeals. He turned away quickly, but it was too late. He shot a pained glance at Fred.

"Sorry, Johnny," Fred said. He wiped his mouth. "I hoped that, by choosing the Claremont, we'd avoid this sort of thing."

Eliza watched from the corner of her eye as two middle-aged women approached the table.

They jostled one another, nearly knocking each other down to reach the table first, and then stopped beside John.

He acknowledged them with a polite nod. "How do you do?"

At the sound of his voice, the taller one went rigid, her eyes instantly round, while the red-faced one fanned herself with a gloved hand and let out another giggle. "Oh, Helen," she said, never taking her eyes from John. "He's even more handsome in person!"

Helen only nodded, still wide-eyed.

Fred rested his arms across his ample belly and watched John, making little attempt to hide his amusement.

Still fanning herself, the giggly one leaned closer. "Would you be so kind—?"

"It would be my pleasure," John said. "Do you have something I could write on?"

"Oh!" The women gasped at each other and fumbled in their handbags.

"Say, what about these paper coasters, Johnny?" Fred said. "I have two that haven't been used—"

"Oh, we don't mind if you've used it, do we, Helen?"

Helen stared at John and froze again, her mouth now a fully formed *O*.

Eliza wasn't sure Helen was even breathing, which was slightly alarming, because the woman already looked like she was about to have a stroke.

John took the pen and coasters Fred offered. *"To Helen,"* he said, adding his name. He turned to the other woman. "And to . . . ?"

"Lucille, like Lucille Ball. You know, like *I Love Lucy*?" She giggled and covered her mouth.

John signed the coaster and handed the autographs to the ladies with a polite smile.

Lucille clasped her friend's arm and nearly crumpled at the knees.

Eliza could just picture them both fainting right there on John's steak, and hoped like mad that they wouldn't.

Fred thanked the ladies and wished them a pleasant day.

John retained his smile as the women collected themselves and teetered back toward their table, squealing like teenyboppers.

Fred wiped his chin and pushed his plate aside. "Well, on *that* note," he said brightly, "shall we get to work?"

"It's your dime, Fred," John said. "I'm all ears."

"No, *Clark Gable* is all ears." Fred chuckled. "*Johnny Devine* is all charm. And I don't care what you say, you've still got it."

John studied the older man, his face laboring the way it did when he was carefully choosing his words. "Thanks, Fred. But that 'charm' is one of the things I'd rather forget." He folded his napkin and pressed it firmly onto the table. "One of many. And I hope you *do* care about what I have to say, because that's about all I have left."

A solemn quiet blanketed the table.

Eliza felt completely out of place—no, worse than that—an eavesdropper.

With a frown at his folded hands, Fred said, "You're right, Johnny. I was only . . . you're right. My apologies."

John shook his head. "Please, there's no need for that. You know how much I value your opinion. You understand better than anyone what this book means to me, and I know you're taking a huge risk with my story. I admire your faith and courage. And I'm honored that you believe in me."

Eliza tore her gaze from John and studied the spiced apple and mint garnish on her plate, trying to break the magnetic pull of John's presence. The pure grace of his words warmed her, tugged at her heart with a painfully firm grip.

"Thank you," Fred said, tone sobering. "John, I love what I'm seeing so far in the manuscript. It's magnificent work, and I look forward to seeing the finished product, as I'm sure you both are. Now, one of the reasons I'm here is because I've learned about an opportunity I think you'll want to consider. It's up to you, of course. Your agent tells me our book is drawing some big fish. It seems both Universal and Paramount are nibbling at the movie rights."

"*Movie* rights? Sure." John puffed out a laugh. "You've got to be kidding."

"Not at all. Think about the possibilities, Johnny. We'd get first shot at the screenplay, and you've already got a topnotch writer here with a peach of a chance at the contract. And best of all, it's unlimited exposure for your book. I know how you feel about getting your story out. And I'm behind you all the way. Do yourself a favor and think about it."

Eliza's chest fluttered. If John agreed to make his story into a movie, and if she were contracted to write the screenplay, she and John could continue working together.

Fred turned to her. "I'm sorry. Of course, I intended to ask you first, Mrs. Saunderson. What do you say about writing the screenplay?"

"I'd love to, yes. If John is agreeable."

"Absolutely," John said. "I appreciate your support, Fred. Can I think about it?"

"Certainly. Besides, you're on a book deadline now, in case you didn't know." Fred winked at Eliza. "How's it coming, by the way? Are we about ready to fire up the presses?"

"We're in the home stretch," John said. "Thanks to a very talented writer who can take my ramblings and make them sound interesting. We're very fortunate." With a smile, he met Eliza's gaze.

For some reason, she couldn't breathe.

"Didn't I tell you when you had to keep sacking those other typists that the Lord would provide?" Fred turned to Eliza. "Now, Mrs. Saunderson, in case you thought we dragged you down here only to listen to me jaw about Johnny, I have a question for you too."

Eliza forced herself to give Fred her full attention.

"I hear you have a couple of manuscripts that made the rounds at some of the other houses without any takers. Do you have a proposal? If so, I'd be willing to take a look."

Stunned, Eliza gaped at Fred, then at John.

John gave her a single go-ahead nod.

"Well, yes, I do." She swallowed hard. "Are you . . . aware of the subject matter of my work?"

Fred nodded. "I can't promise anything, but I'd like to believe we're a forward-thinking house. What better time to branch out and explore social issues in the light of God's plan for mankind?

Personally, I love the idea of helping people come together in unity and equal footing. Will you send what you have?"

With a joy she could barely contain, Eliza nodded. "Yes, I will. Thank you." She turned to John with a smile so wide it almost hurt.

He smiled in return, eyes shining. John didn't think her writing was a waste of time. He believed in her.

It may have been her imagination, but a ray of honey-colored light broke through the window and warmed her clean through.

> Hope was always just out of reach.
> Like a shadow, I could see it but knew
> I could never touch it.
> ~*The Devine Truth: A Memoir*

18

As John and Eliza waited outside the hotel for their cabs, she heard someone speaking through a megaphone nearby. She looked around to find the source. "Do you hear that?"

John nodded. "Sounds like a rally. That's typical, this close to campus. Although that one doesn't look too promising." He pointed across the hotel lawn. "Pretty thin crowd."

A woman stood on a bench in front of a building, surrounded by about a dozen people, chanting something about equal rights.

"I'd like to hear what she's saying. Do you mind?"

"I don't mind," he said.

They walked north along the hotel drive. Eliza started across Claremont Avenue, but John touched her arm.

"On second thought, I wouldn't go over there if I were you," he said, voice low.

Even through her jacket, her arm tingled where he touched her. "Why not?"

John looked left, then right along the busy street. "Like you, I support the message, but it's not a good place to be seen. Things are shaky right now, with the all the communist scrutiny, and certain topics—such as equality for minorities—are often marked as communist sympathies."

Which Eliza knew all too well. She needed to find out the truth about her parents before anyone else did. She needed to protect her parents—as well as herself—from needless suspicion. "So I've heard," she said finally.

"We should probably get out of here," he said, still looking around. "You never know who's watching. It's just smart to be careful. These days it seems they'll charge anyone on the slightest suspicion—male or female." He shook his head. "How's that for equality?"

Eliza tried to smile at the irony but couldn't. It was too unsettling.

Monday morning, Eliza met Millie at the door with a smile. "I'm glad to see you're back, Millie. Are you feeling better now?"

"Oh, I'm all right, Miz Eliza." She took Eliza's coat and hat. "The good Lord just like to remind me from time to time that I'm gettin' old, that's all." She carried Eliza's things to the closet in the hall.

Eliza had told Millie several times that she

could care for her own effects, certain that the woman had better things to do than to wait on another employee. But Millie refused, saying Eliza had her job, and she had hers. Just wouldn't be right.

Now that the meeting with John's editor was past, Eliza faced a new dilemma. In light of what Fred Wharton had said, she saw her work through new eyes. Perhaps she could explore the idea of equality in light of God's overall plan for mankind—which, unfortunately, she knew nothing about. She needed to talk to Millie about her views on race and gender equality. Her faith and wisdom would lend a very important perspective to the topic.

John met her in the doorway, a book in hand. "Ready?"

Eliza worked at her desk and took dictation from John.

As he spoke, he paced the library, still carrying the book.

Eliza spied the title *Miracles* when he strolled close enough. Perhaps C. S. Lewis had something in his writings about loved ones finding mercy in their final hour and the possibility of seeing them again.

After lunch, John continued his dictation. "The studios were still sending me scores of scripts. They either didn't know or didn't care about the way I was living—showing up on set late, fumbling more lines than I got right. I staggered back and forth between the Roosevelt and the Biltmore, just to keep everyone guessing. The more scripts they sent, the more I drank. I could put down the better part of a fifth without batting an eye. By some miracle, I kept everyone fooled."

He frowned, studying the book in his hands. "No. Perhaps the miracle wasn't that people were fooled—because I'm sure they weren't—but that I had gotten away with it for as long as I had. At the end of that year, Pearl Harbor had been hit and everything changed. The studios weren't buying my sad act anymore. We were at war, and the government wanted to make sure Hollywood was portraying Americans in the best, most patriotic light. Things got a lot stricter on the sets. People were no longer willing to turn a blind eye to a pathetic drunk who fouled up entire scenes. Early in the filming of *The Pride of the Yankees*, I was released from my contract. In a word, fired."

"Oh no," Eliza said. "You must have been very disappointed."

John heaved a sigh and leaned back in his chair. "No. It's crazy, but deep down, I was relieved. Besides, it was for the best. Gary Cooper outdid himself as Lou Gehrig. Earned himself an Oscar nomination."

Eliza shivered as she wrote the lines. She should have worn a cardigan. The ancient room was a little drafty, and now that November was nearing an end, temperatures were dropping.

"You're cold." John frowned. "I'll have Duncan light a fire."

"Oh, thank you, but don't bother him, not if it's just for me. I don't want to drive everyone else out."

"Not at all," John said with a chuckle. "Millie will be happy. She's been complaining of being cold all week."

Eliza watched the old man light the fire. When it was blazing well enough on its own, Eliza went to the fireplace and rubbed her arms.

John returned to his seat, his back to the fire.

"If you don't mind my asking, I've been wondering about Duncan and Millie. How long have they been working for you?"

John shook his head. "I don't know. My grandmother's dying wish was to keep this house open. I only learned of it in her will. This was her dream home, her fairytale come true, I suppose. I don't know why she insisted on keeping the place in the family. But after getting to know Millie and Duncan, I suspected my grandmother kept it going simply to provide for them. Millie once told me that she and Duncan worked here through the Depression, a time when many houses didn't keep help." He turned his head slightly, perhaps so Eliza could better hear him. "I think my grandparents felt responsible for Millie and Duncan and their families."

"And then along came the new landlord." She smiled, secretly admiring his profile from where she stood—a perfect vantage point.

John nodded. "The truth is, I didn't want to live here. I wanted to get much farther away from L.A. But due to a falling-out between my father and his, I never knew my grandparents. I felt it was my duty to make amends by carrying out her dying wish." He shrugged. "So this is it. A big old house and a couple of ancient hired hands is all that's left of the Vincent family. It seemed the right thing to do. Besides, by then things had changed drastically for me. But I'm getting ahead of the story."

Yes, he was, and that wouldn't do. Not that she didn't want to hear the rest of his story; she just wanted to stretch out the telling of it for as long as possible.

"Say, if you're interested, I might have a few pictures of Millie and Duncan when they were younger."

"Oh yes. I'd love to see them."

He went into the sitting room, then returned a few minutes later with a soft, leathery-looking book. He sat down and opened it on his table. "Bet you'll never guess who this is."

Eliza looked over his shoulder at a picture of a man cutting grass using a long-handled tool with

219

a blade at the bottom. "Duncan? Didn't they have push mowers in those days?"

John huffed out a laugh. "Yes. Millie told me that my granddad owned several, but Duncan refused to use them. His father was a chief groundskeeper in Ireland." John switched to an Irish brogue. "And what's good enough for me da is good enough for me."

Eliza chuckled.

He turned the pages and stopped again. "This is my father as a young man." John studied the picture so long that Eliza suspected he'd become lost in a memory and forgot she was there. John's father was also quite a looker.

She smiled at the strong family resemblance.

He turned the page. "Ah. Here's Millie."

Eliza leaned closer to get a better look. The picture was terribly faded, but the petite woman, who looked to be about Eliza's age, was unmistakably Millie. She had that same upward tilt to her chin that Eliza had come to love. "She's such a strong, wise woman," Eliza said softly. "I so admire that about her."

John turned slightly toward her, inhaling slow and deep.

Eliza froze. The man had no idea what his nearness did to her. And unless she wanted to lose her job, he could never know.

He turned toward her a little more.

She could feel his eyes on her cheek, like heat

grazing her skin. Against her better judgment, she looked at his face.

Slowly, John's gaze rose until it met hers. The air between them stilled. Something in his eyes took hold of her, made it impossible to breathe.

Move. Now!

She stepped back and nearly stumbled into the fireplace. What a fool, putting herself in such a spot, getting so close to him.

What was she thinking? What must he think?

She gathered her wits and scurried back to her seat, stunned by the intensity of her feelings. Feelings she needed to extinguish immediately, before her heart got burned.

> I remember thinking that my father
> and brother died to give us freedom,
> and this is what I do with it. Work hard
> to make people believe a hopeless
> illusion.
>
> ~*The Devine Truth: A Memoir*

19

The bus ride to Richmond Heights on Thanksgiving gave Eliza plenty of time to count her blessings. She had her health. Her rent was paid up, and she'd been socking away money for the in-between times. She had a job with a shot at some extra work if the movie deal worked out.

Then she spent the rest of the trip stewing about the possibility of spending more time with John. The sooner she distanced herself from John David Vincent, the better off she would be.

Easier said than done.

God, can You help me? The way I feel about John needs to stop. It's pointless, not to mention completely absurd, and will only leave me crushed when the work is finished. I can't continue entertaining these feelings.

It was time to tell Betty about her situation.

Eliza didn't care how her sister took the news. In fact, the more violent her reaction, the better. Eliza needed all the help she could get.

Ed Cunningham met Eliza at the bus stop and drove her home in his new Packard. As they approached the house, Betty waited in the doorway, Sue Ellen and Eddie Jr. peering out from either side.

"Darling, so good of you to come," Betty said in her cheeriest voice. She spied the bouquet in Eliza's hand. "Daisies, how simple." She gave her an almost-kiss on the cheek. Then she stepped back and examined Eliza's pale-blue dress and pearls with an approving nod. "And gloves. Perfect."

Eliza waggled her fingers at Sue Ellen. "Better safe than sorry."

Eddie Jr. squeezed around his mother. "Auntie Liza! I got the latest model in the Heavy Bomber series. It's a Boeing B-29 Superfortress. Wanna see it?"

"Eddie Jr., what have I told you about hounding guests with your airplanes the minute they walk in the door?" Betty tsked.

Eliza smiled at her nephew. "I'd love to see it."

Eddie Jr. tugged her by the hand and led her to his room down the hall, chattering the entire way about the different kinds of bombers. In his bedroom, model airplanes of various sizes covered the bureau, the windowsill, and the nightstand. The newest one was in late stages of assembly on his desk.

With a smile, Eliza glanced around the room as her nephew showed her his newest acquisition, describing it in detail. Not a thing in the room was out of place, which was no surprise. She studied the airplane. "So this bomber was used a lot during the war?"

"Yep. My pal Jack only has the light bombers, but the heavies have the most power and can fly the farthest. Look at this."

As Eddie took a different one down from the bureau, a framed photo beside the model plane caught her eye. Eliza picked it up.

It was a faded photo of a young man in an olive-colored uniform. He wore a belted military jacket, pants, and a cap with a small red star in the center. Something about the man's broad-shouldered build drew her closer to study his face.

It was Papa as a young man. She was sure of it.

"Eddie Jr., where did you get this picture?"

He looked at the picture, then at her. He chewed his bottom lip. "I found it."

"Where?"

"In the attic."

Eliza's heart raced. "Are there any more photos like this in the attic?"

The boy shrugged, already finished with any

interest in the photo, now absorbed with adding small pieces to his new plane.

"Thank you for showing me your planes, sweetheart." Eliza returned to the living room with the framed photo.

Betty was in the dining room directing Sue Ellen on proper place settings.

"Betty, can I see your attic?"

Betty frowned. "Whatever for?"

Hoping she wouldn't get her nephew into trouble, she showed Betty the picture. "Did you know about this?"

Betty took it from her and stared at it. "He must have found this in that old steamer trunk that Mama had us store for her when Ed and I married. I forgot all about it."

Had her parents wanted it stored in order to hide it? "I'd like to look at the trunk, if you don't mind." Eliza pulled off her gloves.

Betty opened her mouth to protest, then closed it. She studied Eliza's feet. "Take those off, then. You can't climb the ladder in heels. Come on, follow me."

The attic's single light fixture offered a dim glow that didn't quite reach the corners where the roof sloped. The amount of dust made it clear that Betty had not been up here in a long time.

Brushing aside cobwebs and trying not to breathe in the dust, Eliza followed Eddie Jr.'s footprints to a steamer trunk in the far corner.

There was very little of interest inside, just an old wool coat, a framed picture, books, a wool scarf, an ivory shawl, and two envelopes.

Eliza held up the envelopes and gave Betty a long look. "Do you trust me with these?"

Betty's red lips pressed together, then she shrugged. "You have as much right to know what's in it as I do."

"I promise I'm not going to harm our family's name, Betty. If anything, I'm trying to clear it. This may be just what we need to do that."

Betty nodded. "All right. Go ahead."

Eliza opened one of the envelopes and drew out a thin, faded letter written in a language she didn't recognize but suspected was Russian. She scanned the lines, hoping for something that would make sense.

The letter appeared to be in feminine handwriting. Perhaps a love letter.

Or top-secret information?

She opened the second envelope.

This letter looked as if it was written in the same language and was addressed to the same person. But the second one was not the same handwriting.

Eliza checked the sender. The signature was not very legible, but she could see that it was not the same person, due to the length of the name and the difference in handwriting.

What did these letters contain? This was such

a potential find, and yet so useless in her hands.

"I need to find someone who can translate these. Even if it's just a simple correspondence or a love letter, at least it will help us know more about them. Mind if I take them?"

"Please, go ahead. Just be careful." Betty brushed the dust from her hands with a grimace. "You don't want those getting into the hands of that G-man. He sounds positively bloodthirsty."

For once, Eliza had to agree with her sister.

Stuffed with turkey, sweet potatoes, and a sliver of pumpkin pie that came close to being as good as Millie's, Eliza leaned back with a groan and pressed a hand to her stomach.

Sue Ellen's eyes widened.

On second thought . . . Eliza sat up straighter. She didn't want to be the sole ruination of her niece's etiquette training.

"Ed," Betty said sweetly, "why don't you tell Eliza what Stanley said when you told him she was coming for Thanksgiving."

Ed took a bite of his pie, frowning. He finished chewing, then wiped his mouth with a cloth napkin and set it down. "I don't remember. Why don't you tell her?"

Betty's smile almost disguised the miffed look in her eyes. "Oh, but you remember, don't you, dear? Stanley said she was a lovely girl, and he simply could not understand why she wasn't married yet."

Ed narrowed a gaze at his wife. "I believe it was more along the lines of 'it's odd that she's still not married after all this time.' " He shot a brief glance at Eliza, then stabbed another chunk of pie.

Betty wore a flat, humorless smile.

As annoying as the sisterly interference was, Eliza actually felt sorry for Betty. "Don't worry, Betty. The right one may still come along."

"*Right* one?" Betty sniffed. "Any man with a decent job would do at this point. You're not—"

"Getting any younger, yes. Thank you for reminding me." Eliza glanced at her niece and nephew. "So, how is school this year?"

"Sue Ellen, Eddie Jr.," Betty said, "it's time to wash up and find something quiet to do in the other room." As her children left the table, she turned to Eliza. "I know you don't like to discuss this, but, darling, you must. Your rocky marriage is already one strike against you. And you are getting past the age that a man wants in a wife."

Eliza stared at her sister. "A strike against *me?* Are you saying our 'rocky marriage' was *my* fault?"

Ed quickly wadded up his napkin.

"Let's be sensible. It takes two to make marriage work. But that's neither here nor there, as I'm sure you've outgrown most of your . . . shortcomings by now. And if you marry well enough, you can hire a maid so you won't have to worry about your cooking."

Eliza drew a calming breath, then another. Neither one did the trick. "Betty, you have no idea what it was like being married to Ralph. No matter how hard I tried, he was not to be pleased. He humiliated me daily. He was unkind, uncaring, and unfaithful. And silly me, I kept smiling and giving and trying harder. What more would you have had me do?"

Ed looked like he had just discovered his suit was made of sandpaper. He rose and excused himself.

Betty watched her husband leave, then lowered her voice and leaned closer to Eliza. "But, Eliza, did you really *try?* I'm sure if you would have just—"

"Betty! Do you hear yourself?" Eliza's heart thumped so hard it hurt. "Do you have any idea how degrading it is to tell a woman who lives to be pleasing, day after day, that it's her fault when her husband cheats on her? Do you have any idea how demoralizing that is? How can you, a woman, even consider letting a lying philanderer off the hook and say that a man's dissatisfaction—or anything for that matter—justifies sleeping around?"

Betty stiffened and stared at Eliza as if seeing her for the first time.

"Can we just drop this, please?" Eliza hissed,

her body trembling from the adrenaline coursing through her.

"Yes, of course."

Did Betty really understand? Because Eliza couldn't understand her sister's way of thinking. Did Betty really believe a woman was to blame for a husband's choices and men were not to be held accountable? Were men not capable of being kind and considerate out of mutual respect? Had Betty forgotten their father? He not only showed kindness to Mama, but love and affection. Was Papa a rare exception?

Betty took Eliza's plate and carried it to the kitchen.

Eliza didn't join her. Forget love and affection. Was it too much to ask for simple kindness or a little approval once in a while?

The intensity of her own emotions shook her more than she thought possible. Too long had those feelings festered. Too deep had the pain been driven.

Will this anger and hurt ever go away, or will it keep bursting out of me again and again? Will I ever be free of this?

Ed returned to the dining room, followed by Odella with a tray of coffee. Ed was probably trying to think of a good excuse to take Eliza to the bus stop early, and she couldn't blame him.

Odella offered Eliza a cup, which she accepted with a slight tremor in her hands.

"So how's work these days?" Ed said. "I hear you're doing some kind of book collaboration."

Betty returned to the table and took her seat. Her blue eyes were dark and rimmed in red.

Eliza's heart sank. *I bet they're glad I came. Happy Thanksgiving, everyone.* She eased out a smile. "I'm collaborating on a memoir."

"Memoir?" Betty tried to smile, but her eyes weren't joining in. "How interesting. So you're typing someone's diary?"

"No, Betty," Ed said. "A memoir is particular events in someone's life, told with a point. A lot of famous people write them." Ed turned to Eliza. "So who is he? Don't tell me—Winston Churchill." He chuckled.

"As a matter of fact . . ." Eliza said. This was it, now or never. "I'm working on the memoir of Johnny Devine."

Betty's eyes widened.

Ed stared. Then he laughed. "Funny, for a minute I thought you said Johnny *Devine,* as in the famous movie star." Still chuckling, he shook his head.

Eliza nodded. "That's the one."

Ed's face sagged, losing all traces of mirth. "You can't be serious. *The* Johnny Devine? That guy was all the rage. Legendary ladies' man. What's writing his story like—copying notes written on ladies' undergarments and cocktail napkins?" He laughed at his own joke.

Fingering her pearls, Eliza tried to keep calm. After all, Ed didn't know John. Which made his flippant remark all the more aggravating. People could be so callous, so quick to assume and judge people they didn't even know.

Was this the kind of reception John's book would get when it went public? Now, more than ever, she wanted the book finished and filling the shelves of every bookstore in the country.

"That would be some trick, wouldn't it?" Eliza mustered a weak smile. "No, I transcribe notes taken from dictation. I edit the notes as needed and then type the manuscript." She stole a glance at her sister.

Betty caught her glance and held it, her churning thoughts almost visible on her face. "And *who* takes dictation from him?"

"I do."

More shocked stares.

"Jiminy," Ed said, his face thoughtful. "Looks like we'll have a celebrity in the family, Betty." His eyes lit up. "Your name's going on the cover, right?" He leaned forward on folded arms. "What kind of, uh . . . royalties are you going to be pulling in?"

"Well, it doesn't work that—"

"Where?" Betty said. "I mean, where does this *dictation* take place?" She said the word as if it fouled her tongue to say it.

Here it comes. Eliza met her sister's questioning

stare head-on. "We work in the library at his gated home. There's a maid and a gardener there at all times."

Betty reddened. A thick silence settled over the table.

Ed's gaze shifted between Eliza and Betty. He looked as though he'd just stepped into a nest of something best left undisturbed.

"Darling, I don't mean to be negative," Betty said, tone cautious, as if Eliza's previous outburst had been a lesson to her. "But are you aware of this man's reputation?"

"Yes." *As a matter of fact, I hear it, write it, read it, and type it. Every day. You could say I know him by heart now.*

"Should you really be working for a man like that?"

Eliza studied her hands in her lap. No wonder John had a hard time forgetting his past—no one else could. "He's perfectly professional, Betty. He treats me with utmost respect. I can assure you he has never, nor will he ever, make a pass at me." A dull ache settled deep into her chest. "And what you don't know—at least, not until the book comes out—is that he's changed. That's the reason he's writing—"

"Changed? Please. He's an *actor,* Eliza. It's an *act.*"

Eliza broke from Betty's gaze to avoid another scene. One outburst per holiday was Eliza's limit, and her earlier tirade would be remembered for holidays to come.

All she had to do was keep her wits about her for another half hour, then she'd be on a bus back to Oakland.

"Betty," Eliza said as evenly as possible, "may I remind you that I was desperately in need of a job. This one pays me well enough to put away a tidy little nest egg."

"And may I remind *you* that you wouldn't have to work if you would only—" Betty clamped her lips.

"Get married? Yes. You've reminded me."

Odella moved through the dining room without making a sound, coffee urn in hand. "More coffee, ma'am?" she asked Eliza.

"Oh yes, thank you, Odella." As the woman poured, Eliza turned to her. "By the way, Odella, do you have a family?"

Odella didn't make eye contact. "Yes, ma'am." She concentrated on the urn.

"Are they waiting for you to get home so you can have Thanksgiving dinner together?"

The woman's gaze lifted slowly until it met Eliza's. "Yes, ma'am." With a sideways glance at Betty, Odella collected dishes on her tray and left the room.

Betty spooned three lumps of sugar into her coffee with a clang each time her spoon hit the cup. "Of course, you could just *marry* Johnny

Devine. Then you would never have to work again." She stirred her tea with a vengeance and picked up her cup without meeting Eliza's gaze.

Marry John? Her sister must have pinned her curls too tightly and pinched her brain. "Don't be ridiculous, Betty. He doesn't see me that way. At all. He's an award-winning movie star with scores of fans who swoon over him and smart, glamorous friends whose beauty would take your breath away. I'm nobody."

As the last two words left her lips, they tore something from her, leaving a hollow ache.

Betty set her cup down and leaned closer, blue eyes flashing. "Good. I wouldn't marry that skirt-chasing gutter trash if he were the last man on the planet. There. How's that for not letting a cheater off the hook?"

Anger seized Eliza's lungs. "You're wrong about John," she said with all the calm she could muster. "That's not who he is. Not at all. Not anymore."

Betty studied her long and hard. "Oh, Eliza," she said, shaking her head. "You'd better watch yourself. You're treading on very dangerous ground, in more ways than one. You need to end that situation pronto. I see nothing but heartache on the horizon for you."

Don't I know it.

> A confession can be made to one person or to many, but either way, dark deeds must be exposed to the light and acknowledged for what they truly are.
> ~*The Devine Truth: A Memoir*

20

The first thing Eliza noticed when she woke Friday morning was that her favorite clock had suffered some kind of malfunction. Even though Kit-Cat's tail and eyes were moving back and forth in unison, the time read one thirty. Eliza rolled out of bed, stumbled to the bureau, and checked her watch.

The clock was right. She'd slept into the afternoon. Good thing she had the day off.

A heart-stopping rattle on her door made her realize this wasn't the first time someone had knocked.

Eliza closed her eyes with a groan. No more questions. No more insinuations. No more trying to defend herself and her parents to people who would not listen.

"E-*liz*-a? You alive in there?" Joan's voice carried through the door.

Tucking back a stray curl, Eliza went to the door and opened it a crack. "I think so."

"Good. I know you said no calls, but it's a gal. Says she's your sister."

Was there some rule in Emily Post's etiquette book that said she *had* to take her sister's call? Eliza sighed. "Thank you, Joan, I'll be right down." She wrapped her robe around her and belted it, stepped into her slippers, and tiptoed down the stairs, praying no one would see her. Pressing the receiver to her ear, she tried to smile and failed. "Hiya, Betty."

"Do you know what you've started?" Betty's voice squeaked.

Eliza's head pounded. Aspirin. No, coffee. With two lumps of aspirin. "What's wrong?"

"I was just paid a visit from a *friend* of yours from the house of UN-American something or other. We'd left the picture of Papa in uniform on the coffee table, and the man questioned me about him. At length!"

"What?" Eliza shook her head, only making it hurt more. "You let him in your *house?*"

"Of course I let him in, Eliza. I have nothing to hide."

"What did he say?" Heels clicked down the stairs, and Eliza pressed herself closer to the wall. Apparently the other girls in the building had the day after Thanksgiving off too.

"I don't remember, he asked all sorts of questions. About the red star on Papa's uniform, which the man said was the uniform of Lenin's

Red Army. He also insisted on seeing my birth certificate. How did he know about that, Eliza?" The pitch of her voice bordered on hysteria.

"I don't know, Betty. Probably the same way he knew how our parents died. How do these people know anything?"

"I don't know. You tell me." A huff rattled across the line.

"What—you think *I* told him?"

Silence.

This was too much. With her only living family member against her, there was no one on Eliza's side.

"He insisted I tell him why all the lies and secrecy and what subversive activity this family is hiding." A muffled sob. "My children had to hear that."

This was not good. If Sue Ellen and Eddie Jr. were nearby, they were probably afraid their mother was losing her marbles. "Betty, where's Ed?" Eliza asked gently, hoping her tone would calm her sister.

"I can't reach him. He's at a big lunch meeting with a bunch of engineers."

Eliza tried to think. There wasn't really anything she could do for Betty in this moment. The harassment needed to stop, that was all there was to it.

But the only way to end it was to find some kind of proof that she and Betty were not

238

involved in anti-American activity. If only there *was* such proof.

"Betty, I'm sorry this happened. I know you're upset. But I'm sure he won't be back. Just try to calm down."

"Calm *down?* He said I should be prepared to go to their headquarters in downtown Berkeley for questioning. Why? I haven't done anything, and I don't know anything. I shouldn't have to endure all this questioning, Eliza. I've worked too hard to have a good standing in the community. Whatever you've gotten yourself into, you need to drop it. It's upsetting my family and I won't have it."

Eliza started to answer but was interrupted by a disconnect tone.

Saturday, Eliza spent most of the day in the library reading everything she could find about Lenin's Red Army and what had been taking place in Russia during the years prior to Betty's birth. The Red Army had been made up of young volunteers who believed in the promises of Lenin's new communist regime, and who hoped to be paid for their service in food rations, since the country was facing one of the worst famines in history.

She also tried to find record of her parents' arrival in America. Betty's birth certificate listed the name of a hospital in Queens County, New York, as her birthplace. Eliza got the hospital's number and called to see what records they had on file, but nothing turned up. So far, every scrap of information she could find had only led to a dead end.

Sunday morning, Eliza half hoped that John would invite her to his church again, even though it wasn't a good idea to continue being seen with him. Going with him the one time had probably raised questions, and he certainly didn't need that, or to give the appearance that he was gadding about with women, not with his book coming out soon.

By Sunday afternoon, most of her distress over Betty's call had dissolved. Though there was no reason to be so hysterical, Eliza couldn't blame her sister for being upset over a visit by Agent Robinson. And though she hadn't admitted it to Betty, Eliza suspected she was to blame. Who knew how long the agent had been watching Eliza? He had probably found Betty by following Eliza to her home. It was fortunate—or perhaps providential—that Eliza had removed the Russian letters from Betty's house. Those people were probably experts at finding anything they wanted to.

Which made it all the more urgent for Eliza to find out who her parents were before that agent did.

John was quieter than usual when she arrived to work Monday.

Eliza took her cue from him and waited at her desk, notepad in hand.

John rose and paced the room, stopping to examine a picture on the wall. "This is under the heading *1942*," he said finally. "Being out of work for the first time in two decades, I was finally forced to face what my life had become. That happens when you've lost your friends, your work, and your self-respect." Frowning, he peered out the window at the rear of the library. "By then, I'd become an expert at avoiding the truth with enough Scotch to drown a horse."

"What truth? Of who you had become, the puppet of studios, that sort of thing?"

John shook his head. "No." With a deep frown, he studied the floor. "Something I haven't been able to talk about, but . . . since I've revealed just about everything else now, I guess I can't withhold this."

More confessions? Her heart twisted. "Are you sure it's necessary to include in your book?" If only she could spare them both any more of his difficult memories. Hadn't he confessed enough?

John's face tilted skyward. "I do believe God has forgiven me. And I want people to understand that there is nothing He can't forgive. But . . . it's still hard to forget some things and go on carefree, as if no harm was done. There are things I've done that some people will never be able to forgive and will certainly never forget."

Unfortunately, she had just learned this first-hand at her sister's house. There would always be people who would never let John forget what he once was. "The truth shall set you free," she said, remembering Jesus's words.

John pivoted and studied her from across the room, perhaps surprised that she knew a Bible verse. He turned back to the window. "What if the truth that sets one person free only imprisons others?"

He said it so quietly, she wasn't sure he meant for her to hear it. She set her notepad down and stood. "Why don't I get us some coffee, give you a chance to collect your thoughts."

He nodded vaguely.

She went to the kitchen, but Millie wasn't there, so Eliza started the electric coffeepot. While it percolated, she went to the doorway to see if John was ready to resume.

He just stood in the library, leaning more heavily on his cane than usual, looking defeated, burdened too long by a weight too heavy. With a sigh, he sank onto one of the nearby chairs. "Jeanette Lovell was young," he said. "Talented, but too green for the politics. Studios collected starlets with a certain daring look, and she had it. 'Studio candy,' they were called. When they weren't going over lines or doing promo shoots, girls like her were assigned to the arm of an actor and paraded beneath the lights of the Boulevard.

This was to make us appear more desirable, you see. Boost publicity. Great for ticket sales."

He studied his cane, twisting it clockwise, then counterclockwise. "Jeanette had married her high school sweetheart."

Eliza nodded, realizing he wasn't dictating but rather remembering aloud and probably needed a sounding board. She stepped into the library so he would know that she was still listening.

"Please, stay where you were. I'd rather not have you looking at me just now."

Pulse racing, Eliza stepped back.

The coffeepot gurgled.

"No one knew. No one but me, anyway. Somewhere deep down, in those rare few moments when I sobered up enough, I saw the whole thing for what it really was. But I couldn't own up to it, so I stayed drunk."

"What happened?"

His hand gripped the cane so hard his knuckles whitened. "When her husband learned of . . . an encounter between us, he divorced her. Immediately." John hung his head. "I don't blame him. Poor Jeanette was completely devastated. This sort of thing wasn't a habit of hers, you see. That's the thing. I . . . I should have known that. Not that it should have made a difference."

Eliza glanced across the room at her notepad, but she didn't need it. He wasn't composing—he was confessing.

"At the time, I chalked it up to bad luck. Tough break, doll face, these things happen. Hollywood is no place for your heart. To work in this town, you have to pack light and keep moving." He groaned, as if the memory pained him. "*That* was the extent of my sympathy. My remorse for ruining a marriage and a promising career."

The despair in his tone echoed through Eliza like a melancholy chord. "I take it she never worked in Hollywood again?"

Shaking his head, he leaned his cane against the chair. "No, she didn't. Jeanette had come to L.A. with two things most people only dream of having: young love and huge potential." His voice dropped to a choked whisper. "And I destroyed both. Without even giving it a second thought."

"Surely she could have . . . recovered from her loss eventually and continued acting?"

John hung his head so low she could barely see it beyond his shoulders. "If she'd had a tougher hide or a harder heart, perhaps," he said, voice muffled. "But she had neither."

Eliza stepped into the room to see him better. She was afraid to ask, but also feared he would sink further into despair. "John, what happened to her?" she whispered.

John gripped his head in both hands. "She tried to take her life." His voice broke.

Covering a gasp, Eliza could only stand numb, heart sinking.

"Luckily, a friend found her and took her to a hospital. The press called it a tragedy averted. No one looked for anyone to blame. But they should have."

"No," Eliza whispered. That would have done no one any good.

"She never said a word, and her ex-husband never went public with the truth about the divorce, so no one knew the real reason for her despair. But I knew."

"What became of her?"

John reached for his cane. "She disappeared. Rumor had it she got involved with some real shady types. A few years later, I heard she grew sick and died. Alone and penniless."

Eliza needed to say something, but what? Everything that came to mind sounded so trite.

"I believe she died of a broken heart." His voice faltered. "And it was all my doing." He leaned forward. Silent sobs shook him.

Eliza couldn't move, couldn't breathe. His grief filled the room and tore at her. *Dear God, what should I do?*

John rubbed both eyes with the heels of his hands. "Please . . . don't write that," he whispered. "At least not yet."

The shame in his voice clutched her heart. She went to him and stood beside his chair, aching to console him, and yet, feeling so helpless. "John," she said, "I'm so sorry. But if what you say about God is true, then He wouldn't want you to keep carrying around shame from past mistakes, would He? Yes, her end was tragic, and yes, it's right and honorable for you to accept your share of blame, but it's past and it can't be undone. Nothing good could come from bringing it out in the open now."

He didn't move, didn't respond.

Afraid he wasn't listening, she laid a hand on his shoulder.

John stiffened.

"Admitting the truth is a very brave and noble thing. Maybe you *did* need to confess this aloud to someone, like me. But perhaps you don't need to tell it to the whole world."

His eyes drifted closed, forcing tears down his cheeks.

Her heart thudded. He looked so broken—in spite of the solid strength of his shoulder beneath her hand.

She pulled her hand away. "I'll check on that coffee." She slipped into the kitchen, still trembling from having come dangerously close to pulling John into her arms.

> By the end of '42, I had hit rock
> bottom. When I wasn't blind drunk,
> I was depressed and ailing from
> years of reckless living. And though
> I lived in Hollywood's busiest hotels,
> surrounded by parties day and night, I
> was completely alone.
>   *~The Devine Truth: A Memoir*

21

Eliza finished typing what little notes she had
taken and went home early at John's insistence.
He was done for the day.

She didn't blame him.

Eliza arrived home early enough to call the
university, hoping to find someone who could
translate the letters from Betty's attic. At first,
when she said she was looking for someone
who could translate Russian into English, the
receptionist sounded suspicious. Eliza politely
explained these were old family letters that were
all that she had left of her parents. The woman
finally agreed to put her through to the linguistics
department. With a sigh, Eliza explained her
mission again, getting the feeling she was
meeting another brick wall. She was transferred
to a Russian literature professor, to whom she

told her story yet again. This man said he would be willing to look at the letters, but only by appointment.

And the only time he had available was Wednesday at noon.

Crossing her fingers, Eliza made the appointment, hoping John wouldn't mind her missing a day of work. When she arrived at his house on Tuesday, Eliza asked about taking the next day off and explained it was for personal family business.

He hesitated. "I was hoping we could speed things up. I'd like to finish the book as soon as possible."

Eliza nodded, disappointed that he was in such a hurry, but not surprised after his painful confession the day before. "Of course, I understand. I will just call back and change the—"

"But if it's the only day you can take care of your family business, then you should take advantage of that, by all means. I'll spend the day writing as best I can."

"Thank you," she said, feeling guilty for delaying the book when he wanted it done. The publisher's deadline was the end of December, which was still four weeks away. "Do you want to finish the book before Christmas? Or did you mean even sooner than that?"

John straightened the books on his table without looking up. "As soon as possible."

Still trying to catch her breath, Eliza knocked on the faculty room door on the third floor of Stephens Hall. She'd gotten off the bus at the wrong stop. When she finally figured out where the Slavic Studies department was located, she ran the entire way and arrived a few minutes late.

As she waited at the door, she checked to make sure the letters and her steno pad were still in her bag.

The literature wing was located in an older part of the building—the part built before modern heat had been invented, apparently.

Eliza wrapped her coat a little tighter.

The door opened and a gray haired gentleman greeted her. "Mrs. Saunderson? I'm Professor Grant. Come in."

She stepped inside a room containing a few small tables with chairs and a black-and-white-checkered floor.

"Please, have a seat," he said. "Can I get you coffee or tea?"

She couldn't hide her shiver. "Coffee sounds wonderful, thank you."

The professor brought two steaming mugs and got straight to work, sipping the black liquid as he read the first letter. He squinted and brought it close to his face a few times. "Some of the writing is hard to distinguish, the lines have blurred and faded. But I believe I can piece it together through context. Would you like me to read it now?"

Eliza nodded, not sure she could trust her voice. These letters could be her parents speaking from the grave. She readied her pencil to transcribe the letter in shorthand.

"This letter reads, 'Dearest Vasily, Do you still have terrible cough? Please stay warm and promise you will not refuse food. I know your comrades are also hungry, but you must be well. Think of our son.' "

Eliza gasped. "Son? Please, can you check and see who the letter is from?"

Professor Grant checked the signature at the bottom. " 'Your Loving Wife, Lara.' "

She swallowed hard. Her parents had a son? "Please, continue."

" 'Your Mama is still ailing, so I stay with her and make her eat broth, though she tries to say she is not hungry. But I do just as you say and do not hear her protests. See, it is not only the old wives who are wise with persuasion, my love.

" 'The fuel and food have all run out now. The villagers are very hungry and cold and there is a look in their eyes that I fear. I believe it is the look of death. When you and your comrades receive your rations, please send some home quickly.

" 'I think baby Ivan is finally getting stronger now, but it is hard to know because we are all so cold. Anything you can send will put this mama's heart at ease. Our son depends on you, my love.' "

The professor lifted the paper higher and angled it in the light. " 'I am so proud of you, Vas. Be strong. Your Loving Wife, Lara.' "

Eliza finished transcribing, thoughts whirling. Her parents had a *son?* She had a brother?

She could picture the scene, though she didn't want to—a stark Russian winter and starving villagers. A sick baby boy weak from cold.

Eliza clapped a gloved hand over her mouth to stifle a sob, but the tears rushed to her eyes unchecked.

Professor Grant offered her his handkerchief. "Russia has seen some very difficult times. Do you know when this letter was written?"

Shaking her head, she tried to calculate her parents' ages. They were in their early twenties when Betty was born in 1919. "I wonder if Ivan was a family name," she said. "Perhaps that would help me trace my parents' history."

Professor Grant shrugged. "That is possible. It is a good, strong name. It is the Russian form of John, which means, 'gracious gift from God.' "

John, a gracious gift from God . . .

"Did you say you had two letters?" the professor asked.

Shaking herself from her stunned reverie, Eliza handed over the second one. "I think the handwriting on this is different from my mother's."

The professor nodded. "Yes." He peered at the writing, then held the paper up to the light. "This one is more difficult to piece together. I will read what bits are legible."

She readied her pencil. Whose voice from the grave would she hear now?

"I can't make out the first paragraph, save for a few words like 'Mama' and 'soldier.' Let me see . . ." He scanned the lines closely, scratching his forehead.

" 'I can stay no longer, brother . . . too much for my heart . . . first Mama and now my beloved Anatoly, only days before we were to marry . . . find work as nurse . . . cannot tell you where.' "

His face relaxed. "This next part is clearer. 'Yes, I will help, but you must never speak of this to anyone. We will never see each other again, Vasily. Be brave, my brother. You have . . .' " The professor tilted the paper again, shook his head. "I think it says 'beautiful wife . . . child coming soon. You can do this. Do it for them. Do it for me. Your beloved sister . . .' "

Eliza leaned forward, in some crazy hope that her proximity would help him read it. "Is there a name?"

Professor Grant squinted, shaking his head. "Just a moment, I'll be right back." He left the room with the letter.

Eliza's heart raced. He wasn't thinking of calling someone and turning it over to the authorities, was he? She'd heard rumors of professors being forced to sign some kind of loyalty oath.

Maybe the HUAC had ordered universities to be on the lookout for anti-American activity.

When the professor returned with her letter and a magnifying glass, she eased out a pent-up breath. He held the letter and the glass at varying angles, squinting, for what seemed like half an hour.

"I think I can make out the first three letters. 'Kat.' "

" 'Kat?' Is that an actual name?"

He nodded. "There are many Russian female names beginning that way. Katja, for example. There are also Katerina, Katenka, Katjusha." He smiled. "I hope that helps, Mrs. Saunderson. I am truly sorry I could not tell you more."

Eliza jotted the names on her pad. They stood, and Eliza offered her hand. "You've been extremely helpful, Professor Grant. I appreciate your time. Thank you so much."

On the bus ride home, Eliza read her transcription again. As stirring as it was to hear her mama's voice, the letters only raised more questions.

She and Betty had a brother? And an aunt?

What other relatives might they have? What had Aunt "Kat" promised to help do, and why was she resigned to never see Vasily again?

Was Kat still alive? If so, how could Eliza find her?

Eliza took out the envelope containing Kat's letter. She couldn't read Russian but could tell it had a return address. What were the chances that there was still someone at that address who knew Kat, Lara, or Vasily Petrovich?

She needed to talk to Betty.

When she reached her building, Eliza stopped at the telephone.

Ivy was using it, but gave Eliza a nod and, after a moment, wrapped up her call.

Eliza thanked her and gave the operator Betty's number.

Odella answered. "Cunningham residence."

"Hello, Odella, this is Eliza. May I speak to my sister, please?"

A heavy sigh reached across the line. "Miz Betty . . . indisposed, ma'am. Would you like to leave a message?"

Indisposed my foot, Betty. Sticking your head in the sand won't make this go away.

"Yes. Please tell my sister she might like to know that we had a brother."

A hesitant silence. "Yes, ma'am. One minute please . . ."

The sounds of muffled talk through rustling

254

cloth confirmed Eliza's suspicions about her sister's *indisposition.*

"Eliza?" Betty's voice. "What's this? Who has a brother?"

"We do. Or, it seems, we did." She explained about getting the letter translated.

"Will you read it to me, please?" Betty's voice sounded oddly distant.

Eliza read the letter from Mama first, her voice catching again at the mention of baby Ivan. "What do you think happened to the baby?" she asked when she finished.

A heaviness drifted across the line. "It sounds like he was very sick. What do *you* think?"

Eliza tried not to picture the infant but couldn't help it.

A tiny boy, weak and gray. Mama looking into the face of her child, desperate to see signs of improvement. Coming to America without him.

"I don't know, Betty." Tears clogged her throat. "I'm afraid he may have . . . died in the cold."

The phone line went silent. Or at least it seemed so at first, but then Eliza heard the sound of weeping.

"Poor Mama," Betty whispered. "She always did seem sad."

"Yes. And poor Papa," Eliza added. "How awful to be stuck in the army somewhere far from his family, knowing they were struggling to survive and not able to help them."

Betty sniffled. "Eliza?"

"Yes?"

"Please find out what happened to them. I don't care if you have to break down the door of the Russian Embassy with a Sherman tank. Do whatever it takes. Please."

"I'll try." She swallowed hard. "I love you, Betty."

Betty sniffled. "I love you too, sis."

Back in her apartment, Eliza wondered about the address on Aunt Kat's letter. Could the home have survived the war? Was it even inhabited? And if someone did live there, what were the chances the residents knew of her family? Was it possible that there were relatives or people in the nearby village who knew the Petrovich family? Eliza had to try. What was the worst that could happen if she sent a letter to that address?

Eliza put a clean sheet of paper in her typewriter and settled in to write her letter. She explained who her parents were, mentioned baby Ivan, and said she was looking for any relatives of the Petrovich family, particularly a woman whose name began with "Kat."

Once she was satisfied with the letter, she carefully copied the return address onto a new envelope and sealed the letter, then hurried to the post office before it closed for the day.

And the truth shall make you free.

Those words had a way of turning up at such inconvenient moments. Yes, perhaps the truth *would* free Eliza. Unless the nagging fears about her parents were true.

Because in that case, the truth would only make matters worse.

> By then, my life was sliding closer to
> the chasm at my feet and I couldn't
> stop. And yet, because the façade was
> so convincing, fans adored Johnny
> Devine more than ever before.
> ~*The Devine Truth: A Memoir*

22

Russian Embassy? Would the Russians know about her parents?

As ridiculous and possibly dangerous as a visit to the Embassy would be, what if Eliza *could* get information there?

Was it worth the risk?

Yes. She needed to know the truth, no matter the cost.

After mailing the letter to Russia, Eliza called the Soviet Consulate in San Francisco and found out that all requests for information had to be made in person. No information was given over the telephone. And since the consulate was only open on weekdays, she would have to ask John for another day off, or more likely two, according to what she was told. But because of John's urgency to finish the book, it was a request she dreaded to make.

After his gut-wrenching confession about

Jeanette Lovell's tragic death, anyone could understand why he wanted to put the memoir behind him. He had to be weary of reliving his past and facing the full emotional brunt of his troubling memories.

Yes, she understood his urgency. It was just that the thought of their time together ending tore at her insides and stole her appetite. But once the job was finished, she would find a way to move on.

She had to.

Thursday morning, Eliza hurried to John's house, spurred on by a gusty breeze that matched her own swirling emotions.

Millie didn't meet Eliza at the door as usual.

She let herself in, removed her coat and scarf, laid them on a chair in the sitting room, then went to her desk in the library.

John was also nowhere in sight.

A notebook lay on his table, as she had expected, since he had told her he would spend Wednesday writing.

She glanced around again. A tingle of apprehension nudged up her spine. Where was everyone? She went to the kitchen.

Millie was seated at the table in the corner, her head resting on folded arms across a Bible.

Eliza was about to call out to her but decided against it.

If Millie was asleep, she probably needed rest.

And if she was praying, she probably needed to do that as well.

Back in the library, Eliza took John's notepad to her desk and looked at his latest pages with an editorial eye. He had continued on from where they had left off. As good as his writing had become, she would have no trouble typing these pages and adding them to his manuscript.

The manuscript that would very soon be complete.

Eliza gave herself a stern reminder of Betty's prediction that Eliza was flirting with heartache, then pulled herself together and typed what he'd written.

When the war began, I registered but I somehow missed the first draft and was glad of it. Yet from that moment on, every time I saw the newsreels and heard war broadcasts on the radio, I felt like a coward for not serving when other men were willing to fight and die. The deaths of my father and brother had cast a permanent shadow over my life, a constant reminder of the hero I would never be.

I joined the army of my own accord in February 1943. Fans went nuts over that, naturally. A real true-blue hero, they said. You see, everyone in Hollywood was doing their part for the war effort. If not joining up, then selling war bonds or traveling with the USO and entertaining troops. When I joined up, the studio (the one that fired me, as it happens) milked it for every drop of publicity they could.

You might think I joined as a way of following in my father's and brother's bootsteps, a way to be like them, a way to gain some measure of honor. And I may have entertained a thought like that. But the truth is, I carried a deeper, darker hope. I could think of nothing I wanted more than to meet a German bullet and end it all. Die in battle. Put an end to what my life had become.

But when I left Sicily and returned to England unharmed, it seemed God had other plans for me.

One of the guys in my division—Red Cahill—was religious, and though the guys in the unit gave him grief for it, he took it without complaint. He carried a tiny, pocket-sized Bible that he would often read with a penlight at night. One day, I did a bunk check and noticed Red had left that Bible on his pillow. I knew he'd be stuck with latrine duty if the lieutenant saw it, so I decided to do Red a favor and put it away. I took it to his

261

footlocker, but then I stopped. What was so special about the Bible that would make a guy risk being caught with it on his bunk? I hunkered down and started reading, just to see what the big deal was. I leafed through and saw the Gospel of John—seemed as good a place to start as any. I didn't find anything mind-boggling, but I kept reading anyway. I'd read ten chapters and was just about to toss the thing, but decided to read one more chapter.

It was the chapter in which Christ raised a dead man back to life. Ironic, because I was as good as dead. I deserved to die, and I had come prepared to do just that. But seeing how Jesus brought that man back to life did something to me. Gave me a flicker of hope, something I hadn't felt in a long time. What if God could give me new life too? What would it hurt to ask? I had nothing left to lose.

I didn't know what I was doing, didn't know how to pray. I had just read the part about the need to repent of my sins— that part was easy. The problem was that I couldn't possibly list them all. But I figured God knew more of my sins than I did and could fill in the blanks. Alone in an airless barracks tent, I gave my life, whatever it was worth, to Christ. And I was pretty sure it wasn't worth the boots on my feet, but I'd let God sort that out.

I soon became friends with Red Cahill, and I also talked to the chaplain whenever I could. I don't know how or when it happened—some of it was instant, some gradual—but God began to change me. Change my heart, give me hope through His promises. And hope, something I'd long forgotten, tasted sweeter than anything I'd ever known.

Until June 1944. In His kindness and mercy, God had helped rid me of a lot of things, and without all the booze and late nights, and in spite of a raging war, I was getting healthier, stronger. I'd begun to hope, to believe life was worth living. But when final orders came for us to storm that beach in Normandy, I had a feeling that the punishment I deserved had only been delayed, my past couldn't be made right by simply turning my life over to God. That just seemed too easy. Omaha Beach would be my payment, the squaring of things between me and God, once and for all. It made sense that he would take me out at that point. After all, that was the reason I'd joined up.

The only problem was, I'd changed my

mind about wanting to die—I wanted to live. I had found grace and mercy, and I didn't want it to end, not yet. "My Father," I said, borrowing a prayer from Christ, "if it be possible, let this cup pass from me: nevertheless, not as I will, but as You will."

As part of the 1st Infantry Division, Red and I were in the first wave to hit Omaha Beach, just before daybreak on June 6. As we neared the beach, gunfire peppered the water all around us.

We waded toward the beach, but machine-gun fire rained on us from every direction and pinned us down. Red was hit and couldn't go any farther, sinking in two feet of murky water. I tried to fire back, but my gun jammed. One of our tanks lobbed a shell in the direction of the assault. A sniper shot from somewhere above the beach and hit my helmet. I dropped down into the water next to Red, who had passed out. I screamed for a medic. Shells were exploding all around us. I hunkered down and covered him, kept his face above water, and prayed hard.

About that time, a shell from a German 88 exploded near us and knocked the wind out of me. It should have killed me, but instead, the shrapnel only hit my right hip and knee. I yelled for the medic again, not sure if Red had taken shrapnel too. The water around us turned bright red. All I could think about was how the blood from one man's body—God's Son—was somehow enough to save every man on that beach and then some.

Red was still unconscious, and I didn't know what else to do but pray. The Germans kept pinning us down, and things looked bad for our guys on the beach. Someone dragged Red and me out of the water. That's when I blacked out.

When I woke, I was lying on a stretcher at an aid station. I asked about Red, but no one knew where he was. I passed out again for several days. Later, while recovering in an army hospital, I got a letter from Red. He was going to be okay and was headed back home. His letter came wrapped around a small, pocket-sized Bible.

I still have that Bible.

And I still have the wounds I received on D-Day. The scars have mostly faded, but the pain lingers. I walk with the help of a cane now, a blessing in disguise. It reminds me of how I tried to throw my life away and how God, in His mercy, took hold of me. Like Jacob, who dared to wrestle with God, I was only touched at the hip and sent back, left with a limp and a reminder that God is sovereign. I should have died that day. In fact, everyone who saw that 88 shell explode said I should have been dead. Maybe in a way, I did die that day. I know I've never been the same.

Though I lived most of my life not believing in Him, God never stopped believing in me, and because of that, I've never wanted to live more than I do now.

With a deep sigh, Eliza took out the last typed page and added it to the stack. She should proofread the last few pages before moving on, but she couldn't. Her eyes were blurred with tears. John had done an incredibly heroic thing by shielding his friend with his own body—offering his own life, in fact. Why was it easy for him to point out how terrible his mistakes were, but dismiss his noble acts?

The sound of John's cane approaching filled her with a mingled rush of emotion.

He came into the library, but when he saw her, he stopped. "What's wrong?" His brows gathered into a *V*.

"Nothing. I was just going over these latest pages of yours."

"But something has upset you."

Eliza shook her head. "Not at all." She wiped her cheek and tried to smile, but after what she'd just read, a smile felt so inadequate.

John still didn't look convinced.

She tried her best for a lighthearted tone. "Don't you know a teary-eyed reader is a good sign?"

He swallowed, forcing his Adam's apple to bob, but still didn't say a word.

"Your story is deeply moving. And nearing the end, it would seem."

John examined the floor. "Yes, it's almost finished. I only hope someone will find it useful."

Useful? John's story had changed her in ways she never would have believed possible. Eliza simply nodded, unable to trust her voice.

The sky had grown quite dark by the time she boarded the bus. December always seemed so impatient, the daylight hours so short, as if to remind her that time was quickly slipping away. Without a single peep of protest from her.

And what did she have to protest? That she had fallen in love with John? What possible good would that do? He had no such feelings for her. And why would he? She was a typist for hire. A nobody. *Eccentric,* as Betty had so kindly noted. If there was room in John's heart for love, that place was probably being filled by the one woman he still wasn't talking about in his book. And if his silence about Deborah Marlow was because there had been no off-camera relationship— which Eliza found hard to believe—then why did he receive letters from her?

She closed her eyes to avoid seeing her fool-hearted reflection in the dark bus window.

God, it's not wrong to keep quiet about how I feel, is it? Sometimes it's best to keep the truth to ourselves. If John knew how I felt, he would have to replace me.

No, she definitely needed to keep her feelings to herself. Not only that, but she needed to find a way to thoroughly scrub them from her heart.

God, is this something You can help me do?

As the bus pulled away from a corner stop, new passengers made their way down the aisle. An elbow jostled her as someone took the seat beside her.

"Nice evening for a tour of the rich neighbor-hoods, isn't it?"

She knew that voice. Eliza rubbed the knot forming at the base of her neck and turned to him.

The glee in Agent Robinson's eyes matched his broad smile.

"I have nothing more to tell you."

"That's odd." Delight dripped from his voice. "I should think you would find working with John David Vincent, a.k.a. Johnny Devine, to be as fascinating a topic as I do."

Was there nothing this man *didn't* know about her?

"Time to cut the innocent act." He made a sweeping glance at the other passengers. "I know about your father's service in the Red Army and all the lies about your parents' identity. We have reason to believe your parents were selling information to the Soviets. And I think you and that sister of yours know who the contacts are."

"There were no contacts, as I've told you. And even if there were, my parents are dead and neither my sister nor I know anything about it. We only just recently discovered that our parents were Russian."

"Is that so?" The agent smiled. "Funny thing is, the more time I spend looking into your family, the harder I find it to believe in the growing number of coincidences. Like your association with John Vincent. His Red file keeps growing too."

Eliza turned to him, stunned. John had received calls asking him to name Hollywood colleagues who were communists, sure, but were they now accusing *him* of communist activity?

"But that's another topic. I won't waste your time by laying out the details of our investigation."

"Really? Then what *does* qualify as a good reason to waste my time?"

He shifted in his seat to face her.

At such close proximity, Eliza could see the tiny red veins in the agent's eyes. Along with a disturbing amount of zeal.

"Just so you know, I've received special commendations from McCarthy himself for flushing out commies. Want to know why? I *watch,* Miss Peterson. That's how I find subversive activity. A classic rooskie tactic is to infiltrate nice neighborhoods. Slip in quietly, looking like every other American family. Kids, dog, whitewalls on the Buick, the works."

That picture could describe thousands of families in neighborhoods all across the country.

"It's my job to know who you are. But . . . let's say I take your word for it and stop asking about your family."

Eliza would take the bait, of course—if not for his expression. As if he was setting a hook to reel in the biggest catch of his career. "And what do you want in exchange for leaving us alone?"

"You're sharp. I almost forgot about that college degree of yours." He opened a briefcase, took out a large manila envelope, and handed it to her. "This is addressed to me. It's even got postage, see here? You provide me with a copy of Johnny Devine's full manuscript, including the names of his colleagues, his subversive activities, and commie associations, the whole ball of wax. And this is just between us—he doesn't have to know. Then I make a note in your file about your cooperation on this. That you've shown your willingness to do your patriotic duty. Add some solid points to your defense."

Give this man a copy of John's manuscript? All that flatfooting must have scrambled his brain. "You couldn't be more wrong about him."

With a wave of his hand as if her opinion was of no consequence, the agent shook his head and smiled. "No need to confuse your pretty little head with complicated details. Just send the manuscript, then you and your high-strung sister will be seeing a whole lot less of me."

23

Friday morning, Millie opened the door for Eliza and ushered her inside. Millie's gait seemed a bit slower and the catch in her step more pronounced. Probably from the change in weather. Winter was only a few weeks away.

"I sure hope that book gonna be finished soon." Millie took Eliza's coat.

"Why is that?"

Millie peered into the library, then turned to Eliza with a somber headshake. "He just ain't been hisself. Bringin' up all those old memories like to do him in, I 'spect."

So even Millie had noticed the toll it was taking on John. Yes, completing the book and moving on would be best. For everyone's sake.

She went to her desk. John was not in the room, but she hadn't really expected to see him. As much as she hated to admit it, they had made tremendous progress with him doing more of his own writing. And that was good, considering her latest dilemma. Of course she would never consider giving a copy of John's book to that lunatic. As if duplicating an entire manuscript without John's knowledge was even possible. And if the agency did get his book, who knew what those fanatics would read into it? Robinson seemed to be on some kind of personal mission that went beyond standard investigation. Besides, she could never do that to John.

Perhaps it was time to let him know what was going on. He wasn't going to like the fact that the HUAC was now linking the two of them together.

John had left his notebook on her desk with two new pages, which she typed in no time.

She was just finishing the last few lines when John came in.

"Ah, I hope I haven't left you in suspense." John seemed more relaxed than he had been in a while. He even smiled, which sent goosebumps racing along Eliza's arms.

"No, you're just in time," she said. "And I'm glad you're here. There's something I need to talk to you about."

"Of course. Are you all right?"

Eliza nodded, warmed by his concern. "For a while now, I've been followed and questioned by an agent from the HUAC."

John came to the settee near Eliza's desk and

lowered himself onto it, facing her. "You too? Why didn't you say anything?"

"I haven't mentioned it before because he keeps trying to say my parents were . . . spies, and I've been trying to uncover the truth about them before he does. I'm . . . not sure what I'm going to find." She winced. This was harder than she thought, hearing herself doubt her own parents aloud. She went on about the agent following her and the things she had learned about her parents, including the letters.

"Is there a way to find out if your aunt is still alive?"

"I've sent a letter to the return address in Russia. But her letter was written at least thirty-five years ago. The country has been so war-torn, and since Kat said she was relocating, I don't expect anything to come of that. It's just a shot in the dark."

"We can pray," John said. "God can add divine guidance to your bullet."

Eliza nodded. "That brings me to one of the things I need to tell you. I'm hoping the Soviet Consulate can help me locate any relatives in Russia who knew my parents. I don't know how else I can clear their names and get the agents to take me and my sister off their list."

John nodded. "Good idea. Do you think the consulate has the information you need?"

Eliza shrugged. "I don't know, but I hope so.

I spoke to someone who said I must come in person. The trouble with *that* is . . ."

"You can only go to the consulate during the week."

"I'm afraid so." She studied his reaction, but his expression remained even, as usual. "The good news is, it's in San Francisco. The bad news is, the process could take several days."

"By all means, take as much time as you need. Do you want to stay near the consulate? Do you need help paying for a hotel?"

Blushing at the idea of him paying for her hotel room, she shook her head. "Thank you, but I can manage."

"All right." John studied her. "So you'll go first thing Monday?"

"Yes, if you don't mind. I'm sorry, I know you want to finish the book as quickly as possible."

"Don't give it a second thought. I'd want to be doing something too, if I were you. I know the kind of pressure those maniacs can apply. Believe me, I understand."

Which was probably a good time to tell him that their files were now strapped together in Agent Robinson's briefcase. She looked him in the eye, but couldn't get the words to come. No matter how she said it, he was sure to be upset. Maybe even blame her.

No. John was nothing like Ralph. He was quite different. In fact, he was so—

John's concerned expression returned. "What is it?"

"There's something else, and you're not going to like it."

"Go on." His eyes never left her face.

"I'm afraid that I've . . . led them to you."

He frowned. "To me? What do you mean?"

"The agent cornered me on the bus last night. He knows I'm working with you on your book. He . . ." She stared at her fingers intertwined in her lap. "He asked me to give him a copy of your manuscript." She steeled herself for his response and then looked up.

"I see." He glanced at the pages stacked on Eliza's desk.

"Of course I would never do it," she said in a rush.

John met her gaze. "I know that," he said. With a sigh, he rose and went to the window. "McCarthy's lost his mind. He thinks *everyone* is a communist until proven innocent. He and his minions will twist anything into evidence. And it's only gotten worse since the Rosenberg executions. Those agents are like sharks. Once they taste blood . . ."

So the threat was worse than she thought. "I'm truly sorry for getting you tangled up in my troubles."

John turned to her, face softening. "You did nothing of the sort. They've been badgering me for months. And don't worry, there's nothing in my book that will implicate me or anyone else." He reached over and ruffled a corner of the stack of typed pages, then shrugged. "Maybe I'll just have Fred send them a copy."

Was he serious? Eliza could just imagine Agent Robinson taking some minor detail in the book out of context and twisting it into evidence against John.

"Listen, if it will make you feel better, I'll talk to Fred Wharton. He'll get his lawyers on it. They know how to handle these guys. And in the meantime, try not to worry. Okay?" He seemed so calm and confident.

If he wasn't worried about the added scrutiny, there was probably no sense in her worrying, either. She studied his expression, just to be sure. "All right, I won't worry." She forced more confidence into her smile than she felt.

His gaze fell to her lips and lingered for a moment, then another, then dropped to the floor.

Her heart skittered. How unfair that he could do that to her without even saying a word.

"I need to attend to something," he said, his brow furrowed. "Perhaps we could just resume when you return next week. Do you mind?"

"Of course not," she said. With the book so close to completion, was he no longer in a hurry to finish it?

With a single nod, John turned and left her.

．．．

That afternoon, Eliza picked up a transit schedule to plan her trip into San Francisco on Monday. It felt good to be doing something proactive.

She spent Saturday working on her new proposal, though she couldn't finish revising the book until she talked to Millie about her views on equality. As disturbed as Eliza was about prejudice, was she truly showing the plight of the oppressed accurately? Being a white, middle-class American, could she really understand?

Eliza called Betty and shared her plans to visit the consulate on Monday.

Betty was all for it, especially after she'd explained the mission to Ed, who gave his stamp of approval. It was good that Betty sought her husband's opinion and approval. But sometimes, Eliza wondered how happy her sister and brother-in-law actually were. Of course, they always *appeared* happy, which was of critical importance to Betty. Eliza just hoped her sister had other goals in life besides keeping the garden club ladies' tongues from wagging.

Sunday morning, Eliza woke to Mr. Darcy yowling at her door, apparently miffed by the fog. She hurried to let him in, chuckling. "A little spoiled now, are we?"

The cat headed for his bowl, purring. Being the night owl that he was, he'd become content to sleep in the center of her ironing board during the day. He'd developed a habit of sleeping with one eye open, and whenever she walked past the ironing board, he would reach out a paw, and if she stood close enough, he would tug her closer.

What was a little cat hair on her clothes when such affection was to be had?

> Full surrender is frightening. It's like taking a blind leap into a deep hole, headfirst, hands tied behind your back. And yet, ironically, total surrender to God brings peace, because His love and mercy are bottomless.
> ~*The Devine Truth: A Memoir*

24

Armed with her transit schedule, Eliza boarded the west-bound electric train Monday morning and settled onto a seat by the window. The last time she'd been near a train of any kind was the day her parents' bodies were delivered home for burial. What a tragic irony. They left the railway station on one train and returned a week later on another, as though they had simply taken a trip and come back home as planned.

She passed the time by watching the city transform as the train traveled through Oakland and approached the bay. In the distance, fog blanketed the surrounding hills. But as the train crossed the Bay Bridge, the fog dissipated and sunlight shimmered on the water's surface like confectioner's sugar in sparkling motion.

The transit station in downtown San Francisco was a beehive of rushing people, oily machinery smells, shouts, steady chatter, the squeal of gliding wheels, and the *ding-ding* of electric train bells. Wishing she'd worn her saddle shoes instead of heels, Eliza set out for the nearest cable car terminal, hoping her route information to the Soviet Consulate was correct. She spent the next half hour on a packed car going into west San Francisco. The car pitched down steep streets toward the marina and the Pacific Ocean. Eliza took in the city—the multiple lanes of honking cars, the pedestrians, the marine smell of wharf and sea and fish frying, the colorful apartment buildings with bay-style windows jutting out from each story.

She got off the car a few blocks from the consulate and walked the rest of the way, glad for the fresh air and a chance to recover from being squashed between two large people in the cable car. She arrived just before noon, which should give her enough time to request her information and get the process started. If she was lucky, maybe one day was all it would take.

A guard wearing a visor cap and a dark-blue overcoat with gold bars on his shoulders stopped her at the door. He said something in Russian.

Eliza stilled. "I'm sorry, I don't understand."

"Papers."

"Papers? No. I'm afraid I don't have any."

The man examined her face and her clothing. "State business."

Eliza swallowed hard and thought fast. "I am here to get help finding my relatives in Russia. My parents were from Russia. I guess that makes me Russian. Sort of." She smiled. The people on the telephone hadn't said anything about needing papers.

"Wait here," the guard said. He gestured to another guard, who went into a small booth and used a telephone. Moments later he returned and spoke to the first guard.

"Go to front desk." He gestured toward the entry door.

"Thank you." Eliza hurried inside.

Two more guards stood at attention inside.

Since they didn't stop her, Eliza studied her surroundings.

A woman in royal blue sat at a desk in the lobby. About a dozen people stood in line to see her.

Eliza got in line, took a book from her handbag, and waited.

When the person ahead of Eliza finally finished his business at the desk, the clerk wrote for a long time, then added a page to one of the stacks of paperwork surrounding her.

Eliza checked her watch. It was nearly two o'clock.

Without looking up, the woman said something in Russian.

"I'm sorry, I don't—"

"May I help you?"

"Yes, I hope so." She drew her aunt's letter out of her handbag. "I am looking for my relatives in Russia. I was hoping to get some help finding them, or at least to get in touch with the officials in this village."

Frowning, the woman took the envelope from Eliza and squinted at the return address, then peered at Eliza. "What is purpose of contact?"

Eliza smiled. "I recently learned I have an aunt in Russia. Or had, anyway. I want to find out if she's alive and if I can make contact with her. Her name is Kat, perhaps short for something longer, and her maiden name would have been Petrovich."

The woman's frown deepened. "One moment." She picked up a telephone and spoke quickly in Russian. She nodded as she listened, watching Eliza.

She fought the urge to fidget. Surely these people would understand her desire to find a lost relative?

"What is political interest in Soviet Union?" the woman asked.

"None. That is, I don't have any political interest there. I—I only want to find out if my aunt is alive."

The woman tapped her pen against the desk. "You are not able to prove political interest?"

Eliza shook her head. "Since I don't have any,

I don't see how I could prove it." She frowned. This wasn't going the way she'd hoped. An idea struck. "Wait—maybe you can read this letter. It was written to my father, Vasily Petrovich, from his sister."

The woman heaved a sigh, glanced beyond Eliza, then unfolded the yellowed paper. She pulled it closer as she read. Then she glared at Eliza above the page. "Where did you get letter?"

Dread raced down Eliza's spine. Had she just made a terrible mistake? Could the information in the letter possibly get someone in trouble? Her aunt may have come under suspicion all those years ago. Papa never mentioned that he had a sister—perhaps that was because Kat lived in hiding and needed to stay that way.

Forcing a calm, polite smile, she slowly reached for the letter. "It belonged to my parents." She licked her suddenly dry lips. She tugged the letter out of the clerk's grasp, silently thanking God the woman hadn't confiscated it, and stuffed it into her bag.

"We cannot give information. If you cannot state political allegiance, I must ask you to leave consulate."

Eliza's heart pounded. "But—"

The woman motioned for the nearest guard.

"No, I don't need an escort, I'm leaving."

She hurried out of the building, half expecting to feel the clamp of a hand on her shoulder and handcuffs on her wrists. It wasn't until she reached the sidewalk outside the gate that she caught a full breath. Why did she feel like a criminal?

Her own government was suspicious of her for being Russian. Now Russians were suspicious of her for being an American.

She walked a few blocks to catch the next cable car back to the train station. There was no point hanging around San Francisco if the Russians weren't going to do anything but treat her like some kind of political enemy.

But where could she go where she would *not* be treated like an enemy? And why should she be seen as an enemy? For simply being born to her parents, for being opposed to injustice, for wanting to find the people to whom she belonged? What was so subversive about that?

When Eliza returned home that evening, although her toes and calves throbbed, she stopped at the telephone and gave Betty a report.

"That's inexcusable. They should have been more helpful. Imagine, treating an American citizen that way! I'll have Ed call them and give them a talking-to."

Eliza smiled, and it felt good. It was her first

genuine smile all day. "Thanks, Betty, but they made it very clear that they don't give out information to just anyone. We have to have some official reason for the request, backed by paperwork."

"Well, at least you tried. You're coming for Christmas, aren't you? Ed brought home an aluminum tree, and we're putting it up now. You should see it. Ours is positively the most stylish tree on the block."

Eliza rolled her eyes. "What color?"

"Flamingo pink!" Betty said. "It's going in the front window."

After they said their goodbyes, Eliza climbed the stairs, feeling as if someone had attached a wrecking ball to each of her legs. Inside her apartment, she kicked off her shoes, peeled off her coat and scarf, and fell onto her bed. The heaviness in her heart matched the fatigue in her body. What more could she do? She wasn't about to give Agent Robinson what he asked for, so now she was left to face further investigation and maybe even a trial. As ridiculous as a trial sounded, Eliza was beginning to believe it was possible.

What else would the agent uncover? What if he found Aunt Kat before Eliza did? And what if her parents had truly been in some kind of political trouble? Could the HUAC use it to incriminate Eliza? People were being tried for treason on flimsy evidence. Who knew what was in Eliza's file?

Too weary to think anymore, she fell into a fitful sleep, hounded by dreams of running from a lurking figure following closely on her heels.

> I once hoped the 'legend' would eventually disappear and I could just be a man forgiven, but it was a fanciful hope. The reality is that a man may be forgiven, but a legend is never forgotten.
> ~*The Devine Truth: A Memoir*

25

Tuesday morning, fog covered the Berkeley hills like quilt batting, making her walk slow going. It didn't help that each step was a reminder that the book was nearly finished and her time with John was about to end.

Eliza arrived at the villa twenty minutes later than usual. But since John wasn't expecting her until at least Wednesday, perhaps her arrival time today made no difference.

Millie's wrinkly forehead gathered into a puzzled frown when she saw Eliza. "Thought you wasn't comin' today."

She smiled to mask her disappointment. "The task didn't take as long as I expected." She smoothed her curls and went into the library.

John was on the telephone and beckoned her in.

As he resumed his conversation, Eliza went to

her desk and looked for his newest pages, since he'd had all day Monday to write. She found nothing there, so she went to his table, saw a notebook, and took it back to her desk. She put a clean sheet of paper in the typewriter and opened his book.

The latest page contained only one dated, unfinished paragraph.

<u>December 7, 1953</u>
So is this the penalty I've brought on myself? Her touch still haunts me. Is this some kind of test? Do You know the agony I feel knowing she's so near and yet I can never have her? How difficult it is to keep silent? Do You know what it's like to feel your heart leave your body and watch it walk out that door day after day? Do You know how empty my life will be when she's gone? If this is my punishment, I don't know how much more I can stand. I can't keep

The meaning of the words soaked in like water on sand. Numb, she stared at the page again, at his familiar handwriting. His words. His feelings.

For her?

Some part of her brain registered that John had gone dead silent.

Eliza looked over her shoulder.

John was no longer speaking into the telephone, but was staring at her, the receiver in his hand falling slowly to his side.

. . . the agony I feel . . .

Heart pounding, she stood and faced him.

He still hadn't moved, but simply stood watching her.

. . . difficult to keep silent . . .

Yes, keeping silent had been painfully difficult for her as well. Now they could both say what had been held in check.

But he didn't speak. Didn't come to her.

Why not?

He didn't know her feelings, of course. John would never make advances without knowing she wished him to.

He needed to know she felt the same way.

Forcing her legs to move, Eliza crossed the library.

John watched her approach with a look of dismay that deepened as she came near. When she reached him, he wore a stark expression she didn't understand.

"John?" It was no more than a whisper.

He turned his face away.

She stepped closer. "Those things you wrote . . ."

John's chest moved in a shallow, rapid rhythm, but he would not look at her.

Please look at me—you need to know . . .

With a strange boldness, she placed a trembling

hand on his cheek and gently guided his face back to her.

Slowly, his gaze rose until it met hers. There, in his eyes, were things she'd never dared hope to see. Raw things, like longing. Suffering.

Love.

John loved her.

She couldn't feel her legs.

"I feel the same way," she whispered. She stepped closer and closed her eyes. His warm breath fanned her skin, sending a delicious ripple through her. Her lips tingled in anticipation.

Sensing a shift in him, Eliza opened her eyes.

John was backing away.

Panic crept in. Weren't his words, his agonized longings about her? Or—

Had he been writing of someone else?

Of *D.M.?*

"John? Were you not—?" She couldn't stop the rising panic. "Were you not writing of *me?*"

He stiffened and turned away again.

Which could only mean one thing: Eliza had just made the most embarrassing blunder of her life.

"Oh my goodness, I'm so . . ."

Stupid.

". . . sorry." She dashed out of the library and gathered her things, barely seeing what she was taking. Passing a confused-looking Millie in the sitting room, Eliza hurried out the front door, down the steps, and across the stone walk, her humiliation compounding with every step.

What he must think of her, throwing herself at him like that . . . no different from all those silly, swooning women . . .

She stumbled twice and nearly fell in her hurry to get away from the house. The gate at the end of the drive was a blur through her gathering tears.

What did it matter what John thought of her? She wasn't coming back.

Between her tears and the cloying mist, she could barely see. When she reached the gate, the dam burst. Crying, she tried to push the button for the gate but couldn't find it.

A door slammed against the house, startling her.

"Eliza!"

She jumped at the sound of his booming voice. She felt for the button again, frantic.

"Eliza, wait!"

Heart hammering, she turned. She had never felt more ridiculous or more alone. She waited, trapped.

John rounded the bend, working his cane as fast as he could.

Must he fire her in person? Couldn't he just call the agency? Tears dripped from her chin, soaking the collar of her dress. *So stupid. I should have listened to Betty . . .*

When John reached her, his eyes were black

pools of misery. "Yes," he said, his deep voice ragged. He grasped the back of her neck, pulled her close, and crushed his lips to hers.

Stunned, she wavered like a sapling reed, suspended between earth and heaven, nearly collapsing at the knees. Couldn't think. Couldn't breathe. But she could feel. And what she felt was . . .

Loved.

His lips lifted a fraction and hovered beside hers. "Yes, I was writing about you. Yes, I am in agony when you're near. Yes, I have to leave the room because of you."

Am I dreaming?

He kissed her again, gently but urgently, his lips soft yet searing, shooting pure warmth straight to her core.

Her tears flowed again, but this time from blissful release. John loved her—Eliza, a quiet, penniless woman of no renown.

With a stifled groan, he let go and backed away. "No, no . . ."

"What?"

"Dear Lord, what am I doing . . . ?"

"John? What's wrong?"

"I shouldn't have done that. I'm so sorry. You left so hurt and I couldn't let you leave thinking—" He scowled, then turned away. "I only meant to stop you. I'm sorry, Eliza. I shouldn't have kissed you. That was wrong."

"Wrong?" She stared at him, waiting for his words to make sense, but they didn't. "What are you saying?" She shook her head to clear the confusion. "What about what you wrote?"

He dragged a hand down over his face. "You weren't supposed to see that."

"But . . . didn't you mean those things?"

For the longest time, he just stood there, motionless. "I meant every word," he whispered.

Then say it. "I love you, Eliza." Just say it.

But the words didn't come.

John turned to her, eyes red. "But it doesn't matter, because I can't do this, Eliza. Not to anyone. And especially not to you."

"Can't do what?"

He shook his head. "I can't love."

"*I* can."

His gaze fell to the cobblestone between them. "I know you can, and you must. Just . . . not me." He scowled at his cane. "Kissing you was purely thoughtless. I'm sorry."

Why couldn't he love her? Why couldn't he—? "John, if you're worried about your past, none of that matters."

He shook his head, face grave. "You may not think it matters now, but it will. Believe me, it will. You still have a bright future ahead of you. My past and reputation will trail me like a stench for the rest of my life. People *never* forget. And there's not a soul I would ever ask to share such a burden." He lowered his voice. "Especially you."

"I don't care what people think."

He looked beyond her, as if searching for reinforcement in the gate, then shook his head again. "I can't."

She braced herself for the risk she was about to take. "John, if you don't want me, then say so. But if . . . if you love me, then please don't let me walk out of your life."

He didn't move, didn't answer. Instead, he stared off in the distance, his stance rigid.

Her chest burned with a crushing ache she hadn't felt since her parents died. "I see." She lifted her chin in a pathetic attempt at dignity while her heart plunged in a free fall. "I guess that's my cue to leave."

"Please, don't do that," John said. "I understand why you want to leave, and you have every reason to, but if you could . . . find it in your heart to stay a little longer, I need . . ." He scowled at his cane and wouldn't meet her gaze. "I need to finish the book, and I can't do it without you."

That stung. He needed her, just not enough to put aside what kept him from loving her. He needed her skills, nothing more.

What Eliza needed was to turn around. Open the gate. Walk through and keep going.

Turn, Eliza. Move.

But not one of her limbs would cooperate.

What would Betty do? That was easy. Betty wouldn't have gotten into this position in the first place.

What would Mama say?

Strange, but the only person coming to mind was the compassionate, extraordinary Man in a story she couldn't forget. The One who offered acceptance and hope to a humiliated woman.

Hope? No. Her only hope was to turn around and leave and never come back, as painful as that would be.

If you let Me, I will make you new.

Or . . . she could summon the courage to stay and finish what she had begun, but only because she was a professional with many hours invested in a book that deserved her best effort to see it through to completion.

"Very well," she said, her voice surprisingly calm. "I will stay until the book is finished."

It took everything she had to mask her broken heart and walk back into that house.

> Solitude is a small price in exchange for what God has done for me. If I had to choose, I would rather be an unknown son than a famous orphan.
> ~*The Devine Truth: A Memoir*

26

Millie was waiting inside, rooted in the front room like a tiny gray flagstaff, her feather duster poking out from her tightly crossed arms. She frowned at John, then inched closer to Eliza and examined her closely.

Eliza must have looked a fright with her frizzled hair and tear-stained face. She gave her cheeks a quick swipe.

"Ma'am, I'll just take that coat of yours—again," Millie said softly. "That is, if you gonna stay a spell this time."

"I'll stay." *But not for long.* Eliza didn't look at John.

Millie took Eliza's coat and left them, humming a tune. Halfway to the kitchen, she added lyrics to her song. "O what peace we often forfeit . . . O what needless pain we bear . . . all because we do not carry . . . everything to God in prayer."

Eliza quickly took her seat at the desk, still

reeling from hurt and confusion and a growing realization that staying may not have been such a wise idea.

It's only one more day, two at the most. Then the book will be on its way to New York, and I will be finished here. Soon John and Millie and all of this will be nothing but a memory.

No. The past two months would never be just a memory. No matter how heartbreaking things had turned out, the time she'd spent in John's home had changed her life.

With the book so close to completion and both of them anxious to wrap it up, Eliza spent the morning trying to write John's concluding thoughts, but met with little success.

After an hour of intermittent dictation, John leaned back and massaged his forehead with both hands. "I'm sorry. You're trying to finish and I'm useless."

He wasn't the only one struggling to concentrate, but Eliza kept that to herself. It also didn't help matters that every time she looked at him, John was holding his head in his hands, glaring at his feet.

He was angry with himself—she knew him well enough to know that.

It also didn't help that Eliza was still numb from that kiss, and from what it meant. But the more she tried to make sense of the things they had said to each other, the more she realized how pointless that was. John's mind was made up. Begging had even crossed her mind but was, of course, out of the question.

By lunchtime, they were both ready for a break, though the idea of eating anything—even Millie's cooking—turned Eliza's stomach.

Millie served pork chops with roasted potatoes and chocolate cake in the dining room. Her trips to and from the kitchen took longer than usual. But who wouldn't be tired, working so hard at her age?

Eliza eyed the thin layers of chocolate separated by ribbons of shiny brown frosting and could only imagine how frightful the thing would have turned out if she had attempted it.

John said grace for the meal.

When he finished, Millie said there was a telephone call for him.

He frowned. "Who is it?"

"Says he's your *attorney*," Millie said, one brow low, the other lifted high. "Want me to tell him the same thing I tell them government agents?"

John removed the napkin from his collar, grabbed his cane, and rose. "No, I'll take it." He turned to Eliza. "You're welcome to listen in if you like. It's probably about the book."

Eliza followed him to the telephone in the library.

"Hello." He listened, then frowned. "Subpoena

the *manuscript?* That won't be necessary. I already told them they can see it. I have nothing to hide." He turned and met Eliza's gaze. "I'm not surprised. Do you know why they're finished talking to Oscar? He can say things that sound so good you forget he hasn't answered a single question." He huffed out a laugh. "Sure, but I still don't see what difference it will make. They already have names of party members. What do they want from me?" He listened for a few moments more. "Fine. I won't lie, and besides, it's no secret. I've worked with known party members, including Carnovsky, Lawson, Odets, and"—his voice fell low—"Marlow."

Eliza barely stifled a gasp. *Deborah* Marlow? She had tried to forget about the pink letters. But now, all of her previous questions and assumptions came rushing back.

Would Deborah's name finally come up in the conclusion of the book? In what capacity?

Did Eliza really want to know?

But then, what did it matter?

"Let them try," John said, his tone more determined than before. "I'm not worried. I have faith. The truth will prevail."

Later that evening, Eliza glanced at the telephone as she passed through the hallway, half tempted to call Betty. If ever Eliza needed a sympathetic ear, it was now. But Betty probably wasn't the best shoulder to cry on, especially since John was the source of Eliza's misery.

The note taped to the telephone that said *Absolutely NO Calls for Eliza* had been littered with doodling and phone numbers. With a sigh, Eliza went to her mailbox and took out her mail, sorted through it, and stopped.

A heavy linen envelope, addressed to her, bore a United States emblem that included the letters HUAC.

With hands that shook, she tore the envelope and took out a single paged letter.

November 30, 1953

TO: Mrs. Eliza Jane Saunderson
FROM: House Un-American Activities Committee, Berkeley Branch

Your presence is hereby requested at a special panel query convening at the HUAC provisional agency headquarters located in the Whitecotton Room of the Shattuck Hotel at ten o'clock a.m. on Thursday, December 10. Your cooperation in this matter will be noted. Failure to appear and answer questions to the panel's satisfaction will result in a subpoena. You will be asked to provide truthful information pertaining to your business dealings with the "American Women's Alliance" and their anti-American and communist associates.

Would they even listen?

In the days of the Salem witch trials, the whole town believed absurd accusations, even the magistrates. People were convicted and death sentences were carried out based on unfounded rumors.

HUAC agents thought she was a spy.

Eliza closed her eyes and willed herself to stay calm.

Ivy and another girl in bobby socks whispered to each other, their glances wary.

Yes, this was far too much like old Salem for Eliza's taste. She moved toward the stairs, but her encounter with John combined with this letter pressed on her like a half-ton weight. The idea of being alone in her empty room was too much.

Betty's shoulder was better than nothing.

Eliza took the telephone and dialed the operator. "Richmond four nine two seven."

"One moment, please," the operator said.

With every ring on the line, Eliza's pulse quickened another notch.

"Cunninghams." Ed's voice, irritated.

"Hello, Ed. May I speak to Betty, please?"

A pause. "Betty is seeing to dinner, but I'm

sure, since you're calling at dinnertime, it must be important."

Eliza winced.

"You're not in any trouble, I hope?"

"No, no, nothing like that. Perhaps I should just call back another time."

"Of course not. Just a minute."

As he went to fetch Betty, Eliza checked her watch with a grimace.

"Eliza?" Betty sounded anxious. "Did you find out something about Mama and Papa? And baby Ivan?"

"No, I'm afraid not," Eliza said. "I'm not sure where else to look. But don't worry, I'll keep trying. Maybe I should find the town that the letters were sent to and start placing ads in some local newspapers in the area."

"Is that a good idea? Aren't they watching you?"

"Yes, you're right. That's probably not a good idea." Eliza caught her lip in her teeth to keep from crying. "Actually, that's why I'm calling."

"Oh?"

Eliza glanced around to be sure no one was listening. "I just got a letter asking me to come to HUAC headquarters on Thursday to answer questions. It's an *invitation,* but it's pretty much a summons. Betty, it looks like they've found a link between the American Women's Alliance and the Communist Party. They want me to answer a bunch of questions about my . . . *association* with them."

The only sound Eliza heard was her own heartbeat.

"Betty, I'm scared." *Please don't lecture me about my writing, please . . .*

"Well, of course you're scared, darling. I think it's time to call a lawyer."

"You know I don't have that kind of money."

Betty's end of the line sounded muffled, as if she was covering the mouthpiece so she wouldn't be overheard. "Would you . . . like me to ask Ed if we can help with that?"

Ed Cunningham was a decent man, but he certainly would not be happy about taking on the legal expenses of his spinster sister-in-law. "Betty, that's swell of you to offer, but no. You and your family don't need that kind of burden." She drew herself up straight. "I'll just go to the hearing and see what comes of it." Would she be taken into custody?

"You do that and then call me right away, okay?"

Eliza nodded, unable to answer. Even Betty's thin offering of sympathy cracked the fragile grasp Eliza had on her crumbling heart. With tears streaming, she broke down and told Betty about reading John's journal by mistake and how he had stopped her at the gate.

"I don't understand," Betty said. "Why didn't you just keep going?"

Good question. "I . . . wanted the things he said to be true."

Seconds ticked by. "Oh, Eliza."

She fought to keep from crying, then told her about the kiss and the things she and John had said to each other.

Betty listened to it all.

"And then I said, 'If you love me, then please don't let me walk out of your life.' "

"And how did he answer?"

A fresh crop of tears filled her eyes. "He didn't."

The hurt that had been building all day spilled over. By the time she finished talking, her head ached and her palms were wet from wiping her face.

"Oh, darling, I *am* sorry, really. But . . . let's be honest. It's better that it ended before it began, isn't it?" Betty's voice coaxed. "Just think how truly awful you would've felt if that little game of his had gone on until irrevocable damages were done. Now you can walk away relatively untainted."

Sniffling, Eliza could still see the desperation on John's face when he hurried out to stop her. The way he kissed her. She shook her head. "It was no game, Betty."

Silence.

"John's not like that."

More silence. "Oh, Eliza. Don't you *know* what men like him are capable of? They'll do and say anything just so they can . . . well, you know. I'm sure he's positively convincing, given his background. Don't you realize he only wants one thing? And the next thing you know, you're damaged goods that no decent man will want."

Decent? Eliza's jaw clenched. Hanging up would relieve the sting of Betty's words—for now. But something in Eliza rose up, an outrage that would not be so easily set aside.

Blind prejudice would continue as long as no one spoke against it. Silence would not be the last thing Betty would hear.

"Betty, you don't know John. He's nothing at all like what you think. He is a good man. An honest, God-fearing man. But I don't expect you to value that. You can't value anyone who doesn't look like you. And that makes me sad for you, Betty. Because if all you want is outer appearances, then that's all you will ever have. There is a moral strength and a humble grace to John that you'll miss because you're too busy arranging your furniture to impress bridge club ladies you don't even like."

An audible gasp shook the line.

But then again, perhaps silence would have been the better choice this time. "I'm sorry, that was unkind," Eliza said.

No answer.

Eliza could see John in her mind's eye, determined to give people real hope that God was his rescuer and faithful friend. "John deserves a chance to be heard, Betty. I just hope, when his book comes out, you'll do the right thing and give him that chance."

They ended the call with dull goodbyes, leaving Eliza feeling even emptier than before. With a heavy heart, she climbed the stairs to her room.

Later that night, as she drifted in and out of sleep, the hiss of the radiator turned into whispered echoes of Betty's words. Dream Betty reminded Eliza that smooth-talking men were clever enough to say whatever a girl wanted to hear. When Eliza replied that she wasn't listening anymore, her sister took a pencil and wrote a message to Eliza.

On pink stationery.

27

Eliza arrived at John's house on Wednesday
morning battling a headache. Nothing like
tackling the final pages of a book after a night
of tossing and turning. Denying love was hard
enough when she was the only one feeling it, but
now? How could she put John out of her heart
knowing how he felt?

*You just do. And then you go on with your life.
That's all.*

No one met her at the door, so she let herself in.

The thump of John's cane came from the north
end of the house. When he entered the front room
and saw Eliza, he stopped.

"Good morning." He looked like a man who
hadn't slept in days.

As she removed her coat and hat, John just
stood there. "Is something wrong?" she said.

John shook his head. "No. I'm . . . just surprised
you came back. Thank you." He headed toward
the library.

"John, if you have a minute, there's something
I should tell you."

He stopped and turned to her. His gaze lingered on her lips briefly and then fell away. "What is it?"

"I've been summoned to the HUAC headquarters for a panel query. Tomorrow morning, actually. I thought you should know, in case they question you about me. You know, since Agent Robinson was asking me about you."

He shook his head. "This is getting completely out of hand."

"Yes, it is," she said, hoping to mask the tremor in her voice.

"Are you worried?"

"I don't know what's going to happen. They want me to admit that I wrote articles I sold to the American Women's Alliance." She looked around for Millie and quieted her tone. "I wrote them under a pen name, and until now, I haven't admitted to writing them. I guess I wanted to hold on to one last bit of security. But now, it looks like they may have found a real connection between the AWA and the Communist Party. Which I honestly knew nothing about."

John frowned and it dawned on her—she had probably just made a mistake by telling him. He would very likely be asked what he knew about Eliza.

"*Were* you hired by communists?" John said.

"No. And I don't write propaganda. At least not intentionally."

"Then you have nothing to worry about."

"If this were still the good old USA, I might believe that. But with this Red Scare spreading so fast, I don't know what to think. I *am* worried. Not because I'm guilty, but because paranoia seems to have robbed everyone of their common sense. Anything can be considered communist behavior, and it seems impossible to prove you're innocent."

"Like the Salem witch trials," John said.

Eliza nodded, taking little comfort in the fact that McCarthy's obsession had reminded both her and John of the same thing. "I want to tell the truth, but I'm afraid they'll just twist it."

"God knows you're innocent, Eliza. He would want you to be truthful. Tell the truth and leave the rest to Him."

Leave it to God? That was like asking her to jump into a bottomless pit headfirst. How could John be so certain?

He offered a faint smile. "With God's help, we'll fight this to the end."

"We?"

John's smile faded. "I didn't want to mention it before, but they've already asked me about you."

Eliza gasped. Not only were they harassing John about his former colleagues, but now they were asking him about her?

"What did you tell them?"

John shrugged. "I didn't answer."

"What happens if you don't?"

"If I continue to refuse to answer, I could be subpoenaed to testify under oath."

Dread pricked her heart. "Oh no, I'm so sorry—"

"Don't worry, Eliza. You're going to tell them the truth, as I have, and sooner or later, they're going to give up." He looked into her eyes with a strong, steady calm. "The truth *will* prevail."

If only she could find a way to draw from his strength and confidence.

"Would you like me to go with you?" he asked.

"No!" She felt her eyes widen. "I mean, thank you, but don't you think that would be dangerous? They already have us linked in their 'Red' files." Eliza pictured the zeal in the agent's eyes and shuddered. "Agent Robinson already thinks he has the next Julius and Ethel Rosenberg in his sights. I certainly don't want to feed into his delusions any more."

John nodded. "You're probably right."

Duncan came down the hall from the kitchen, his bent gait doubled. "Please, could you come quick?"

"What is it, Duncan?"

"It's Millie." He hurried back the way he came.

Eliza and John followed close behind.

In the kitchen, Millie sat slumped over the table.

"I thought the old girl was asleep." Duncan wiped his brow with his sleeve. "But I can't wake her."

Eliza gasped.

John leaned down and spoke Millie's name in her ear.

The woman moved but didn't wake.

Eliza reached for Millie's wrist and felt her pulse. It was a bit weak, and her skin felt odd, like damp cheese. Stroking Millie's forehead, Eliza spoke, raising her voice.

Millie stirred, made some muttering sounds, then opened her eyes. She swept a glance around the kitchen, face dazed. "My, but you early, Miz Eliza." She looked up at John and Duncan, her eyes hazy with confusion, and then back at Eliza. "I was just havin' a little prayer time, that's all. Never know when you need to be extra prayed up."

Eliza smiled. If Millie needed extra prayer *or* a nap, she certainly deserved it.

"Good." John nodded. He gave Millie's shoulder a pat, then went into the library.

Duncan also left.

But Eliza lingered. "Millie, are you sure you're feeling all right? You seem tired lately."

Millie smiled. "Bless your heart, child. When you seventy-nine, 'tired' already waitin' for you when you wake up. Beats not wakin' up at all, though." She chuckled. "But just between us, bein' absent from the body mean I be dancin' with Jesus, and I'm ready for that."

Eliza studied Millie's gentle smile. Was she serious? "If you're feeling tired," Eliza said carefully, "maybe you should take some time off. I mean, at your age, should you really be working so hard?"

"Aw, Miz Eliza, I appreciate your kindness. But I already had this out with Mr. John. Many times. And you know what? I *still* win. Every time." Her broad smile forced deep ripples into her face. "And that, child, is *always* worth gettin' up for."

Eliza returned Millie's smile, but a shadow crossed her heart. The book was practically finished. This could be one of the last times she would see Millie.

On impulse, she gave the woman a hug.

Millie hugged her back and patted Eliza's arm.

As Eliza entered the library, John rose from his seat and met her. "I have some pages here. I . . . thought perhaps writing it down would be better than me stammering in your ear." Avoiding her gaze, he held the pages out. "I do believe this is the last of it."

She took them, and, without thinking, looked into his eyes. His nearness, the scent of his cologne, and the love he refused to feel struck her with a wave of longing.

He pivoted away. "When you've finished,

I'd like to know what you think." He crossed the room and stood by the fireplace which was already aglow with a small fire.

She sat down and read.

Epilogue

George MacDonald said, "The one principle of hell is—'I am my own.'" The truth is, being my own master meant being master of nothing at all. It was all an illusion, and not just Hollywood. Now I am no longer my own, but God's, and this brings me greater peace than I've ever known. With each surrender of my will, I find myself a little freer in my soul, a little less chained to myself, a little closer to God, a little more like Him.

My friend, I would like to leave you with this one final thought: We think we're alone. You and I pass each other on the street and exchange smiles at the façades we've created, but deep down, we long for someone to peel back the mask, see us, and accept us as we really are, flaws and all. People look at the outward appearance, but God looks at the heart.

Eliza stared at the words, nodding outwardly but also agreeing in her heart. Yes, she knew that feeling well, wanting to be known and accepted unconditionally for who she was and not for what someone wanted her to become.

> I've bared my soul to God and surrendered all I am to Him. Because of this, I have not shared everything with you. I don't want to burden you with things too troubling to read. Some confessions can be a useful lesson to many, but other things, perhaps not so useful, are best confessed in the safe company of one compassionate, trusted friend.

Eliza covered a gasp. Knowing that John valued her as a trusted confidante warmed her, filled her with joy. But was 'trusted friend' enough?

It would have to be.

> I cannot tell you how grateful I am for God's boundless mercy, His unfailing love, and His power at work in me, making me a new man. I've tried, but I don't know if I could ever give Him the thanks He deserves.
>
> My friend, if nothing else, I hope you will take this one thing from my story: No one is beyond God's loving reach. I wasn't. And neither are you.

"Yes."

John turned from the mantel and stared at her. "What?"

"Your message and your gratitude are very clear. And you've given God all the credit for the good things in your life now. Beautifully done." She nodded. "I applaud you."

He went to the window and faced the bay for the longest time, as if he was translating her words into a language he could better understand.

"Your book makes me believe that with God, there is hope for anyone," she said.

John turned and searched her face, eyes glistening. "Thank you, Eliza," he said. "I'd rather hear that than a lifetime of applause."

28

Eliza settled into the lone chair and wiped moist palms on her skirt. She should have worn gloves.

The Whitecotton Room on the top floor of the Shattuck Hotel was nearly as classy as the Claremont. Ornately trimmed, arched windows surrounded her on all sides; their white-linen curtains tied back to give a clear view of the tops of buildings nearby and the buzzing city beyond. White pillars spanned from floor to ceiling throughout the room. Wallpaper of black filigree over gold covered the wall directly in front of her.

Behind a long table, four empty chairs faced her.

She had heard about congressional hearings involving the HUAC, but as far as she could tell, this panel was only a query and would not be as formal as that.

Things must be bad if a girl was tempted to lie simply because no one would believe the truth.

She closed her eyes.

Dear God . . .

Would He hear her clumsy, silent prayer?

Did she have a choice?

John says I should tell the truth and leave the rest to You. But there is a catch, isn't there? I know what You want in return, but I've given up enough of myself already. Too much. I don't think I can do that again—

Four men, including Agent Robinson, entered the room.

Heart hammering, she watched the men take their seats at the table, her mouth instantly cotton.

Agent Robinson opened a folder and stared at her as he spoke to the man beside him.

Eliza rubbed her palms on her skirt again.

This is it. Tell the truth or lie?

A strange calm stole over her, along with a very real sense that she was not alone.

God . . . is that You?

"Please state your full name."

Eliza started at the unexpected voice. "Eliza Jane Saunderson." She met the agent's gaze with all the confidence she could muster.

"What other names have you gone by?" the agent asked.

"Just my maiden name, Eliza Peterson."

The two men in the center spoke quietly to each other while Agent Robinson, on the far right, stood.

He looked her in the eye. "Miss Peterson, are you now or have you ever been a member of the Communist Party of the United States?"

"No." She cleared her throat. A glass of water would have been swell.

He leaned to one of the others and gestured at

something on the table. The man on the far left rose and brought a packet to Eliza. He opened it and handed her five photographs.

Robinson stepped around the table. "Please tell the panel what you're doing in these pictures," he said.

She sorted through all five photographs, heart sinking. "These appear to have been taken the day I visited the Soviet Consulate in San Francisco." She wanted to go on and tell them about her visit, but perhaps it would be wise to only answer the questions asked.

"What was your business there?" The agent drilled her with a look.

How much should she tell them about her family? "I was hoping someone there could help me find out if I have any relatives living in Russia. I recently learned that my parents—"

"Who are your contacts in the Soviet Union?"

Eliza fought to keep from glaring at Agent Robinson. "As I've told you before, I don't know anyone there." *Yet.* She frowned. "You also have me on record as saying I am not a communist, right?"

No one answered.

Easy does it, Eliza. Let them ask the questions.

"What are your parents' names?"

Eliza scrambled to think of how to answer. Perhaps it would be best to tell them only what she knew to be true. "I knew my parents as

Laura and Wesley Peterson. I've recently seen a document that makes me believe they may have also been known as Lara and Vasily Petrovich."

"Why did they lie about their identities?" Agent Robinson read the folder in his hands.

"What makes you think they were lying?"

He looked up at her, eyes narrowed. "They changed their names."

"That's not lying. It's common for immigrants to change their names to sound more American."

"No. Immigrants change their names upon arrival. According to your sister's birth records, she was born in New York to parents with Russian names. Names they later changed. Why?"

"I don't know why they did it later. Perhaps the birth of my sister happened so quickly on their arrival that they didn't have a chance to take care of it until after she was born."

"Regardless of what happened when, they were clearly hiding who they were. What were they hiding?"

"I don't know. As I said, I've only recently learned that they might have been known by any other names."

"What was your father's rank in Lenin's Red Army?"

"I know nothing about that. All I know is that my father was a literature professor."

The other three men bent close to confer, while

Agent Robinson studied her. "Do you expect us to believe that you lived with your parents for"—he glanced at the file—"eighteen years, and yet you knew nothing at all about your parents' lives in the Soviet Union or your father's involvement in Lenin's communist regime?"

Eliza lifted her chin. "That's correct. My parents never talked about their lives before my sister and I were born, other than the fact that they came from Europe."

"Do you also refuse to answer questions about your father's political activities in the United States?" Even from across the room, the gleam in the agent's eye was impossible to miss.

Eliza was going to get trapped if she wasn't careful. "I haven't refused to answer anything," she said. "I honestly don't know. If my father held political beliefs, communist or otherwise, I'm sure he had his reasons. My parents were very good people."

"So, since you were raised by communists, doesn't it make sense that they had a guiding influence on your current political viewpoints?"

"They weren't communists. And my . . . viewpoints are more of a personal nature than political."

Agent Robinson picked up something and came toward her with it, but she already had a good idea of what it was. He held out an issue of *A.W.A.R.E.*, the American Women's Alliance's newsletter. "Please read to us the byline credited to the article on the far right."

"E.J. Peterson."

"Did you write that article?"

God, I'm going to tell the truth. If You're there, please don't leave me all alone. "I did."

"Did you write sixteen other articles for the AWA and also"—he looked in the file—"twelve articles for the League of Women Voters' publication, *Action*?"

She resisted the urge to close her eyes. "I did."

"If your articles are only meant to explore *personal* interests, then why do you write on subjects that are highly inflammatory and politically charged in nature?"

Eliza frowned. "By inflammatory, do you mean to say that there are people who don't like to hear about social injustice? I am not being subversive or slandering the government—or anyone else for that matter. I'm just trying to help others understand how unfair it is that some people are treated unjustly simply because of their gender or the color of their skin."

"You're saying you didn't slander anyone in particular?" The man on the left said, sitting up straighter.

Had she? She tried to remember exactly what she'd written. "I have not."

The stiff man read aloud. "I quote, 'Performers such as Sammy Davis Jr., Lena Horne, and

Nat King Cole cannot stay in, or even eat at, the venues in which they perform. Davis was a headliner at the Frontier Casino, but after earning the casino a large sum of money, he was forced out the back door and made to stay at a boarding house on the west side of town. He was not allowed to gamble in the casino or dine in the hotel restaurant, simply because of the color of his skin. Louis Armstrong headlined at the Flamingo Hotel to a sold-out crowd, yet was forced to use the service entrance and was kicked out after his performance.' "

Eliza nodded. "Yes, I wrote that. It's all true, after all. Am I not free to repeat truth?"

"Anti-American propaganda is often signified by its inflammatory tone and particularly its focus on championing minorities."

A sharp string of replies came to mind, but Eliza held her tongue. *Wait for a question . . .*

"Who put you up to writing and publishing those articles?"

"My conscience."

"Your conscience?"

"Yes. How can I, in good conscience, enjoy a glass of iced tea and dip my toes in a sparkling hotel pool while another woman just like me, perhaps of the same age and education, is not allowed to drink from the same kind of drinking glass but has to use a paper cup, and if she dips one toe in the pool, the hotel will drain it, simply because of the color of her skin?"

The men conferred again.

Agent Robinson examined another sheet of paper. "How much Red money have you received for writing propaganda?"

She shook her head. "I don't write propaganda. I write about the gross injustice of racial, ethnic, and gender inequality. Not for anyone's agenda, but because I believe this kind of bigotry is wrong and should be exposed for what it is— shameful."

Robinson held the paper higher and raised his volume to match it. "I hold in my hand documented proof that the American Women's Alliance has received funding from the Communist Party of the United States. You have received payment for your articles from the American Women's Alliance." He stepped close enough for Eliza to see the veins pulsing in his neck. "Let me ask you again," he said. "How much Red money have you received for your articles?"

Eliza lifted her chin. "I sold my articles to a women's publication in hopes that women who suffer from injustice might read them and find a common thread of support, so that if they are in an unjust or oppressive situation, they will know they are not alone. I wrote those articles to encourage women and minorities. The AWA paid me for them. I accepted the money and didn't ask them where it came from. If the AWA has communist ties, I wasn't aware."

Robinson strode back to the table and the men resumed their discussion, shuffling papers.

After a minute, the man on the left end looked at her. "What is your relationship with the actor Johnny Devine, also known as John David Vincent?"

There was no telling how far this query would go. "I am a collaborator on a book he is writing."

"What do you know of Mr. Vincent's longtime association with the Hollywood Ten?"

"Everything I know about Mr. Vincent's dealings in Hollywood is included in his book." Eliza lifted her chin. "It will be available soon. You should buy it. I think you'd really enjoy it."

Actually, she knew of one Hollywood story that John had left *out* of the book—the young starlet's tragic life. Which was simply none of their business. Surely they wouldn't ask Eliza about Jeanette Lovell . . . would they?

Please, no questions about her. I can't do that to John. Please.

"And where do you . . . collaborate?"

The way one of the men in the middle said it made Eliza's skin crawl. And was it really necessary for him to ogle her like that? "In Mr. Vincent's home."

At once, all four men gave her their full attention. One raked a gaze over Eliza's skirt.

Cheeks burning, she tugged the fabric forward to make it cover as much leg as possible. Betty surely would've chosen an ankle-length skirt.

"And while in Mr. Vincent's home, have you seen anyone coming or going, such as actors, screenwriters, directors?" one agent asked. "Any telephone calls, correspondence, visitors, anything like that? Have you heard him discuss meetings or mention names?"

She kept her expression even. If she hadn't been so nosy, she would *not* have noticed the arrival of pink stationery on more than one occasion. But then again, she didn't actually *see* a name, and didn't know for sure if it qualified as correspondence. It could have been tickets to a film premiere. Recipes for Millie. A wedding invitation. How was she to know what was inside?

While she was deciding how to answer, the man on the left spoke. "You are aware that your full cooperation today will go a long way to making our file on you . . . go away."

Whether their tactics qualified as bribery or coercion, the idea that they would simply stop investigating her in exchange for information about John stunned her, though she shouldn't have been surprised. How unethical. A perfect example of injustice and oppression at its worst. She had half a mind to tell them so.

John was right—an entire department was

infected with this paranoid insanity. Someone needed to drive the HUAC out of business.

Eliza sighed. "Listen. I don't know anything about Mr. Vincent's friends, but what I do know is that he's not a communist. You're wasting your time on him."

Agent Robinson spoke to the others and then, with a nod, he wrote something in the folder.

"Is that my file?" Eliza asked. "What are you writing?"

The agent didn't bother looking up. "You're being placed on the hostile witness list."

29

Eliza wasn't sure if John was expecting her to come to work after the panel query, but the distance from the Shattuck to his home wasn't far, and the day was still young. It wouldn't take long to finalize the manuscript, and, barring anything unexpected, Eliza could have the memoir finished and ready to mail to New York by the end of the day.

As the bus jockeyed its way through the city, Eliza focused on the sights—the vigor of traffic, the milling pedestrians, and the majesty of Sather Tower standing tall against the western horizon of merging sky and shimmering water.

Couldn't the bus get a flat tire or run out of gas? Even better, couldn't it turn around and go back in time to the day she first met John?

She let her tired mind wander. What would she do differently if she could go back to that day? If she had known the things she knew now, would she do it again?

Eliza leaned back against the seat. She'd been part of an amazing book that would offer hope to many people. Her heart had been awakened, and she'd known love and friendship. She had grown.

Yes. Even if the outcome was the same, she would do it all again.

The bus left the Berkeley campus and began its winding ascent between the fragrant evergreens lining the route leading to John's fairytale home. There was no point fantasizing about delaying the end. John was eager to be free of it. And Eliza had no desire to prolong the inevitable.

Yes, I do. I want to drag it out for another week or two, or a hundred and fifty-two.

No. Once the book was done, Eliza was no longer needed.

But he does need me. And I need him.

True or not, it wasn't up to her. It was up to the man who refused to share the burden of his past with her, a refusal that had kept Eliza awake at night, her heart ripped in half. One half burned in frustration at John's resolve, while the other half loved him all the more for wanting to protect her.

She didn't want to be protected. She wanted to love the man.

Maybe it's not about what you want.

Eliza closed her eyes and waited, listening for any other input from that Voice that was not her own. John had said there was a purpose to their lives that they couldn't always see, a larger picture, and he was at peace with that. Millie often talked the same way.

Well, if God had a larger purpose for Eliza's life, it would have to wait. Right now, she needed to catch a break in solving the mystery of her parents, and she desperately needed to clear her name.

Maybe God could help with *that*.

"You're here." John met her at the front door. He looked even more battle-worn than he had the day before. He stepped aside, beckoning her. "I'm sorry, please come in. How did it go?"

"Not well, I'm afraid." Eliza removed her coat and then gave him a summary of the morning's inquiry.

John listened without comment.

When she finished, she examined John more closely. He looked pale. "John, what's wrong?"

"It's Millie." He grimaced.

Dread seized her. "What is it?"

"Her grandson Nathaniel called. She's had a bad spell of some kind." John met her gaze and held it. "They think it was her heart."

Eliza could barely breathe. "Oh my goodness, is she—?"

"The last I heard, she was alive." John's mouth tightened. "But unfortunately, it took Nathaniel so long to find a hospital that would admit her, it's hard to say how she will fare."

Eliza's handbag fell from her hand and hit the floor. "Oh dear! Poor Millie!" Her eyes filled with tears. She sank onto the nearest chair.

John offered her a handkerchief, which she took absently.

"I should have known," she whispered. "Yesterday wasn't the first time." She shook her head. "I should have taken her to the doctor right away when I found her like that. Oh, why didn't I—?"

"No. If anyone should have done something, it's me." John shook his head. He lowered himself to the chair beside her. "I've tried to get her to stop working, but she refused. Said this house was her responsibility, she'd been taking care of it more than half her life. I told her she would have a good pension. She said it wasn't about the money. I think it was about her pride."

Eliza dabbed at her eyes. "She told me you two had words over her staying on and she always won." She glanced around the room at the spotless furnishings. "She's quite proud of that."

"If Millie worked herself into a heart attack, I'll never—"

"No." She looked into John's troubled eyes. "You are not to blame. And there's no point in either of us wishing we could go back and change what's done."

He looked around the room. "She's always been here, a part of this home. A stabilizing force."

"Yes."

"Perhaps we could pray for her."

With a nod, Eliza bowed her head and listened as John placed Millie into God's care. The sound of his deep voice, rich with compassion and sincerity, warmed her, and her tears flowed again. Somehow, Millie had entwined herself around Eliza's heart. She didn't know how or when it had happened, it just had.

In the silence, she realized John was watching her.

She wiped her eyes again and wished she could see Millie's face. Wished for her comforting arms. Wished she wasn't walking out of John and Millie's lives today for what could very well be the last time.

"There's nothing more we can do now but wait," John said.

"Yes, I suppose you're right. I've come to finalize your manuscript and send it to New York."

John stood and offered her a hand. "Yes, of course. Thank you."

Eliza went to work, and for the next several hours, John kept to another part of the house, which was fine with her since the final touches didn't require his input. By four o'clock, the manuscript was packaged, addressed, and ready to mail. It seemed such an anticlimactic finale to the weeks of laying John's soul bare.

Eliza gathered her coat and bag and then waited in the library a moment. Should she wait, ring for John, or go in search of him?

After a few moments, John came in. "You're finished?"

She nodded, unable to trust her voice.

He stared at the package. "So, that's it." He checked the clock on the mantel. "And still enough time to post it today."

"Yes, I believe so."

"A tremendous amount of work has gone into this book. I believe it's only right to give it a proper send-off. I was thinking of celebrating. With dinner."

She ignored the ridiculous rush of hope his words stirred. "That's a good idea."

He set his cane against a chair and buttoned his jacket. "Since it wouldn't be possible without you, it's only right that you should celebrate as well. Would you care to join me?" he said, not meeting her eyes.

Her heart clenched. Prolonging her time with him—yes. Prolonging their last goodbye—no. Going out with him in public—well, what did that matter now? It would be the last time.

"Yes. I'll join you." Betty would have kittens. In fact, Eliza would have to agree with her sister this time. Dining out with him was foolish and would only make saying goodbye harder.

But how could she resist?

They took a cab and headed for the west side of town, with a brief stop at the North Berkeley post office. That didn't take long. While Eliza waited, John dealt with the clerk, then turned away from the counter with a shrug. No fanfare.

The book was out of his hands, that was that.

By the time they reached a restaurant near Fisherman's Wharf, the parking lot was full, surprising for a Thursday. Though the sky was growing dark, the lights of the city sent a golden shimmer across the rippling bay. Inside, the host led them to a dimly lit corner table at a window overlooking the water. Partially enclosed by dark wooden lattice draped with ivy, the table was set for two with a tapered candle casting a mild glow over deep-red linens.

John swept a guarded glance around the room and then pulled out Eliza's chair.

"Thank you," she said.

John seemed especially quiet, which was odd, since it was his idea to celebrate. He was probably thinking of Millie.

Thoughts of Millie had tugged at Eliza all day.

A phonograph played Billie Holiday's "The Very Thought of You."

Swell. Nothing like a romantic love song to awaken hushed longings.

When the maître d' came with a bottle of wine, John declined with a wave and a "No, thanks," but as soon as the waiter left, John turned to Eliza. "I'm sorry, force of habit. I didn't think to ask if you wanted wine. Do you?"

She smiled. "No, thank you." No telling what effect even a little wine would have, and it was best to keep her tongue and her wits about her tonight. Eliza studied her menu, but the items were not connecting with her brain.

John was handsome to distraction in his black coat and tie. Of course, the man would be handsome in old coveralls and a ratty fishing hat. The picture brought a faint smile to her lips—a welcome diversion. She needed something to get her mind off the finality of the day and the uncertainty about Millie.

A shadow fell over her menu.

"Hello, there." Oscar Silva smiled down at them. "I saw you two from across the room and figured I'd better pop over and get an autograph."

"Hello," Eliza said. What an odd coincidence that Oscar was here.

John rose from his seat and shook Oscar's hand.

"Congratulations on finishing the book."

How did he know? John must have telephoned him. Which meant his appearance here was no coincidence after all.

Oscar gave John's shoulder a clap, and then leaned down close to Eliza. "You think I'm kidding, but I really do want your autograph." He offered her a pen and a paper. "Would you mind?"

Eliza smiled. "How exciting, my first. And probably my last," she added with a chuckle. "And to whom shall I make it out?"

Oscar laughed. "To Oscar, the *second* best agent on the planet."

She humored him, cheeks aflame. People were staring now. Maybe that was Oscar's plan. He was probably getting a head start on generating press for John's book.

"Oscar, mind if I have a word with you?" John gave Oscar a pointed look and turned to Eliza. "If you'll excuse us."

Eliza nodded, not sure what to think of this odd exchange.

The two men walked around a corner and out of sight.

Above the dining room chatter, Nat King Cole sang "Almost Like Being in Love." If the next title was his "There Goes My Heart," she would have to ask the waiter to play something else.

While the two men were gone, Eliza received curious glances from several of the diners. Ignoring them, she tried to study her menu again, but nothing sounded appealing.

How badly had Millie suffered? Would she recover?

When the men returned, John avoided Eliza's curious gaze and took his seat.

Oscar gave her a gallant bow and spied her autograph. "Ah, yes, I can't leave without that. This is going to be worth a mint when that book hits the bestseller list." He kissed Eliza's hand, gave John's hand another firm shake, and then left.

When the waiter came for their order, Eliza chose clam chowder, hoping it would tempt her appetite. John handed over his unopened menu and asked for whatever the chef recommended.

A woman approached the table for an autograph.

John was polite but wrote quickly and bid her a good evening, barely short of shooing her away. Then he met Eliza's gaze with a wince. "Sorry. I'm used to this sort of thing, but for you, it's probably—"

"Hiya," a middle-aged woman said, voice breathless. She beamed a giddy smile at John, then at Eliza. "Can I have your autograph?"

John signed the back of her coaster.

Then the woman turned to Eliza. "And yours?"

Eliza opened her mouth but couldn't think of a thing to say.

John rested his chin in one hand, hiding a smile.

"Thank you, but I'm afraid I . . ." Eliza scrambled to think of how to let the woman down gently.

"Oh, and I'm sorry to intrude on your meal, but could you tell me which picture was your favorite to make?"

The woman was looking at her, not John.

Eliza's eyes widened. "Picture?"

"Oh yes, I'm your biggest fan. Just ask my

husband, he'll tell you. I've seen every Gene Tierney film."

Eliza looked to John for help, but he was sipping his water—and taking a very long time to swallow. A smile curled beyond the edges of his glass.

What should she say? The woman would be mortified if Eliza corrected her now. She turned to the woman and smiled. "What is your name?"

"Evelyn." Her shoulders nearly touched her ears as she clasped her hands.

"Evelyn, what a lovely name. Tell me, what's *your* favorite film?"

"Oh! Gracious, there are so many!" She turned and whispered loudly at the man behind her. "Oh, I know," she said, turning back. "*Leave Her To Heaven*. That was breathtaking! And if you don't mind my saying, they really should have given you the Oscar."

Eliza avoided John's face. "To Evelyn, with love," Eliza said as she wrote the message, then signed a loopy signature that she hoped no one would ever be able to read.

"Thank you!" Evelyn smashed the autograph to her bosom and grinned at John as if she'd just won a jackpot, then returned to her seat.

Unfolding her napkin, Eliza shot a furtive glance around the room and hoped no one else was getting the same idea. Then she caught

John's smile. She dropped her gaze to keep from laughing.

John signed four more autographs by the time their meal arrived, leaving them little time for conversation. Not that either of them were feeling talkative.

A nagging foreboding about Millie had returned. When the chowder came, Eliza's stomach rebelled at the thought of eating. She stirred the soup, then set her spoon down.

John poked at his Lobster Thermidor. He nodded at Eliza's bowl. "You don't like it?"

"I'm sorry. I probably shouldn't have come. You wanted to celebrate, and I'm no help."

"Are you not feeling well?"

"I'm fine, I just can't stop thinking about Millie. It's so unsettling, knowing how she must be suffering and not knowing what's happening and whether or not . . ."

"You're right." He stared at his hardly touched meal. "I can't very well celebrate while Millie might be lying somewhere holding on by a thread."

"I wish there was a way to know."

John placed his napkin on the table, then grabbed his cane and stood. "There may be. If you'll excuse me."

Eliza watched him go, sorry that she had ruined his celebration dinner but grateful that he understood.

Ten minutes later, John returned, looking more optimistic than when he left. "I phoned Nathaniel's house and spoke to a neighbor who is staying with his children. She's at St. Luke's Hospital."

"How is she?"

"The neighbor didn't know."

Millie was alive, at least. But in what condition?

John rose and offered her his hand. "Come, our cab is waiting."

She stared at his outstretched hand. So that was it, the evening was over. "I'm sorry to have ruined your—"

"To take us to St. Luke's," he said. "That is, if you'd like to go."

"Oh yes!" She collected her things, took his hand, and stood. "Thank you, John."

He avoided her eyes.

As they left the restaurant, Eliza's heart swelled at his thoughtfulness, but she quickly put her gratitude aside. It was just one more thing she loved about him that she would miss.

30

At the hospital, Eliza stood by while John asked the desk staff about Millie, but no one seemed to know where she was. After about fifteen minutes of waiting, he and Eliza were directed to the basement wing.

The *basement*. Because of the color of Millie's skin.

Pressing down her anger, Eliza joined John in the elevator. "I hope they at least gave her a bed," she muttered.

John glanced at Eliza without a word, just stuffed a fist in his jacket pocket and watched the lights change until the *B* glowed.

Nothing could have prepared Eliza for the sight of Millie's room. From the doorway, she counted seven occupied beds—the patients all colored—crammed into the room like puzzle pieces. Men and women of varying ages surrounded one bed.

Soft murmurings quieted when she and John walked in.

Swallowed by a giant, white pillow, Millie looked like a small, sleeping child. Her hair was a misty, gray halo, her skin nearly the same color.

Dear God, she looks so frail . . .

As John moved toward the bed, a few of the

people shifted as best they could to make room for him.

One young woman in a maid's uniform gave Eliza a polite smile. Everyone else remained somber.

John leaned down and spoke quietly to Millie, but she didn't respond. He turned toward Eliza, his expression as uncertain as she felt.

Is she dying?

John straightened and spoke in low tones to a younger man—probably Millie's grandson Nathaniel. The two men maneuvered through the people and left the room.

Eliza moved closer and reached for Millie's hand, tears brimming. "I'll pray for you, Millie." To Eliza's ear, the words sounded so presumptuous, as if her clumsy prayers could fix the woman. "I . . ." It felt like everyone in the room was listening. She leaned down, kissed the old woman's forehead, and whispered, "I love you."

Millie smiled faintly but didn't open her eyes.

Eliza looked to John, who beckoned to her from the doorway. She excused herself and slipped away to join him.

John glanced at Millie's family, then leaned down to speak into Eliza's ear. "It's her heart. The doctors don't expect her to last much longer," he said. "They don't even know how she made it this long."

Eliza's eyes drifted closed. She wept soundlessly.

A strong arm encircled her, and she leaned into the comfort of John's embrace.

As the cab carried Eliza and John toward her apartment, she knew she should try to make conversation, but it seemed her heart had swollen until it pressed against her lungs and stole her ability to speak.

Perhaps John didn't mind her silence, since he was also quiet. He was probably thinking about things that he didn't need to, like what he might have done differently for Millie. Which was pointless. Millie had made choices for reasons of her own, and it was unlikely John could have dissuaded her.

Another blanket of fog had settled over the city while John and Eliza were inside the hospital, and the thickness enveloped them now, closing in, cutting them off from the world. Normally, fog wouldn't be so troubling. But today, the idea of losing both Millie and John at once left Eliza feeling more isolated than she had felt in a long time.

After the cab stopped at Eliza's apartment building, John opened her door and offered her an elbow. "I'll see you to your door."

Biting her lip, Eliza glanced at the building. "Thank you, but I am sure the girls living here will start a small riot if they see you. Besides, it's . . . not necessary."

"All right, then. As you wish."

Eliza swallowed hard. "Goodbye, John. It's been . . ." Words couldn't describe what her time with him had been. Raising her hand in a wave, she turned and walked away. It was all she could do.

"Eliza?"

She turned. In the haze, she could barely see his face in the glow of a nearby streetlamp.

He took a few steps toward her, then stopped and drew a deep breath. "I owe you an apology. The other day, at the gate, when I . . . it was incredibly thoughtless of me to kiss you like that. I had hoped I was no longer that kind of man."

Her tongue turned wooden. He wouldn't make her relive that day's humiliation, not today of all days, would he?

John took a step closer.

She kept a steady vigil on his chest to avoid seeing his eyes. She had worked too hard to put that kiss and his confession behind her to dredge it all up now.

When he didn't speak, she looked up and met his gaze. This time, he didn't look pained and conflicted. He looked desperate.

"I tried to tell myself I didn't dare hope," he said softly.

Her heart raced. "Hope for what?"

"You." He swallowed hard. "Eliza, you're a beautiful, kind, intelligent woman. You have your whole life ahead of you. You deserve a good, honorable man, one without a scandalous reputation. A man who isn't . . ." With a frown, he lowered his gaze to his cane. "You deserve a whole man."

"Yes, I do," she whispered, dizzy from her heart beating out of control. "And I'm looking at one now."

He searched her eyes.

If he was trying to see into her heart, she would make him look no further. "You're a very good man, John. And you're far more 'whole' than anyone I know."

"You can say that after everything you've heard?"

She nodded. "I know exactly who you are. You don't pretend you're something you're not. You don't put on a false front. You live each day in humble faith with a moral strength that's genuine."

His voice softened. "You see all that?"

"John," she whispered, afraid her voice would break. "You're the most honorable man I've ever known."

"Honorable?" His expression crumbled. "I've never felt honorable in my life." His dark eyes locked onto hers, filled with the same turmoil she'd seen the day he kissed her. "I ache for you,

Eliza. There. Do you still think I'm honorable?"

A tear fell as she nodded, caught up in the wave of bliss rippling through her.

Gently, he stroked the wet trail, then touched his lips to her cheek.

Her eyes drifted closed.

"I ache to hold you," he whispered against her skin, "and tell you how much I love you."

She finally forced her eyes open. The look on his face made her forget how to breathe. "I love you too, John," she whispered. "With all my heart."

He pulled her close and held her tight. When he finally released her, he leaned down and met her with a kiss so gentle and so full of love she feared she was dreaming.

She wrapped her arms around his neck as she returned his kiss, saying without words what she had desperately longed to say.

He said her name and kissed her again, warming a path to her heart, filling a place that had long been vacant.

This was love, right and real. A joy like nothing she'd ever known flooded her, filling her more than she ever believed possible.

When they finally parted, John pressed a solemn kiss to her forehead and released her. He reached into his pocket and took something out.

A small jewelry box.

He looked into her eyes. "Eliza, even though

I believed God had forgiven me, I feared I still owed penalties—like the inevitable consequences of our mistakes. So when you came into my life, I thought the time had come to pay my dues, that perhaps falling in love with you was part of my punishment. But a good friend reminded me that God doesn't work that way. That sometimes God, in His mercy, shields us from penalties we deserve and gives us joys we don't." His voice fell low. "Unexpected and unimaginable joys."

He looked at the box as if it might help him proceed.

Eliza's breath caught.

"That day at the gate, you asked me not to let you walk out of my life." His gaze met hers. "Eliza, I believe God brought you into my life, and I can't imagine living another day without you. Please don't ever walk out again."

Was she dreaming?

He opened the box and turned it around. Nestled in a satin crevasse, a large, oval solitaire glittered. "Sweetheart, this thing has been burning a hole in my pocket all evening." He searched her eyes. "I hope you can forgive me for not doing this on bended knee. Will you marry me?"

Eliza gasped. "Oh, John." She wrapped her arms around his neck and kissed him again, heart bursting. If this was God's doing, then He deserved her deepest thanks.

As they parted, John chuckled. "I'm going to take that as a yes."

She smiled, tears blurring her vision. "Yes! Yes! Yes!"

Smiling back, John heaved a sigh.

"So what good friend shall I thank for convincing you to give love a chance?"

"Oscar," he said. "I owe him more than I can ever repay. We'll probably have to feed him dinner every night for the rest of his life now."

Eliza winced. "Okay. But there's . . . something I need to tell you."

His expression sobered. "What's that?"

"I'm afraid I'm not much of a cook."

A slow smile spread across his face and he shook his head. "Scandalous," he whispered in mock horror.

Eliza hugged him tight.

31

Eliza awoke with a jolt. Had last night been a dream?

She checked her hand and smiled. No, she hadn't dreamt it. She was engaged to be married. To John David Vincent, the man she loved.

She felt something warm and soft at her shoulder. At some point in the night, Mr. Darcy must have decided that Eliza was his new pillow. How would he like living in a huge storybook house with a cottage garden? Hopefully, John liked cats.

A knock at the door startled her. She slipped a robe over her nightgown and cracked the door an inch.

Ivy peered through the crack. "Say—for a girl who's not taking any calls, you sure get your share of 'em. I wish I were as popular as you." She tucked a bus transfer slip through the door and pointed at the scrawled writing on it. "One of them called twice. And then there's the fella who called just now. Of course, I told him to buzz off." Ivy tilted to better see Eliza through the crack. "But he didn't sound like that other guy. This one . . ." Ivy fanned herself. "Oh my stars, but he sounded dreamy. If you toss him back, *I'm* throwing out a line." Ivy frowned. "He

didn't leave a number. He said you'd have it."
She raised an eyebrow.

John. Eliza smiled. "Thanks bunches, Ivy. You're a doll."

"Mm-hmm," Ivy said.

Eliza let Darcy out, then dressed quickly. On her way out the door to telephone John, she spotted the transfer slip. She picked it up and frowned at the message. She'd been called twice by someone at Flushing Hospital in Queens County, New York.

The hospital listed on Betty's birth certificate.

Eliza hurried down the stairs to the phone.

The operator reminded her that this telephone was restricted to local calls, and authorization for long-distance calls was required.

Eliza groaned. She dreaded going to the super, but then he wasn't known to pass up a chance to add his "finder's fee" to tenants' phone charges.

Once Eliza had authorization, the operator placed the call to the hospital. Eliza gave her name to the desk clerk. She waited several minutes before someone came on the line.

"Is this Mrs. Eliza Saunderson?"

"Yes. I had a message that you called." *Please, tell me you know something about my parents.*

"I'm Margaret Carter, head nurse. I oversee our hospital volunteers. Mrs. Saunderson, I called because you contacted us about a patient who gave birth here in 1919. Is that correct?"

"Yes, I did. Do you have any information about Lara Petrovich and her child?"

"No, I'm sorry, I can't help you with that."

Eliza's hope deflated.

"This may sound rather unusual, but the reason I'm calling is that when I gave your information to a candy striper to file as you had asked, I was told that you are not the only person who has contacted this hospital about that particular patient. This other person also asked us for any information about that patient and infant, and left his name on file. It seems the man has been looking for the Petrovich family for quite some time. The candy striper found his information when she filed yours."

Eliza gasped. Her body felt wooden. "Was his name Ivan?"

"No. His name is Vlad."

Vlad? Who was that, another brother?

"I believe his full name is—let me see if I can pronounce it—Vladimir Tishchenko. He called a while back and asked to be contacted if there was any new information about Lara or Vasily Petrovich or the infant born to them. We don't give out patient information, but I didn't see any harm in telling you that someone else has also been looking for your family. He is Russian, but I believe he lives in West Virginia. Would you like his number?"

"Yes, please." Eliza hunted for something to

write on and found a pencil stub, no paper. She tore the *no calls* note off the wall, turned it over, and wrote the telephone number. She barely remembered to thank the woman, whose name she'd already forgotten. Then she stared at the name and number.

Who was Vlad and what was his interest in her parents? Was he a relative? A friend? An enemy? Or perhaps . . . a spy? Could this person be the reason her parents left Russia and changed their names?

Had they been hiding from this Vladimir?

Eliza stared at the telephone number, then at the receiver. She needed to know and had no choice but to risk the call. She didn't have to give her name.

But she did have to get another long distance call approved. Once the call was placed, a woman answered in Russian.

Eliza's hopes fizzled. "Hello," she said, hoping the woman understood English. "I'm calling for Vladimir Tish-chenko?" Eliza winced, certain she had destroyed the pronunciation of the man's name.

"Vlad is not home. Who is calling, please?"

Until she knew why the man was interested in her parents, she would not reveal her identity. "I am calling because Vlad left his telephone number at Flushing Hospital in New York, and the head nurse gave it to me."

"The hospital told you to call Vlad? Why?"

"Because I also called the hospital. About . . . a family named Petrovich."

The line went silent. "Petrovich?"

"Yes." Perhaps the nurse's information was incorrect.

The woman spoke in Russian, then English. "Wait. I have Vlad telephone you from work. You wait for his call, da?"

God, should I trust these strangers? Do I really want to know what connection this man has with my parents?

If this contact with Vlad *was* God's way of helping her, then perhaps she should trust it.

"Yes, please ask him to call me. My name is Eliza." She gave the telephone number and ended the call, then stared at the receiver.

Had she done the right thing?

Minutes passed. She was about to give up and call John when the phone rang.

Hands trembling, she answered. "Hello?"

"Eliza?" A male voice.

"Yes."

"May I ask who you are?" His Russian accent was heavy, but his English was good.

Not so fast, mister. "The hospital in New York gave me your number. It seems you and I are both looking for information about the same family."

A few beats of silence followed. "Do you know

Vasily and Lara Petrovich?" he said slowly. "And their child?"

Eliza's pulse raced. "Perhaps. Will you please tell me why you are looking for them?"

A slow exhale played out across the line. "I need to know what you will do with information. Is your interest personal or political?"

"Personal." Eliza willed her rigid shoulders to relax.

"Ah, good. Then, in that case, my mother has lifelong friend who lost contact with Vasily when he left Russia. This woman searched many years for him. She knew that Vasily set sail for New York in late 1918, but nothing more. I live in United States now, so she asked my mother for my help. I contacted many New York hospitals and clinics until I found hospital where Lara Petrovich gave birth. Like finding . . . needle in haystack as they say, da?"

"Yes," Eliza whispered. *And the woman searching is . . . ?*

"Now I ask who *you* are," the man went on, "or do you still have questions for me?"

"One more. What is the name of your mother's friend?"

"Katerina Petrovich."

Eliza gasped. "She's my—I mean, she never married?"

Vlad let out a sigh. "No. She was promised to my uncle Anatoly—my mother's brother. They were all childhood friends, you see, very close. But my uncle died same winter. I was only infant. I never knew him."

"So you never knew Vasily and Lara?"

"No."

Eliza's heart sank.

"Now, may I ask why you also want to find Vasily and child?"

"Vasily and Lara are my parents. I am their second daughter. The first daughter, the one born in New York, is my sister."

"*You* are Vasily's child?" Vlad exclaimed something in Russian. "Your parents and sister, they are well? I must send telegram to Katerina at once. She will be overjoyed to find brother!"

Eliza's eyes stung with tears. "Vlad, I'm sorry, but my parents died in a train accident many years ago. My sister and I are the only ones remaining."

A pause stretched for several seconds. "I am so sorry to hear this. You must miss them very much."

"Yes."

The super passed through the lobby and gave her a slit-eyed look. She turned her back to him and lowered her voice. "Vlad, my parents didn't tell us where they were from. Or why they left Russia. I would very much like to speak with Katerina and to know why my parents came to the States and changed their names. They never spoke of it to us."

"You do not know?"

Eliza stilled. "No. Do you?"

"Da."

She gasped. The truth was here. Now. It would either set her free or add to her troubles.

"My mother told me story. During Russian Civil War, commoners were cold and starving from fuel and food shortages. The harsh winter claimed many lives and famine continued. Since payment for military service was rations and fuel, Vasily joined Red Guard. Lenin fooled people with talk of new regime. But after Bolsheviks took over Petrograd, Red Guard was used to wipe out imperialists. It was a time of much terror and bloodshed. Vasily witnessed atrocities he never imagined. He wanted out, but deserting Red Guard meant execution for Vasily and entire family, as well as relatives, friends—all people connected to him."

Entire family . . .

"There was an infant son. Do you know what happened to him?"

Vlad sighed. "Da. They had son named Ivan. But sadly, the child became sick and died."

"That's what I was afraid of," she said, her voice breaking.

"Vasily was desperate to save family and break ties with Lenin and communist regime. But the only way was to take wife and leave country. If he told any family where he was, they would be in danger. Deserters and those harboring them were executed. To protect family, Vasily took pregnant wife to Switzerland, on foot and under cover of night. Katerina arranged for Vasily and Lara to go from there to America hidden on cattle boat. To protect him and family, Katerina told Vasily to change name and disappear forever. She did not want to know this new name so she could not . . . be forced to give her brother away."

You mean tortured. Eliza let the story sink in, stirring up new images of her parents and the heartbreak, cruelty, and injustice they had suffered. Her parents were not communist spies. They were two people who abhorred violence and injustice and risked their lives to protect their loved ones. They were grieving, young parents who fled and began a new life in a strange, new land where they knew no one. How hard they must have worked to conceal their nationality, all to protect those they loved.

"Thank you, Vlad," Eliza said. "You don't know how much this means to me to finally know their story. I am greatly indebted to you for this."

"No owing, no debt. I am pleased to find you at last. There is someone else who will also be most pleased. May I send telegram to Katerina?

She must know you and sister are alive and well."

"Yes, I would be very grateful. Thank you so much."

"I am certain she will send telegram, but she does not speak or write English. If you permit me, I will call you and translate her message for you."

"Yes, please." She felt no reason not to trust him with this information. He had just given her the most precious gift—the last pieces of the puzzle of her parents' lives.

The pieces she had challenged God to provide.

As soon as she ended the call, she phoned Betty. As she told Betty the story, she could hear her sister crying.

"Betty, this was no coincidence. All these things leading us to the story of our parents and to our aunt. I think . . . maybe God is helping me."

Silence. "Well, it doesn't matter how it happened, I'm just glad it did. Promise me you'll tell me just as soon as you hear any word from Aunt Katerina, won't you?"

"Yes, of course. And now that I know why our parents were hiding their identities, I can put a stop to this HUAC harassment once and for all."

"Oh, darling, I hope so. What a nightmare!"

Eliza glanced down at the ring on her finger

and smiled. She had one more important piece of news for her sister. But perhaps Betty had heard enough for now. Eliza's engagement news could wait one more day. Tomorrow would come soon enough.

32

Eliza went back to her room, still reeling from what she had learned. Telling Betty she would set the HUAC straight was just an impulse, but the more she thought about it, the more certain she felt. The truth would prevail, as John always said.

She returned downstairs and phoned John.

"Ah, Eliza, thank goodness. I was half afraid last night was only a dream."

Eliza smiled. So she wasn't the only one.

"I love you," he said, deep voice thrumming across the line. "In case I forgot to mention that."

She caught her lower lip with her teeth, but that did nothing to contain her smile. "I love you too. And you *did* tell me, but I don't mind hearing it again."

"That's good," he said. The line went quiet for a moment. "Say, I spoke to Nathaniel this morning. Nothing has changed. Millie is fading, sweetheart. I don't think she has very long."

Her stomach twisted. She was so helpless, just like the day she learned about her parents. Was there nothing she could do to keep from losing Millie too?

Eliza told him what she had learned about her parents, and how she hoped to hear from her aunt soon.

"That's excellent news," John said. "You can rest easy now."

"I'll rest a lot easier when I see the look on Agent Robinson's face after I tell him he was wrong about my parents. In fact, I have half a mind to go to HUAC headquarters and tell him."

"Is that so?"

The amusement in John's tone sealed the deal. "Yes. As a matter of fact, I think I'll go right now. Why not put a stop to all this bullying?"

Another stretch of silence. "I'll come with you."

"But aren't you afraid of them seeing us together?"

He laughed. "With you armed and ready to do battle? I'm not afraid of anything."

"Meet me at the Shattuck in two hours," she said, grinning.

Eliza waited outside the Shattuck Hotel for John's cab to arrive. A small army of photographers were camped around the hotel's entrance. Had they somehow learned John was coming? She went to one of the men and asked what was going on. The man, wearing a press badge, told here there were rumors that the HUAC was preparing to make an announcement, and he was there to get the scoop.

She went inside the hotel lobby to wait where

she could see the street from the windows, out of sight of the cameras.

John's cab pulled up out front. When he exited, several of the photojournalists rushed the cab and snapped shots of him.

John smiled and waved at them, ignoring their questions. He met Eliza in the lobby and hurried her toward the stairs.

A kiss would have to wait.

At the reception desk outside the Whitecotton Room, Eliza asked for Agent Robinson and was directed to the lobby on the mezzanine, as the panel was in session. She and John waited at the far end of the smaller upper lobby, as far out of view of passersby as possible. Being with someone as recognizable as John would take some getting used to.

Finally, a clerk called Eliza's name and led her and John inside. Four men were seated at the long table today, but only two of them were from the day before. And no sign of Robinson.

"Eliza Saunderson?" one of the men asked.

"Yes. I'm here to see Agent Robinson."

"Agent Robinson is not here." The man took a folder from the other man and spoke in low tones, then turned to Eliza. "What is the nature of your visit?"

Disappointed she couldn't tell the agent directly, she went ahead. "I was here yesterday and was questioned at length about my family.

I'm here today because I've just learned the truth about my parents and the reason for their name change and move to the United States from Russia. I would like to go on record with this information."

The men studied her.

One of them spoke to John. "And you are?"

"John Vincent."

"Also known as Johnny Devine?"

"Yes."

"What is your interest in Mrs. Saunderson's case?"

"I am here for moral support." John smiled at Eliza.

As one man shuffled through a stack of folders, the other one told Eliza to proceed.

She told them the story of her father's desertion from the Red Guard, her parents' risky defection, and the reason for changing their names. She explained that her father wanted nothing to do with communism after seeing Lenin's regime firsthand.

One man wrote, while the other continued to look through folders.

Finally, the one writing looked up at Eliza. "Do you have anything else to say?"

"Yes." She glanced at John to bolster her courage, then faced the men. "I want to say that, as an American citizen, I am appalled by the way this committee has handled these investigations.

This is a country for which freedom and liberty were hard-won by the lives and deaths of patriots, and yet a branch of our own government makes false accusations and is prepared to pronounce guilt on its own people, which is both damaging and unwarranted. If I have a political position, it is that I am revolted by injustice. But that revolt makes me neither a dissident nor a communist. I am a proud American patriot who has something to say and nothing to hide."

Breathe. You did it.

"Mrs. Saunderson," one man said, "I will make a note of this in your file. You may be interested to know that Agent Robinson is no longer with this agency. Our new field director, Charles Hamilton, will be reviewing Agent Robinson's case files. If we need any more information from you, we will contact you. But at this point, you may consider yourself no longer a person of interest in these investigations. You are dismissed."

Eliza drew a sharp breath. "And my sister?"

"What is her name?"

"Betty Cunningham."

The man peered at the folder in front of him and shook his head. "Your sister is of no interest to us."

She heaved a sigh and turned to John. "It looks like God answers prayer."

"He certainly does." John smiled. "Shall we go?"

"Mr. Vincent?" The other man held a thick folder in his hand.

"Yes?"

"We do have a few questions for you. If you please."

Oh no. What had she gotten him into?

"Fine," John said. "I also have nothing to hide."

"What is your relationship with 'D.M.'?"

Eliza froze.

John didn't say a word. His stony expression was impossible to read.

The agent scanned the contents of the folder in his hand. "We have reports that you receive regular correspondence from someone we suspect is actress Deborah Marlow."

No. This can't be happening.

John stood silent.

God, make him tell them it isn't true, please . . .

"Mrs. Marlow has admitted to attending Communist Party meetings with her husband, Douglas Kelley, and their lifelong friend, John Garfield. I ask again, are you in regular contact with Deborah Marlow?"

John's gaze remained fixed on the agent.

Heart breaking over his silence, Eliza held herself still. His silence could only mean one thing: he still had feelings for the woman and didn't want to admit it in front of Eliza.

"Would you like me to leave?" she whispered.

John shook his head, his eyes never leaving the agent.

"Do you refuse to answer the question?" the agent asked.

John's lips tightened. "Any communication I've had with Mrs. Marlow does not concern this committee in any way."

Eliza couldn't feel her legs. So it was true. The letters *were* from Deborah.

The men spoke in low tones to each other, then one turned to John. "We'll need more than that."

"I'm sorry, but I am obliged to say no more."

"You will be subpoenaed to testify."

"I understand."

Eliza's heart sank. Was John withholding the details of a political association, or a personal one? Was protecting his relationship with Deborah worth facing a Congressional hearing?

"We will also be forced to subpoena Mrs. Saunderson."

John cast a pained glance at Eliza, then squared his shoulders and faced the man for seconds that felt like hours. "Fine. I'll tell you the nature of my correspondence with Mrs. Marlow if you will promise to leave Eliza out of this. Will you give me your word?"

"We can't make any promises until we've heard more."

John stiffened.

Eliza stared at his profile, willing him to turn and give her some assurance, but he didn't.

"Very well," he said. "In 1948, I wrote letters to people I had harmed or wronged in some way with my . . . reckless behavior in the past. Specifically, to ask for forgiveness. I wrote a letter to Deborah Marlow to apologize for . . . uh . . . compromising her marriage. She wrote back to tell me all was forgiven, and . . . to ask for my forgiveness as well." John's jaw tightened. He cleared his throat. "That's when I learned she'd been keeping a secret. Her daughter, who was seven years old at that time, was not her husband's child." He closed his eyes. "She is, in fact . . . mine."

The room fell silent.

No . . . not again . . . no, this is a bad dream . . . it has to be . . .

But she wasn't dreaming. Once again, the man in her life had given a child to the wrong woman.

She couldn't breathe.

"The girl is now twelve, and both the child and Doug Kelley believe he is her father. Mrs. Marlow believes it would be devastating to the child if the truth were ever known. She made me promise not to tell a soul. For the sake of the child, I was obliged to agree."

The agents talked to each other at length, but Eliza could only stare at him, numbed by the weight of this new truth.

367

"No one is ever to know," John said to the panel. "So I must ask you to keep this strictly confidential. I beg of you, don't destroy a little girl's life by leaking the truth. Please."

The imploring tone in his voice crushed Eliza.

John had a little girl.

He and Deborah Marlow, the woman Eliza had suspected he loved, shared a child together.

"So, all this time you've been *lying?*"

John's eyes closed.

"The truth will prevail, John? Aren't you the one who said God will take care of me if I tell the truth? You persuaded me to admit my family is Russian to a bloodthirsty, anti-Soviet government committee, and all the while you've been keeping a secret like *this?*"

"Eliza," he whispered. "I'm sorry—"

"For what? Getting caught living a lie? For telling me to be honest and trust God when you can't even do that? Or doesn't it apply to you? What other secrets are you keeping—a wife? Maybe you were waiting for our honeymoon to spring that on me?"

John turned to her with a haunted look. "Eliza, please let me—"

"And what about your book? Is that all lies too?" *Yes, stupid girl. You've been duped by a roving cheat. Again.*

Eliza turned and ran.

"Eliza, wait—"

"One moment, Mr. Vincent," an agent said, his voice sharp. "In light of your relationship with admitted communists, we need you to answer some more—"

Eliza left the room and kept going. She crossed to the mezzanine and headed for the staircase in a daze. She needed air, she needed—

She needed her world to stop caving in.

33

Eliza got off the bus at the corner of 35th and MacArthur and headed for home. But the thought of being alone in her empty room made her want to curl up into a ball and cry, so she passed her building and kept walking. She needed to clear her head.

Humiliated not once, but twice. Because men were animals.

Or maybe because you're a gullible girl with pitifully poor judgment.

Driven by a painful truth she didn't want to face, she lifted her chin and kept going, past the market, past a tavern, keeping a brisk pace to stay ahead of the easterly breeze. The few leaf-bearing trees lining the street were barren now, braced for winter. The sun hid behind a dull haze, withholding its warmth. Store windows enticed passersby with Christmas trees and plastic snowmen, their colors faded from too many years on display. A man was hanging a strand of Christmas lights in an insurance office window.

Eliza walked faster.

She and John might have been married by Christmas, if his secret not been forced out of him. When was he going to tell her?

Or was he even planning to tell her at all?

What a complete fool she would have been then. Finding out John had been lying *after* the wedding would have been far more humiliating. It was good that she found out now. The pain and embarrassment would be short-lived with less entanglement. It would serve as a valuable lesson to her.

As Eliza neared Lucky's, a whiff of grilling onions and coffee turned her stomach. Too many times she had ignored her hunger, too many times she had repressed her worries about landing another job.

Worrying was like crying; it never solved anything.

Passing the diner, she pressed on, her shoes striking the sidewalk like the rapid ping of gunfire. Nothing had changed. She was jobless again. And alone.

Are other women this gullible? Or am I the only childless thirty-three-year-old with nothing to my name but an ancient typewriter and a stack of dusty manuscripts?

Eliza's gaze dropped to her left hand. The ring twinkled cheerily in spite of the overcast skies. She kept going, her blurry eyes fixed on the ground while she dodged pedestrians and aimed to stay ahead of the heaviness bearing down on her. A heaviness that threatened to squash the tender hope she'd finally allowed to take root in her heart. There was no one who could help shoulder this burden. Betty would never understand. No one could. No one except—

Millie.

The kind, wise woman had heard only hints of Eliza's deepest struggles, and yet, somehow she understood and had offered comfort and wisdom. If only Millie were . . .

Eliza's eyes filled with tears so thick she could barely see. She stopped at a barber shop window and pretended to look inside, heart plummeting. With all that had happened in such a short time, Eliza had completely forgotten about Millie.

She owed it to Millie to see her, no matter what her state. And if Millie was still alive, Eliza needed to tell her how much she meant to her.

She wiped her face and hurried to the nearest bus stop.

By the time she arrived in west Oakland, dusk had already settled over the city, as if winter's encroaching darkness could be held off no longer. Eliza got off the bus a few blocks from St. Luke's just as the streetlamps flickered to life. She stood on a corner and took in her surroundings. It had taken two buses to get to this place, far from her familiar neighborhood. A shifting breeze tugged at her coat.

Something wasn't right.

Eliza glanced over her shoulder, hairs on her

neck itching. This neighborhood was more neglected than hers, but that wasn't it. One of Millie's hymns trailed across her thoughts.

For His eye is on the sparrow, and I know He watches me.

Except this peculiar sensation of being watched wasn't like *that*. Shaking off the feeling, she pulled her coat tighter and walked quickly toward the three-story hospital.

The entrance must have been on a different side of the building than where she was.

Eliza stepped off the sidewalk and into the alley, hurrying through the dark patches between streetlamps.

God, please make Millie well. You must. She trusts You so completely.

But would God listen to Eliza? Would He hear the prayer of a woman who couldn't bring herself to submit to His rule, who struggled to decide if she believed Him?

What about the guilty woman and Christ's pardon? What about that quiet voice promising to change her if she let Him?

A noise startled Eliza. She looked over her shoulder.

The shadow of a man loomed toward her.

With a gasp, she walked faster but he caught up with her. When they entered the circle of light beneath a streetlamp, she saw his face.

Agent Robinson.

"We meet again."

Her pulse thudded in her ears. His being here was no coincidence. How long had he been following her?

"You no longer work for the HUAC," Eliza said, keeping her voice low to mask the tremor in it. She backed away. "You have no business following me. Leave now or I'll call the police."

"You're mistaken. I have a job to do, and I intend to see it through. See, you commies think you can come here and infiltrate our neighborhoods, influence us with your brainwashing tactics. But you're wrong. I knew exactly what you were the first time I saw you."

"What am I?" She winced, wishing she hadn't asked, but wanting to keep him talking while she thought of an escape.

His narrowed eyes flickered with contempt. "A dirty rooskie spy."

"You're wrong." Eliza trembled. "It's too bad you weren't at headquarters today when I told the panel about my parents' innocence. But since you no longer work for the HUAC, it's none of your business."

"Oh, I'm sure it was a touching tale." He stepped closer, bringing him near enough for Eliza to see the fervor in his eyes. "Those scarecrows downtown might have fallen for your little naive act, but I haven't. I'll let you in on a secret. There aren't many who can spot your kind. And you're good, I'll give you that. But I'm better. *Much* better."

"I've told you, I'm neither a communist nor a spy. And you're no longer part of the investigation." She met his steely gaze. "Actually, there *is* no investigation. My case is closed, which you would know if you still worked there." What she had learned from meeting with the panel came rushing back. "In fact, the new field director is reviewing all your case files."

The smugness drained from Agent Robinson's expression. "What would a scheming commie know about my case files?" he said, his voice low.

Eliza tried to swallow, but her throat felt drier than chalk. This was not a man she could reason with. She mentally gauged the distance to the hospital, then turned and ran.

Robinson closed the distance in seconds and hooked her handbag, jerking her to a stop.

Eliza screamed.

He yanked on the purse, causing her to spin around to face him. "I *know* what you are. You're not going anywhere until I have proof! I'll get my job back *and* a commendation. And you'll get the chair!"

"Help! Someone call the police!" She tugged to get away, but her arm was caught in the purse strap.

"*You're* the one who's going to jail. Give me the bag!"

Dizzy from the adrenaline pumping through her, she screamed again. "Help! Someone, help me!" She pulled away as hard as she could.

"You've got to have *something!*" He gave the purse a jerk.

The handle snapped, and Eliza sailed backward. With a dull *thwack,* she hurtled into cold blackness.

34

Pain sliced through her head like slivers of glass piercing her brain.

Eliza forced her eyes open. She seemed to be lying in a brightly lit, swiftly spinning room. Her feet, covered by a white sheet, were the only things she could keep her focus on. At least, she hoped they were her feet . . .

She opened her eyes again.

The light was gone now. The room wasn't spinning, but it was hard to see in the dark. Plain gray walls. Dials and knobs. Her skull felt like it had gone through a tumbler and was then shrunken several sizes and crammed back onto her brain.

Eliza licked her dry lips. *I'm thirsty.*

Maybe if she tried saying it aloud . . .

Sometime later, voices pulled her up from a deep pond, thick as mud. As she approached the surface, she heard a woman's voice.

"A girl scout could fold a better dressing than that. I guess if I want it done right, I'll have to do it myself."

Eliza kept her eyes closed to block the piercing light. "Where am I?" she croaked.

"Nurse, she's awake."

"Get the doctor."

But Eliza couldn't keep afloat anymore and sank back into the mud.

Eliza hoped to stay awake long enough this time to find out where she was. It was a hospital, that much she could guess. But the rest was fuzzy. And excruciating. The harder she tried to concentrate on where she was and how she'd gotten here, the more her head hurt.

"You're awake." An older woman's voice.

Eliza turned her head slightly and saw a nurse's broad shape. "Where am I?"

"St. Luke's Hospital."

"What's wrong with me?"

"You've suffered brain swelling from a blow to the head," the nurse said. "Can you tell me your name?"

"Eliza," she whispered. She squinted and focused on the points of the woman's white cap. "What happened?"

"We don't know. An orderly found you bleeding in the alley. But you're doing far better than doctors first expected. What's your last name?"

"Saunderson." She tried to swallow, but her sticky throat made it difficult. "Can I have a drink?"

A straw touched her lips.

She sucked until cool water trickled down her throat.

"Do you remember what happened?" the nurse asked.

"I was on my way to . . ." The effort to think sent stabbing pain through her head. Eliza gripped the sides of the bed, hoping she wouldn't pass out. But the room spun and swayed, threatening to make her sick.

"We think you were mugged."

"Mugged?" She reached up, turned her head slightly, and felt the stitches on the back of it. Had someone hit her? Or had she fallen?

"Your broken purse was lying several yards away from where you were found, but there was no identification in it. Looks like someone stole your pocketbook."

Stole her pocketbook? Yes, that was it. A fanatic desperate for proof . . .

She could think no more and drifted into blackness.

A new nurse awakened Eliza with a tray of food. She smiled. "Honey, has anyone ever told you that you look like Gene Tierney?"

She swallowed the sudden ache in her throat.

With slow, careful motions, the nurse helped Eliza sit up and then arranged the tray for her. "How do you feel today?"

"Still a little dizzy." Her head no longer throbbed like a steady gong, a marked improvement. "But much better, thank you."

"Good, because there's someone here to see you," the nurse said.

Betty burst into the room. "Eliza!" She rushed to the bed and hugged her.

Eliza winced.

As the nurse left them, Betty straightened and studied Eliza. "Are you in pain? Are they taking proper care of you?" She glanced over her shoulder, then lowered her voice. "The staff here is incompetent. But what would you expect in the slums? I am going to have you transferred to a hospital in Richmond Heights. You'll get much better care there." She looked around the room with a grimace. "Darling, what on earth were you doing in this part of town? And why didn't anyone call me sooner? They told me you've been here for days!"

The sound of Betty's rising tone pierced her brain like a siren. "Please, not so loud."

The nurse was back. "She had no identification, so no one knew her name until she gained consciousness. She suffered acute brain trauma."

Betty gasped. "*Brain* trauma? Good heavens! What happened?"

"We still aren't sure, but it's clear she took a very bad blow to the head."

Betty moved closer to Eliza's side, frowning. "Tell me what happened."

Eliza closed her eyes. "I was on my way to see Millie, but that HUAC agent followed me and caught me in the alley."

"Wait . . . who is Millie?"

"John's housemaid." Tears filled Eliza's eyes. Millie was lying in the basement of this very hospital—*if* she was even still alive. She turned to the nurse. "Can you tell me if there is an elderly colored woman named Millie in the basement wing?"

Betty frowned. "You came to the slums to visit a *maid?*"

Eliza wiped her eyes. Millie wasn't just a maid. She was a wise, kind, saint of a woman who would never judge someone based on her station in life.

"That doesn't matter now." Betty beamed a smile at Eliza. "What's important is that you're going to be okay, isn't that right?" She turned to the nurse.

"Chances are good," the nurse said. "The doctor wants to evaluate her again, but he may release her as early as tomorrow."

"Did you hear that?" She reached for Eliza's hand and squeezed it. And then gasped.

John's ring. There it was, bigger than life, sparkling so bright it sent another sliver of pain to Eliza's head.

"What in heaven's name is this? An *engagement* ring?" Betty stared at the ring and then at Eliza, eyes wide.

"Betty, listen to me, this is important. The man—Agent Robinson—he attacked me. He was fired from the agency, and he's trying to reinstate himself. He's convinced I'm a communist spy. I think he's crazy. He followed me and tried to take my purse. I'm sure he took my pocketbook. He's dangerous, Betty. I want to report him to the police."

Looking bewildered, Betty only nodded, still staring at the ring on Eliza's hand. "Yes, of course, I will contact the police for you at once. But, darling . . . when did you get engaged? And to whom?"

Eliza's eyes drifted closed. "I don't want to talk about that right now."

A single tear rolled down her cheek.

At the sound of paper rustling, she opened her eyes.

Betty had drawn an envelope from her purse and held it up for Eliza to see.

"This was tacked to the door of your apartment. Would it have anything to do with that ring?" Her head tilted as she waited.

Eliza stared at her name on the envelope, written in John's familiar hand.

So he had been to see her.

Betty studied the envelope. "I went to your place to find out how your HUAC meeting went, but one of the girls in your building said no one had seen you for days. And another one complained that there was a fat cat howling on your balcony." She leaned closer. "What's going on, Eliza?"

Going back to the night John proposed, she told Betty everything, including her visit to the HUAC headquarters and finding out she and Betty were no longer under investigation. "But then they had some questions for John," she said. "It turns out he's been . . . keeping a secret."

"Oh?" Betty leaned closer. "What secret?"

Eliza opened her mouth.

But a happy little girl came to mind, a child who loved the man she believed was her daddy, the man she probably looked to as her hero. Eliza would never want any child to find out such news through vicious gossip.

"I can't say. But he kept something from me that a man doesn't keep from the woman he loves." She stared at the envelope, then reached for it. "May I?"

Betty handed it over with a sniff. "Probably full of lies. What did I tell you about men like that, Eliza?"

This was no time for a reminder of Betty's opinion of John. She opened the envelope, drew out the paper, and focused her aching brain on the familiar handwriting.

December 16, 1953

Dear Eliza,
I called and came to see you several times, with no answer. I heard you've

gone away, so I must assume you've left me. I only ask that you hear me out this once, then I will trouble you no more.

I know that my being a part of such a lie is wrong. And you're right to be angry with me for not telling you. I'm so sorry.

If you're still reading, may I tell you now? Her name is Judy.

Eliza flinched and squeezed her eyes tight to block the words, but it didn't help. John had a daughter, and her name was Judy.

Head pounding, she forced herself to read on.

I went along with the secret in order to protect a little girl from pain and public humiliation. And since Deborah would not have let me see Judy in any case, I could not bear to harm the girl by telling the truth when no good would have come from it.

Now so much time has passed, making it all far more complicated. Do you have any idea how difficult it is to know I have a child that I can never see? Do you know what it feels like to be denied any involvement in her life, to have missed her first steps, never allowed to see her grow up? Not allowed to walk her down the aisle?

If you think I should be ashamed of myself, don't worry—I am. I can't even be a proper father. Deborah sends me pictures and reports of her from time to time—I asked if I could at least have that. But I can't send her things. Deborah finally agreed to let me send money for birthday gifts. She tells Judy they're from her. It's the only thing I can do. What kind of a father is that?

I'm asking you to forgive me for agreeing to be part of such a lie. I fully intended to tell you, just not like this. If it's time you need, I will wait, but just so you know, your silence is killing me. I will never forget the look on your face. I should have told you everything before asking you to share my life, I know that now. I guess I was so consumed with telling you how I felt that I could think of little else.

I regret so many things in my life, Eliza. Like a fool, I let myself hope you might actually escape being affected by my past, but I see now that I was wrong. I hope and pray that you will find it in your heart to forgive me. Your faith in me has meant more than you'll ever know.

I will always love you.

John

Eliza blinked tears from her eyes, ignoring the dull throb in her head and an unbearable sense of loss. Had he intended to tell her and simply gotten ahead of himself? While he should have told her before proposing, perhaps he never intended to leave her in the dark, to make a fool of her, as Ralph had.

Was she being unreasonable?

She lifted her gaze above the paper and met her sister's.

Betty sniffed. "He's married. I knew it. So when was he going to tell you about his wife—on the honeymoon?"

Eliza cringed at the reminder of how she had accused him of that very same thing. She stared at John's handwriting again.

How like him to talk openly of his mistakes and face his shame so humbly. This was the John she had fallen in love with. Not a reckless cad, but a man who had struggled for weeks to deny his feelings for Eliza out of a desire to protect her. Despite John's mistakes, he was a good, caring man. And in spite of being party to such a lie, perhaps he was trying to do the best thing he knew how.

"I need to call him," Eliza whispered.

Betty shook her head. "Oh no. You're suffering from brain trauma, darling. Your mind is impaired. Don't do *anything* until you've had time to come to your senses."

Perhaps Betty was right. "But I must find out about Millie," she said. "She's the reason I'm here."

"If you must." Betty sighed. "I'll order a wheelchair."

35

Millie's grandchildren were taking turns keeping vigil, and though she was still holding on to life, the old woman hadn't done more than mutter a few words and then slip right back into unconsciousness.

Eliza rose from her wheelchair and kissed Millie's forehead. She whispered Millie's name, with no response.

The woman's skin was cool and translucent and reminded Eliza of spent leaves turned transparent, drifting through town like thin ghosts.

Eliza wept all the way back to her room.

Tuesday, just as Eliza finished dressing, Betty burst into the room. "Finally! Are you ready to go?"

"Yes." She couldn't wait to leave this place.

At Eliza's apartment building, Betty made Eliza hold her arm and take the stairs slowly, although Eliza was certain she could manage. She'd walked the hospital corridors to the doctor's satisfaction. But she'd allow Betty to mother her anyway, if it would help make her sister feel better about leaving Eliza alone.

A number of phone messages littered Eliza's door. As she sorted through them, her heart sank. None were from John.

But there was one—she gasped. A message from Vlad asking for a return call as soon as possible.

"Oh! This might be about Aunt Katerina." Eliza grasped Betty's arm. "Shall we call him now?"

"Yes, of course!"

Eliza found Vlad's telephone number.

Once the call was approved and placed, a very exuberant Vlad answered. "Finally! I begin to fear you changed your mind. I have received telegram from Katerina. Would you like to hear it now?"

"Yes, please." Eliza motioned Betty closer and tilted the receiver so Betty could hear.

Vlad cleared his throat. " 'Dearest nieces, I cannot describe how my heart bursts with joy to find you and know you are well. I wish to see you. Please write. I also wish to hear of my brother and his life in America. My heart grieves he is gone, but finding you is my greatest comfort and best consolation.' "

Betty stepped away.

Vlad went on. "Kat sends love and hopes to hear from you soon."

Watching her sister, Eliza nodded. "Thank you so much, Vlad. If I send you a letter, can you translate it and send it to her?"

"It would be my pleasure."

Eliza thanked him again, then ended the call and turned to Betty. "What's wrong?"

Betty shook her head. "Nothing. She sounds very kind."

"Yes. And strong." The letter her aunt had written to their father, even if only legible in part, had spoken volumes. "She helped Papa escape, knowing she would probably never see him again. How difficult that must have been for her. I wonder, if she could have foreseen the outcome, if she would have done anything differently."

"I doubt it. What option did they have?"

Eliza shook her head. "I don't know."

"Yes, well, let this be a lesson to you."

"About what?"

"Sometimes saying goodbye is for the best."

Thankfully, Eliza's key hadn't been lost in the scuffle over her purse. She let herself in, looked around, and winced at her unmade bed.

Betty shook her head with a tsk. "You're coming for Christmas Eve and staying over. I insist."

"All right." Eliza smiled. "Thank you for bringing me home. I'm sure I'll be fine. I'll call you if I need anything."

"Yes, well." Betty peered at her. "I don't suppose you want me to stay a little while? Make sure you don't have a dizzy spell or . . . get any silly ideas about calling anyone?"

Eliza's smile persisted. "Thank you, but I'll

be perfectly fine, really. And you still have Christmas shopping to do."

Betty narrowed her gaze. "Don't be foolish, Eliza. A man who will break your heart once will do it again. Mark my words."

After Betty left, Eliza opened the sliding glass door, stepped out, and glanced around.

No sign of Mr. Darcy.

She stepped inside, and as she closed the door, she spied John's letter peeking out of her purse. She took it out and read it again, aching at his humble request for her forgiveness.

A sense of urgency pushed her out the door and down the stairs. She gave the operator his telephone number and waited to be connected. There was no answer.

A little later, she went downstairs and tried again. Still no answer. She tried several more times throughout the evening, with the same results.

The next day, Eliza woke to the realization that it was the twenty-third of December and she hadn't done a single thing to prepare for Christmas. She could not arrive at Betty's empty-handed. Donning her long coat, she headed downstairs, then paused at the telephone.

He had to answer sometime.

"Hello?" Duncan's voice.

"Duncan, this is Eliza. May I speak to John?"

"He's not here, Miss."

"When do you expect him to return?"

"Couldn't say. He left town."

Eliza thanked him, hung up, and headed for the drugstore. Her plan was to find something inexpensive for her niece and nephew. But once inside the store, she found herself roaming the aisles in a daze, sorrow weighing her steps like sandbags. Where had John gone? Perhaps to stay with friends over Christmas. She should have given him a chance to explain himself that day at the hotel, shouldn't have said all those hurtful things that she had. She couldn't blame him for leaving town.

God, please be with him, wherever he is.

She shouldn't have been so quick to compare him to Ralph. John would never knowingly humiliate Eliza.

And on that note, the lingering cloud of humiliation hovering over Eliza's life needed to disappear. John's reckless mistake had resulted in a child. But the child was no mistake. It wasn't Judy's fault that the adults in her life had made poor decisions. A child shouldn't feel as if she were the reason for someone else's shame. Not her parents. And certainly not Eliza's.

If Eliza still felt humiliated over her childlessness, perhaps it was because she chose to feel that way. What was it that Millie had said? "The Lord is the portion of mine inheritance and of my cup." Wasn't that her way of telling Eliza to be content with what she had and stop wasting her energies on anger and longing? Wasn't that the lesson Millie wanted Eliza to grasp?

Dear God, please help sweet Millie. Please heal her body, or else gather her gently into Your arms, whatever is best.

And please help me. I've been so blind.

Eliza chose a small model airplane that she hoped Eddie Jr. didn't already have, and a pink-and-white-striped scarf for Sue Ellen, then took her purchases and headed for the nearest bus stop. She needed to see Millie one more time, if for no other reason than to pay her respects. And most likely to say goodbye.

A young man was stroking Millie's hand when Eliza arrived. People stood on either side of the bed where the tiny woman lay.

The tiny woman whose eyes were open.

Eliza let out a gasp. "Millie?"

"Miz Eliza, bless your heart," Millie whispered. "Come close. Don't 'spect you come all this way to . . . look at my ugly feet."

The young man stepped aside, and Eliza moved as close to Millie as she could.

"How are you feeling?" As soon as she said the words, Eliza wanted to snatch them back. What kind of a question was that?

"My bones feel like dancin'." A slow smile crossed her face.

A man about Eliza's age shook his head. "Grandmama, you can dance later. You gotta rest now, like the doctor said. You hear?"

"Miz Eliza," Millie whispered.

Eliza leaned closer. "I'm here."

Eyes closed, Millie smiled. "You ever hear the story . . . how the Lord told Ezekiel to talk to a . . . valley full o' dry bones?"

Eliza shook her head. "No."

Millie nodded. "He did. And them bones come together . . . with flesh and skin and even eyeballs." Millie drew a long, labored breath. "Then Ezekiel called the four winds . . . and the Lord . . . *breathed* . . . and them bones come to life. Rose up on they feet . . . a vast army."

Eliza waited, but worry tugged at her chest. Shouldn't Millie be saving her strength?

"The Lord used . . . dead men's bones . . . not livin' men." She worked for a few more breaths. "Can't win battles 'less you die first. That's when . . ." She inhaled and looked at Eliza. "The Spirit of the Lord give you breath . . . and then you *really* alive."

A muffled sob sounded behind Eliza. A teary-eyed woman moved in and leaned closer to Millie. "Now, Mama, no need to be talkin' about dyin'."

But Millie only smiled. "Come closer. I can't bite . . . they took my teeth."

Eliza looked around.

Millie meant *her?*

She moved as asked, her face nearly touching Millie's.

"You a beautiful soul," she whispered. "With a kind heart and . . . a way with words." She closed her eyes. "Use that for the Lord, child." She inhaled again. "The Lord use beauty and kindness and words . . . same way He use armies and dry bones and . . . my grandmama's apple dumplin'." Her face scrunched with each breath. "Whatever it take to . . . help this fallen world find Him. You got . . . a heart for them that nobody listen to." She nodded. "You let Him *breathe* into you, child . . . and use those things He give you. He'll help you fight the good fight . . . change the world." Millie's eyes closed and a smile settled on her lovely face.

Tears trickled down Eliza's cheeks unchecked. She reached around Millie, hugged her gently, and kissed her forehead. Then she straightened and turned to Millie's waiting family, struck with a numbing sense of dismay. Had Millie spent the last of her strength on Eliza?

The middle-aged woman touched Eliza's arm. "I think Mama been savin' up to tell you that." Her voice cracked. "She'll rest now. Don't you worry."

Tears blinded Eliza. She nodded. "Thank you for sharing her with me."

· · ·

Eliza only made it halfway to the elevator before she could go no farther, blinded by tears. Millie's faith in Eliza was a gift more precious than any other, like a map to a treasure Eliza thought she'd lost, a glimpse of greater things she had been too obstinate to see.

Significance wouldn't come from fighting to make the world acknowledge her worth. It would come from resting in the knowledge that she was loved by God and gifted for a purpose.

Yes, I surrender. Breathe Your life into me. Change me and make me new. I surrender.

Eliza stood alone in the corridor. She *would* help free the oppressed. Not just those oppressed by injustice, but also those bound by chains of their own making, like discontent. Like shame or shortcomings or a desperate longing for what they didn't have.

Closing her eyes, she offered up a silent prayer. *God, please help John be free of his past once and for all—*

"Eliza?"

She gasped and looked at him. "John?"

"Is she . . . ?" John glanced down the hall at the room where Millie lay, his expression strained.

Eliza collected herself. "She was awake a moment ago. She . . . spoke to me. But . . ." Her voice broke.

John studied her, then looked toward the room. "Will you please wait for me?" he asked.

"Yes, I'll wait."

With a terse nod, he disappeared into Millie's room.

Eliza found an empty chair and sat down, suddenly pressed by the weight of too many emotions and the return of pain in her head. She closed her eyes.

Moments later, the sound of John's voice stirred her awake.

She must have drifted off. She started to rise.

"No, please, don't get up," he said quickly. "You're done in. But I'd like to ask you to hear me out. I won't keep you long, I promise."

Tears swam again. "John, I'm not—"

"Please, Eliza?"

The pain in his voice crushed her. "Yes."

He leaned heavily on his cane. "It was crazy to hope you wouldn't be touched by my past, Eliza. And now it's happened, just as I feared." Remorse filled his eyes. "I'm so sorry for not telling you. Please believe that I never meant to hurt you."

Eliza nodded, unable to speak.

He swallowed hard. "I will talk to the girl's mother and tell her I can't keep being part of a lie. I don't know what will happen, but . . . I promise you I'll do whatever it takes to make this right. I hope you can forgive me, but even more,

I hope this hasn't made you unable to trust God. *I'm* the one who betrayed you, not—"

"John." She stood and faced him. "You told me that Christ gave Himself in order to be held accountable for your sins. So do you think He would want you to keep paying for the same mistake over and over?"

Slowly, he shook his head.

"And didn't you tell me that God forgives and forgets?"

John nodded.

"It's not Judy's fault." Her tears streamed freely, washing away the last traces of her old humiliation. "You've already paid. That little girl shouldn't have to pay too."

"What do you mean?"

"I believe you've tried very hard to do what's right. And that you're doing the best thing you can right now, given the circumstances. But there *is* one thing I would ask of you."

He searched her face. "I'll do anything, Eliza," he said, deep voice faltering. "Anything. Just say the word."

"Will you forgive me?"

His brow gathered in confusion. "Forgive *you?*"

"I'm sorry, John. I love you. I'm so sorry—"

He crushed her to him and held her tight.

36

"I can't believe that lunatic left you bleeding in an alley." John shook his head, jaw muscles rippling.

Eliza sighed. The last thing she wanted to talk about on the way to Christmas Eve dinner at Betty's was Agent Robinson. "The police will deal with him, and he'll get what he deserves. They've been in contact with the HUAC, and he will face assault charges."

"That's good, but he hasn't heard the last from me."

Eliza slipped her hand into his. "My, *this* is a side of you I've never seen."

John squeezed her hand, then frowned at it. "I should have been with you."

"I appreciate your concern," she said. "Anyway, it's over now. And because Robinson harassed me and I brought it to the agency's attention, they're finding I wasn't the only victim, which has launched a full investigation of HUAC tactics. I have a feeling there will be changes soon. Maybe McCarthy and his hounds will be shut down completely."

John leaned close and kissed her temple. "Remind me never to take sides against you."

Eliza studied him. "Now what makes you say

that? I'm just a meek little typist, minding my own business."

He lifted a single brow. *"Meek?"*

She nodded.

John burst out laughing.

The cabbie glanced at them in his mirror.

John tugged her close to his side, still laughing.

Betty outdid herself with a delicious Christmas Eve meal of spareribs and candied yams, a Peterson family tradition. Then she announced that Odella had baked several pies before taking time off for the holiday.

Eliza followed her sister to the kitchen to help serve dessert.

Once they were inside, Betty paused and turned to her. "It's because of you that I gave Odella the extra time off, you know."

"Me?"

Betty inclined her chin. "I'm not as indifferent to the plight of others as you think."

After dessert, the kids took turns reading from *The Lion, the Witch and the Wardrobe* around the Christmas tree. John politely endured Eddie Jr.'s parade of model airplanes and Ed's endless questions about filmmaking, Hollywood scandals, and what was next for John. Although the deal was still in negotiation, the talk of a film based on John's book was likely to become a reality.

Mesmerized, Eliza listened to John's voice and the grace with which he answered questions. Perhaps, in time, Betty would see what kind of man John really was.

As she and Betty rinsed the dishes, Eliza peeked through the dining room doorway at John and then turned to Betty. "Looks like you'll finally get your wish."

"And what wish is that?" Betty wiped her forehead with the back of her wrist.

"That I'll settle down and be a proper house-wife." Eliza handed Betty the last plate for the dishwasher.

Betty set the dish in the rack and closed the door. She took a dishtowel and wiped the counter. "I shouldn't have pushed you."

"What do you mean?"

Betty folded the towel and laid it on the counter. "I tried to fill in when Mama died. I thought I was doing the right thing, steering you into marriage. But—"

"Oh, Betty. I know it wasn't easy filling in for Mama. I appreciate all you've done to look out for me. Really, I do."

Betty's eyes glistened. "Look *out* for you? Ralph was a bully. And I pushed you into that." She turned away.

Eliza took hold of Betty's shoulders and turned her back. "It wasn't your fault. Ralph fooled us all. Some people are just good at putting on the kind of face everyone wants to see."

Betty shook her head. "Not you. You don't worry about what anyone thinks. You can be different. And you're at peace with that. Sometimes . . . I wish I had that."

"You do?"

Betty nodded.

With a shrug, Eliza said, "Who says you can't?"

Betty stared at her, then glanced out the curtained window which offered a partial view of the bare trees encircling the backyard. She mimicked Eliza's shrug. "No one, I guess."

Eliza hugged her. "I love you, sis."

37

A warm spring breeze ruffled the hem of Eliza's dress, tickling her knees. She laid a bouquet of daisies on the flat stone, then tucked gloved hands into the crook of her husband's elbow. The simple stone contained Millie's name, the dates that marked her life, and a single line of inscription:

Blessed are the peacemakers,
for they shall be called the children of God.

She squeezed his arm and spoke lightly to keep her voice from breaking. "I wish I'd had more time with her. Instead, I have to store up everything she said to me like a treasure." She read the inscription again. "What do you suppose she's doing now?"

"Dancing," John said quietly.

Eliza sighed. "She wanted to be with Jesus, so I guess I should be glad for her, but . . ."

"But what?"

She turned to him. "I loved Millie. She was like a mother to me. And I still need her. If I am ever to succeed at the things she believed me capable of, I need her perspective. I need to better understand oppression from her viewpoint."

He stroked his thumb across her cheek. "You still can understand her point of view."

"How?"

"Millie once told me that anyone—including ourselves—can enslave us, but only if we let them. And that true freedom and equality are found in the One who created each and every one of us. In Him, you'll find neither Jew nor Greek, neither slave nor free, neither male nor female. In Christ, we're all equal."

The wind carried his words across the grassy knoll.

"Equal," she said, trying to grasp it. "No one group of people ruling over another, no one kept down simply because of race or gender or class. Do you really believe that?"

John nodded. "I do, but it will take time, prayer, and hard work. You must keep writing, Eliza. Keep making your voice heard."

Eliza stared at Millie's name. "She found a way to speak the truth with grace and forgiveness in the face of tyranny. I don't know how she did it."

"I think you do."

"Well, yes, but she had great faith."

"And you don't?"

Eliza glanced up at him. "I don't know about *great* faith, but . . . let's just say that, since I met you, I've seen what trusting God in the face of difficulty can do. Now, if I could just learn to handle everything as calmly and gracefully as you do."

John's brows rose. "*I'm* calm?"

She smiled. "Well, graceful, anyway."

He slipped an arm around Eliza and tugged her closer. "Millie often said grace takes far more strength than hate does."

"Why is that?"

"Because grace isn't given based on what's fair or deserved. It's an undeserved gift, given deliberately. Maybe that's why it's easier for people to dole out justice than grace. And maybe that's why some of us find grace so difficult to accept."

Eliza looked up.

John's eyes shone with love and something else. Gratitude.

She turned and wrapped her arms around him. "That's quite profound. I wish I'd said it. Can I use it in my book?"

He tilted her chin up and studied her. "You can do anything you want, Mrs. Vincent." The warmth of his smile sent a thrill through her.

"You sure do have a way with words, *Mr.* Vincent," she said lightly. "Anyone ever tell you you're a charmer?"

John shook his head. "Not this lug. What you see is what you get."

She sighed. "Promise?"

He opened his mouth as if to speak, then hesitated.

"What? I'm not kidding," she said. "Your transparency is one of the many things I love about you."

His expression sobered.

"What's wrong?"

"Not a thing." With a sigh, John looked deep into her eyes and smiled. "It's just going to take some getting used to, that's all."

"What's that?"

He leaned down and brushed her lips with a light kiss, then held her tight. "Love. No illusions. Just love."

Author's Note

Senator McCarthy and the
House Un-American Activities Committee
(HUAC)

In February of 1950, in an attempt to ensure his re-election, Senator Joe McCarthy claimed he had a list of more than 200 people in the State Department who were known members of the Communist Party USA. This came at a time when a wave of hysteria known as the "Red Scare" rolled through the nation, fueled by the perceived threat of communists living in the USA.

McCarthy took advantage of the public's fear and established himself as the chairman of the Government Committee on Operations of the Senate. He used his position to widen the scope of the committee to investigate anyone he suspected of being "subversive" or a "dissenter," and eventually became the person most known for heading up the reckless anti-communist crusade known as "McCarthyism." Using hearsay and intimidation, he charged anyone who disagreed with his political views of being communist, including celebrities and film industry professionals, costing many people their jobs and reputations. Government employees, intellectuals, and anyone suspected of being a social or political agitator were scrutinized to determine whether they were sufficiently loyal to the government.

The "Hollywood Ten" was a group of directors and screenwriters who were cited for contempt of Congress and blacklisted after refusing to answer HUAC questions about their alleged involvement with the Communist Party. This led to more than 320 film industry professionals being "blacklisted" and prevented from working in the entertainment industry. People were called to appear before the HUAC to answer questions not only about their own suspected political beliefs, but also to "name names" of friends and colleagues. Panic about these witch-hunts rose, adding to the public's fear of communism.

McCarthy's downfall began in October of 1953 when he began to investigate his suspicions of communist infiltration in the military. Critics countered his accusations and began exposing McCarthy's coercive tactics and his inability to substantiate his claims. McCarthy's reign of terror ended when Senate Committee colleagues formally reprimanded him in 1954. The media quickly lost interest in his accusations, stripping McCarthy of his power. He continued to serve as senator until his death in 1957.

In 1969, the HUAC was renamed the Internal Security Committee. In 1975, the Committee was abolished.

Acknowledgments

This book would still be a half-baked mess if not for my author friend and mentor, Leslie Gould, and her nudges to keep sending new chapters each week. Her encouragement and enthusiasm pulled me past crippling doubt and motivated me to keep pressing forward. Thank you!

Also, I am forever indebted to:

My agent, Rachelle Gardner, for believing in Johnny.

My husband, Dan, and my publisher, Ashberry Lane, for believing in me.

Screenwriting consultant Michael Hauge for his advice on writing a fictional story set in Hollywood.

Author and agency-mate Pastor Bill Giovanetti for his early critique and encouragement.

Authors and agency-mates Sarah Sundin and Keli Gwyn for their insight on the history and geography of Northern California.

The Western Railway Museum.

JoAn (Mom) Montgomery, my favorite fashionista of the '50s.

Carla Stewart, for her steadfast voice of literary wisdom and advice.

And Cary Grant, Clark Gable, and Gregory Peck, for just being themselves.

Most of all, I am grateful to my Lord and Savior, Jesus, for His steadfast love, His deliberate grace, and His shame-cleansing forgiveness, for the dream that inspired this story, and for His help to write it.

Author Bio

Camille Eide lives near the Oregon Cascades. She is wife, mom, grammy, church administrator, bassist and loves Jesus, muscle cars, oldies rock, and the subtle irony of Jane Austen.

She blogs about God's amazing grace at Along the Banks, (www.camilleeide.wordpress.com) reviews books and inspirational TV/Film at Extreme Keyboarding, (www.camilleeide.blog spot.com) and writes faith-inspiring love stories sprinkled with bits of wisdom and wit.

Discussion Questions

1. How close have you come to meeting a celebrity, and how did you react? If you were in Eliza's shoes when meeting the infamous Johnny Devine, how might you have reacted?
2. Eliza's parents raised her to be capable and intelligent, and yet she struggled with a sense of insignificance. Why do you think she felt this way?
3. Was Eliza's desire to be a complete person in her own right realistic for a woman in that era? What, if anything, could she have done differently in her marriage?
4. What did John really hope to accomplish by following Eliza to the gate after her discovery in his journal? Would he have been better off allowing her to believe she'd misunderstood his feelings for her?
5. Since telling the truth can often cause distress or complications, is it ever justifiable to lie or allow others to believe what isn't true? What about when the truth would injure someone like young Judy?

6. Eliza believed her hatred for Ralph destroyed the goodness her parents had instilled in her and that such hatred was unforgivable. Is silent hate dangerous? Why?

7. John wants to tell his story but struggles with reliving shameful details. When are the sordid details of past mistakes helpful to others, and when might they best be kept private?

8. To Eliza, Millie had an unusual attitude about her lot in life. On what did she base her contentment? Have you ever struggled to be content in unsatisfactory circumstances outside your control? What effect did Millie's outlook have on Eliza?

9. Did John's faith in God change the way Eliza chose to face opposition in her own life? Do you see her able to move toward a faith in God of her own that includes trusting Him to see her through future hardship?

10. Millie and Eliza agreed that social injustices and prejudices needed to be abolished, but each one had a different approach to achieve that end. Compare both attitudes and methods. If you had lived in this era and wanted to see change, would you act more as Eliza did, or Millie?

11. Why was John so determined to make sure people knew he wasn't trying to make excuses for his reckless behavior? How did

that conflict with his desire for people to understand how hopeless he'd become?

12. Eliza struggled to understand how an immoral person might have more hope of heaven than a moral person might. Did you sympathize with her? What do you think about the Bible's claim that eternity in heaven is gained by faith in Christ alone, and not in any amount of goodness or righteous things we do? Do you find this difficult to accept, or comforting?

13. John tells his story from the viewpoint of a changed man. But how changed is he? Does he continue to change during the composing of his memoir?

14. John entered the war with a death wish, but just as he found a reason to live, his life was placed in danger. Have you ever been challenged to let go of things you cling to?

Center Point Large Print
600 Brooks Road / PO Box 1
Thorndike, ME 04986-0001 USA

(207) 568-3717

US & Canada:
1 800 929-9108
www.centerpointlargeprint.com